David's Star

DEAN ZAHAV

DAVID'S STAR

Dean Zahav

DAVID'S STAR

iUniverse books may be ordered through booksellers or by contacting:
iUniverse
1663 Liberty Drive
Bloomington, IN 47403
www.iuniverse.com
1-800-Authors (1-800-288-4677)

ISBN: 978-1-4620-6813-5 (sc)
ISBN: 978-1-4620-6814-2 (ebk)
Library of Congress Control Number: 2011960852
Printed in the United States of America
iUniverse rev. date: 12/13/2011

The text face is Simpli designed by Ilia Gruev

For my father

ALAV HA-SHALOM

A conflict begins and ends in the hearts and minds of people, not in the hilltops. — AMOS OZ

And in this respect, the Israeli-Palestinian conflict has been a tragedy, a clash between one very powerful, very convincing, very painful claim over this land and another no less powerful, no less convincing claim. — AMOS OZ

It was not my achievement that I have a foot in the past and a foot in the future, it was my given. I was uniquely placed to comprehend and bridge many worlds, both by historical events and by personal disposition. — RABBI ZALMAN SCHACHTER-SHALOMI

PART ONE

With Huldah

Prologue

JERUSALEM, ISRAEL
30 SEPTEMBER 2019, ROSH HA-SHANAH (JEWISH NEW YEAR)
1ST OF TISHREI, 5780, ACCORDING TO THE JEWISH CALENDAR
THE HEADQUARTERS OF THE TEMPLE MOUNT
AND LAND OF ISRAEL FAITHFUL MOVEMENT

"Is everything set?" The question came from a middle-aged man who had a distinctive white scar on his left cheek. He was no other than Caleb Medan – the notorious die-hard hotheaded chief of the Temple Mount and Land of Israel Faithful Movement. The main goal of the movement was to rebuild the Jewish Temple on Temple Mount in Jerusalem and to re-establish the tradition of ritual sacrifice.

Medan's question resonated in the spacious semi-dark room whose shades were half-drawn to protect its two current occupants from the piercing rays of the stark early afternoon Jerusalem sun. Medan was standing almost menacingly over a timid computer specialist who answered submissively, "Yes, sir."

"Then publish the statement on the website now!" Medan commanded sternly while the young man, eyes locked on the computer screen, began keying rapidly.

Within seconds, the following message appeared on the official website of the Temple Mount and Land of Israel Faithful Movement:

May you be inscribed for a good year!

Dear friends, a new year has begun! 5780 will be the most exciting year in Israel's history because it marks 72 years since the foundation of the modern state of Israel. In 5708 (1948 in the Gregorian calendar) our forefathers began with the reciting of Vehu – the first name of the Shemhamphorasch, the first of the 72 names of God. And so they recited one name of the Shemhamphorasch per year. And so, the years came and went in prophetic succession until 5780 came with Moum – the very last 72nd name of God, which means 'moral blemish'. In 5780 Israel shall finally restore justice by wiping out the moral blemish of exile and destruction of the Temple inflicted upon it. And so it is said in Vayikra, that is, Leviticus 24:20: 'Breach for breach, eye for eye, tooth for tooth: as he hath caused a blemish in a man, so shall it be done to him again.' There were those among us who claimed the re-establishing of the state of Israel equaled to the rebuilding of the Third Temple. They were wrong. The return from 2000 years of exile was the first step. For centuries the Chosen People have been dreaming about the rebuilding of the Temple, the Third Temple, the Temple of Redemption, the Temple of King David's Progeny, The Temple of the End of Days. This dream shall no longer remain a dream. Very soon Israel shall make the second step – the rebuilding of the Temple and this way the dream shall come true. We shall gather here in Jerusalem to mark this act of greatest deliverance.

Once Caleb Medan reassured himself that the message was published, he began reciting in a hushed voice:

"Now, therefore, O Lord our God, impose Thine awe upon all Thy works, and Thy dread upon all that Thou hast created, that all works may revere Thee and all creatures prostrate themselves before Thee, that they may all form a single band to do Thy will with a perfect heart."

1

JERUSALEM, ISRAEL
28 APRIL 2020
DOWNTOWN, OFF THE JAFFA GATE

Palm-tree branches and leaves lay scattered around the main thoroughfares and narrow streets of Jerusalem. The hamsin, the hot, dry wind sweeping down from the deserts in the east, had blown them about the Holy City the night before. It was as if the wind had further sought to acknowledge the arrival of spring, the most pleasant time of year in Israel. A soft rain had appeared from nowhere and the leaves of trees and plants seemed to shake themselves awake and prepare to offer their fruits and flowers. It was a time of trusting the symbolism of spring and of nurturing hope, hope for good causes exemplified by good men.

The view over the Old City's Citadel - The Tower of David, or Midgal David as it is in Hebrew - was dazzling. This ancient fortification has unchangeably been guarding the Western approach to the Old City for centuries.

In the narrow rectangular square running parallel to the Jaffa Road and standing above the Mamilla Mall, a relatively large group of dignified men had gathered. They were speaking to each other in soft tones, everyone in a peaceful mode, waiting expectantly for something to take place. It was a small-scale rally of Peace Now or Shalom Achshav - the well-known NGO promoting peace between Israel and Palestine and appealing to many in the country and far beyond.

A slightly balding man of average height, about 45 years old, wearing black-rimmed glasses above his long caftan, raised his open hand above his head and the gathering of people grew respectfully attentive. They knew this was Ruben Openheim, the forceful head of Peace Now.

"Thank you, each and every one of you, for the immense help you've provided for our cause." He paused and glanced around the plaza as the people shuffled closer, eager to hear every word. "Without the personal efforts of each of you, we wouldn't have been able to complete Safe Haven for Israel - a project costing millions in donations. What a miraculous project this has been! With all of you on our side during the past five years, we have succeeded in constructing many apartment complexes in different countries! In this way we have been able to provide safe havens for Israelis!" Openheim paused for dramatic effect and looked intensely into several faces in the crowd. He was a noted expert in Semitic languages and as such, was also well-versed in the personalities and cultural imprinting of his fellow Israelis.

He nodded in affirmation of his own premise and continued. "Why do we need these safe havens? Because in the event of an attack from allied hostile Arab neighbor states and outlawed terrorist organizations, millions of Israeli refugees can find safety and hospitality in your countries far from their own homes. In a way, I hope we never have to use these shelters; but with them now finished and ready for occupancy, I dare say we are prepared for a second berihah - the mass movement of Israelis from Europe to Israel during World War Two. This time it will be from Israel back to Eastern, Central and Southern Europe. *Toda,* thank you, Szymon Adamczyk from Poland, Matej Horak from the Czech Republic, Peter Novacek from Slovakia, Rabbi Loew, Bogdan Popescu from Romania, Goran Mladic from Serbia, Vladko Radic from Croatia, Ivan Ljubavic from Slovenia and especially the family, Rovine Dilesz from Hungary and Ian Magdev from Bulgaria."

The distinguished names Openheim mentioned evoked murmurs from the people as they nodded to express appreciation of his words. He continued speaking, standing in front of a wall upon which was hung the flag of Israel with its large Star of David in the middle. "Everything has been set. There's only one thing left for us to do now – keep on maintaining peace and fighting for it when necessary. This has always been Peace Now's primary goal. We have to carry on mustering all strength and efforts in maintaining peace in Israel and deliberately and firmly circumvent any danger from impending wars."

Ian Magdev, who had become close friends with Ruben Openheim, rose his hand and said, "On behalf of all the participants in this noble project, I'd like to thank Ruben for letting us give our share to the country we hold dearly." A wave of cheering issued from the people.

In another part of Jerusalem, tucked deeply underground in a decrepit basement and beyond the reach of mobile networks, a group of people was franticly working precisely on the opposite of what Ruben Openheim outlined as Peace Now's primary goal. For these people, war was the means to maintain fear and resignation throughout the region. It was necessary, worse still, vital as they arrogantly claimed.

2

SOFIA, BULGARIA
29 APRIL 2020
LATE EVENING

For Rovine and Ian, the El Al flight back home was calm and uneventful. Sofia bustled with life despite the late hour and the fact that it was Wednesday and not Friday or Saturday night. It was springtime after all and it was pleasantly warm. Their taxi drove by open-air bars and restaurants downtown that teemed with people eager to have a drink outdoors after the long winter. Downtown was quickly over and the brick buildings were replaced by residential compounds. The taxi hit south, down a wide boulevard leading to the foothills of the Vitosha Mountain that guarded majestically the entire southern approach to Sofia. To drive up the mountain meant to reveal a beautiful bird's-eye view over the whole city of lights.

The taxi stopped in front of a two-storey house surrounded by a lush garden full of fruit trees and flowers. Rovine loved them and she had them all over the place.

"Dani, we are back, darling!" The cheerful voice belonged to Rovine as she announced their arrival back from Israel after Ian unlocked the front door. She moved inside the doorway gracefully, her lithe figure almost cat-like, and got in the hallway. She took off her long cashmere scarf and hung it on the hall-stand. She wore her long straight hair pulled back into a thick braid down the middle of her back, this way having her beautiful high forehead revealed. Her lips were parted in a gentle, expectant smile. Rovine was the epitome of the nurturing and gentle mother.

"Where are you, Dani boy? Mom?" Ian, Dani's father, called out while hanging up their jackets. He ran his fingers through his dark curly hair, trying to smooth down the tangles twisted in by the wind and his cap. Ian was slender and physically active. He was a linguist-mathematician who maintained a good measure of spontaneity and unconventionality.

"He's in his room," Maya, Ian's mother, said with a smile as she hurried into the hallway. "Welcome home!" Her voice was that of a very kind and capable grandmother.

"Hi mom, how are you? I hope you didn't have any trouble!" Ian hugged and kissed her.

"I am fine. I'm watching the news. How was the flight?"

"It was perfect," Rovine replied.

"How have you and Dani been getting along?" Ian asked.

"Great, you know him, he's such a sweet boy. Never gave me any troubles."

"And he didn't stay up late?" Rovine pressed on, knowing her son.

"I don't think so," Ian's mother said and smiled.

"That's great because you know how addicted he is to his computer," Rovine explained.

"I know but he's been a good boy," Maya reassured the young parents, smiling to herself.

******

Ian and Rovine hurried upstairs and entered the room of their 14-year-old son Dani. The room was large enough for a single occupant and pretty tidy for a teenager with only a poster or two on the walls. By the window, there was a desk laden with books and dictionaries, a laptop in its middle. Dani's slim boyish figure was leaning forward, his blue eyes fixed on the brightly lit flat screen of the laptop while his fingers tapped rapidly on the keyboard. He stopped and turned around, broad smile lighting up his face at the sight of his parents, a feature he had undoubtedly inherited from his mother. The genes had bestowed the boy with lavish, dark curly hair without a doubt transferring it from Ian's side of the family. Dani jumped up and rushed to greet them.

"Mom, Dad, I'm so happy you are back! How was Israel?"

"A lot of work as usual," Ian said as he hugged his son.

"Unfortunately we didn't have time to go sight-seeing," Rovine said and joined them in one giant hug.

"Will you take me with you next time? You promised, remember?" he asked.

"There may not be another time. We finished the big construction project, Dani," Ian explained.

"So what now? That's it? No more going to Israel?" Dani asked surprised.

"Not for work anyway," Rovine said.

"But you promised we'd visit Aya's family," Dani said with a pleading voice. Aya was the daughter of Ruben and Sarah Openheim.

"Of course we will meet them! But we can visit them anytime. Ruben and Sarah are always happy to have us stay with them," Ian said.

"Great, because Aya asked me when we were going to visit them," Dani said.

"Oh, you are keeping in touch?" Rovine was surprised.

"We're chatting online, occasionally."

"Well, we might visit the Openheims for the summer vacation then," Rovine offered, looking at Ian.

"Why not? That sounds great, actually. We've never been to Israel on holiday," Ian said looking over Dani's shoulder. He spotted a Skype window open on the screen of Dani's laptop, "Are you still chatting with your friends this late?"

"Yea, but we're not just chatting, Dad, we're pigpen writing. And we've gone a step further. We are now also working on pigpen anagramming and monogramming."

"That sounds really interesting," Rovine said and added sternly, "But it's past eleven, Dani! You should have gone to bed by now."

"Mom, you know me, I was just going to bed..."

"Precisely because I know you, Dani, I want you to turn off the laptop, brush your teeth and go straight to bed," Rovine said as she and Ian smiled at their son and left the room.

3

SOFIA, BULGARIA

30 APRIL 2020

Sofia was bathing in the rays of the early morning April sun. Spring had arrived in full swing. It was quite warm outside during the day but the morning air was still cool. In Rovine and Ian's house, the window of their bedroom was half-open so the cool air was gushing in. At exactly seven, the alarm clock went off. His eyes still shut Ian pressed a button to switch it off. He hugged Rovine and kissed her. She kissed him back. They had slept like tired puppies, very contented to be curled together in their own bed. Rovine was slow to force herself out of Ian's hug and to get out of the warm bed, but she knew she had to get Dani off to school. She tied on her dressing gown, shoved her feet in her slippers and hurried downstairs. Ian slid out of bed too and went to wake Dani up.

Within minutes, the aroma of fresh coffee wafted through the house and Ian, shaving while still a bit sleepy, grinned at his reflection in the bathroom mirror.

A bit later and with his bookbag slung over his shoulder, Dani skipped down the stairs two at a time and slid into his seat at the table. "Here's your breakfast, darling," Rovine said as she placed a plate with two sandwiches and a cup of milk in front of him and kissed him on the forehead.

"Thank you, Mom," he smiled at his caring mother.

"Have you prepared yourself for today's lessons?" Ian asked his son, as he joined the family at the table.

"Sure, Dad," he replied biting off a big chunk of the grilled sandwich oozing with cheese and eggs.

"Hun, would you pass me the sugar?" Ian loved calling his wife like that because she was both his sweetheart and she was Hungarian.

"Dad, now that you've finished the Jerusalem project, are we still keeping Israel's flag in the living room?" Dani took a gulp of milk. His parents looked at him quizzically.

"Why?" Ian was puzzled by the question.

"I like it."

"You do?" Rovine asked surprised.

"Yes, I like the huge star in the middle of it. Might as well hang it in my room, if you don't mind," Dani grinned at his parents.

Ian glanced at Rovine and said, "Why not? I'll help you hang it in your room. Now get ready for school, all right?"

"Thanks. See you later!" He jumped up from the table, grabbed his schoolbag, and raced out the door just as the school minibus slowed to a stop in front of the house.

Rovine and Ian were a bit surprised at Dani's request to have the Israeli flag hung in his room. They spoke about it. They had been involved with the Safe Haven project for quite a few years. The flag of Israel had been hanging in their kitchen all along.

"Finally, it makes sense, Rovine. It has to. Dani must have grown fond of the flag with its massive and captivating star in the middle," he concluded looking at her.

"What can I say, he's taken so much after you," she smiled at him.

******

In the evening, after dinner, Dani and Ian carefully removed the Israeli flag from the kitchen wall and transferred it upstairs to Dani's room. There father and son drilled two small holes in the wall, fixed two hooks and mounted the flag on them.

"There you go, Dani!" Ian said as they finished the job. The flag of Israel now hung on the wall across the window and above Dani's bed. The huge Star of David could be clearly seen.

"Thanks, Dad. I'll take a picture of it and send it to Aya."

"Great."

"Yes, I'm sure she will like it."

"It's getting late. You should go to bed now, Dani."

"I've got the feeling you want to ask me something?"

"No, I don't, it's okay, really."

"Night, Dad."

"Good night, Dani."

4

SOFIA, BULGARIA
1 MAY 2020
EVENING

Despite the fact that it was a long and tedious day, Dani didn't feel exhausted. He was sitting on his desk and writing his homework. From time to time he would stop, think for awhile and resume his writing. The flag of Israel hung impressively on the wall across the desk. At one point, his eyes fell on the huge blue Star of David in the middle of it. It was so huge, its lines thick, its structure solid, its rays sharp. All too naturally, Dani's eyes locked on one of those lines and began following it. They got to its end and made a right turn and then went up. A second turn followed and a sharp descent. Another right turn and his eyes went back to the starting point. Almost without realizing it, he had made a triangle. It took a moment for his mind to register and process what had just happened. Then, invariably, it hit him like an oncoming freight train. *I've just completed a triangle.* His eyes began frantically going up and down, making right and left turns. He didn't know how long it took him to do that but after awhile his face froze in amazement. *Wow, there are so many geometric figures.* His expression was one of instant revelation. He hadn't simply discovered geometric figures. He'd just come up with something way bigger. *These are symbols…*

******

"Are you sure you don't need my help with your homework in Bulgarian?" Rovine asked Dani when she had finished going through all his assignments. She had come earlier to his room to help him with some of his homework.

"Sure, Mom, it's already done."

"Great, so you can go straight to bed now. We all have to get up early tomorrow."

"All right, all right, I know... but I want to show both of you something first," Dani said and called out his father.

"Wow, the flag looks really nice, Dani!" Rovine smiled as Ian entered the room.

"It does," Ian said and beamed at his son. In the meantime Dani had taken out a sheet of paper from the top of his desk.

"You remember I told you I was pigpen-writing with my friends and that we'd gone a step further by pigpen anagramming and monogramming?" He was excited.

"Yes, we do remember," Rovine replied, casting a quick glance at Ian. He gave her a reassuring smile.

"As I was doing my homework earlier this evening something about the huge Star of David grabbed my attention. I'm not sure what it was. I was just staring at the star for a long time until I caught myself sketching parts of it in my mind. Then I just put it all down on paper. Look," he said and showed them a sheet of paper upon which he had drawn several Stars of David. Some of the lines were thicker than the others to indicate the parts that had been deliberately made more prominent. And indeed, there they were, four neatly outlined symbols. Ian and Rovine were astounded by this discovery.

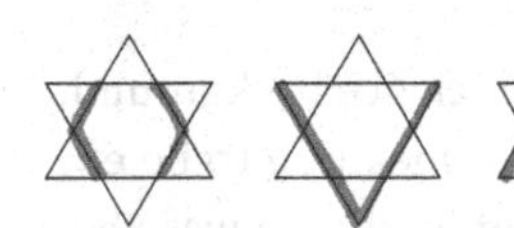

"This way four of the pigpen symbols emerged," Dani explained and showed them the symbols and their corresponding letters, as follows:

<=U; >=T; V=S; Λ=V

"UTSV?" Rovine said, as she sounded out the letters.

"It doesn't mean anything," Ian affirmed.

"Perhaps then TUVS?" she offered.

"The same," Ian said. "And so is the case with VUTS."

"You are right. There is no meaningful combination but it was curious for me to find them interwoven in the graphics of the star," Dani said enthusiastically.

"It is indeed a singular finding, my boy," Ian shuffled Dani's hair.

"Dani, this is really interesting but it's getting late, really late already. Now, turn off your laptop and go straight to bed, please," Rovine said firmly.

Dani shrugged and quietly obeyed his parents but his demeanor was one of longing to stay awake and work on his discovery. *There might be more encoded information. I really want to find it out.*

For a brief moment, his parents exchanged quick glances and then left the room to get themselves ready for bed. Rovine and Ian were caught up in their own thoughts. They were contemplating the possibilities offered by Dani's discovery. From the standpoint of his mathematical linguistics, Ian saw an opportunity for investigating how a set of signs were related to linguistic symbols such as letters. Ian's mind was able to see further than the mere symbols and letters thus also unveiling relations to numbers which, according to him, held many riddles. He had an acute sense for details.

From the standpoint of her cognitive science background, however, Rovine could see a rich field of meaning to be explored. Since she was very diligent in her work, she was able to dig deep into the meaning of words and phrases until she uncovered every possible connotation. Nothing escaped her attention. For the moment however, Dani had only uncovered letters, no particular words. She knew her son wouldn't give up so easily. Once he got on to something he wouldn't stop until he saw the thing through. It was a matter of time.

5

SOFIA, BULGARIA

2 MAY 2020

EVENING TIME

After the evening meal's dishes were done, Rovine, Ian and Dani went into the living room of their house. What made the Magdev's spacious living room so special were not only the bottom-to-top windows opening the space into the garden but also the large number of paintings on the walls. Ian loved abstract and surrealist art and throughout the years he had gathered a decent collection of it. In addition to the paintings, on one of the walls there was a bookshelf with a compilation of books.

Once settled on the long and soft sofa, they spoke about how their day had passed and what each of them had to do the following day. They also checked Dani's homework and Ian helped him with a few mathematical problems he had had trouble solving. It was obvious the three of them had a perfect relationship of mutual respect and much love for one another.

"Mom, Dad, let's go upstairs. I want to show you something." When they entered the room, Dani went straight to his desk and picked up a sheet of paper.

"I think I've discovered something," he said to his parents as he showed them the sheet with some larger letters on it.

"Are these six letters?" Rovine asked with curiosity.

"Yesterday evening I sketched four of the pigpen symbols out of David's Star. Guess what?"

"You've sketched six Cyrillic letters out of it now, as I see it," Ian remarked.

"They are interwoven in the star, Dad. Look and follow my finger," Dani said as he began to describe an A following some of the lines of the Star of David.

"Oh well, you are right. A is indeed interwoven in the star."

"And so are the remaining five letters, Dad. What's more these are the only six letters from the entire Cyrillic alphabet - АДΛСУХ - isn't that odd?"

"I guess we have to find out. Dani, give me a sheet of paper."

"Dad, these are the only six letters. There are no others."

"I see that, son. What I am trying to figure out is whether they'd yield anything meaningful."

"I've already spotted a few words. Look, there is ДУХ meaning *spirit* and СУХ meaning *dry* and ХΛАД meaning *coolness*."

"Then there is СΛУХ for *hearing* and ХУΛА for *obscenity*," Rovine chimed in.

"There's also ΛУД for *crazy*," Ian said and smiled.

"And АД for *hell*," Rovine added.

"Yes, plenty of words, I can see that but nothing coherent has yet emerged," Ian said pensively.

"Maybe there isn't anything coherent at all, just individual words. Think about it. Perhaps it's just wishful thinking on our part."

"But there may be something coherent nonetheless."

"Dani discovered the letters by accident and as though we are now participating in a game," Rovine glanced at Ian.

"Sure, you have a point but who says it's anything but a game and you can't have coherent messages, right? Hun, we're just playing now, relax. Moreover we've got nothing to lose by trying to find something meaningful these six letters might yield."

"Yea, Dad, let's try!" Dani urged with excitement.

"I am intrigued. I think we should give it a try. We've got much to gain if we find something."

"You may even win the game," Rovine said looking at Ian.

"Precisely my point," he replied.

"Yes, absolutely, but it's getting late and I don't think it's the proper time to start something that might lead to many hours of occupation..."

"Mom, can't we stay up a little longer? Come on!"

"Dani, no, it's time you went to bed. We'll talk about this tomorrow," Rovine said and held Ian's arm as they walked together out of Dani's room. He frowned. It was just getting so interesting.

They entered their bedroom without talking and both got ready for bed in comfortable silence. Rovine, wearing a nightgown and robe, noticed Ian looked rather pensive as she brushed her teeth and rinsed her face. She kicked off her slippers and crawled under the covers on her side of the bed; Ian was very preoccupied and seemed seriously distracted.

"Still looking at those letters?" Rovine punched her pillow, put her head down in the middle of it, and turned to face Ian.

"Just scrambling combinations of them in my mind..." he looked at her, his expression solemn.

"And? Have you found anything already?"

"You'd be surprised. Don't think your cognitive science holds all the answers. My mathematical linguistics has a big say, too. Besides, I think those Bible lessons I had in secondary school have finally paid off."

"What do you mean?"

"Look at this perfect pangram," he said as he showed her the small sheet of paper that read С ХУЛДА.

"*With Huldah!* You are right, it is indeed a pangram."

"Exactly," he smiled victoriously.

"It sounds like a name to me."

"And it really is. It's the name of an Old Testament prophetess. Pass me my SkyPhone, please. Thank you," said Ian as he logged online and hit the homepage button. Google's website uploaded in a blink of the eye and they heard the familiar voice of the elderly man saying cheerfully, 'Hi, it's Uncle Google here, ask me anything you want!' The famous search engine had been slightly renamed and advanced to voice-controlled browsing. Ian simply had to say "Who is Huldah?" and in another blink of the eye, Uncle Google supplied a rich list of hits. Ian clicked on the first hit - the one of Encyclopedia Judaica - and began to read aloud. "The name Huldah - חלדה in Hebrew - belonged to one of altogether seven prophetesses mentioned by name in the Tanakh, the Hebrew Bible. She was the wife of certain Shallum who was the keeper of the royal wardrobe during the reign of King Josiah. In II Kings, when Hilkiah found the lost copy of the Torah in the Temple, on order by King Josiah he was sent to consult Huldah about the authenticity of the recovered scroll. It is also known that in addition to being a prophetess, Huldah had her own school established in Jerusalem where she taught."

"Okay, now we've got a very broad picture of who Huldah was but that still doesn't help us very much. I mean, think about it for a moment, Ian. Why would the name of an Old Testament prophetess be interwoven in David's Star?"

"At this point I am as clueless as you are, Rovine. Clearly, this brief explanation won't help us right away."

"Let's try and figure out what With Huldah really means. To do this we will need to place it in its proper context. How do we do that?"

"We may want to consult somebody, an expert in the field perhaps?."

"But who?"

"I'm not sure. Maybe we could call Ruben. He might be able to help us solve this riddle."

6

SOFIA, BULGARIA

3 MAY 2020

Drawn by the aroma of fresh coffee wafting through the house, Rovine headed directly for the kitchen. She found Ian standing by the table and talking on the phone.

"Yes, Ruben, we are all fine here. Thanks for asking," he said and switched on his SkyPhone's loudspeaker to enable Rovine to join in the conversation.

"Hi, Ruben, greetings from me, too," she said and smiled.

"I'm happy to hear you, dear Rovine. It's always a pleasure," Ruben said.

"How are Sarah and Aya?" she asked. The two families had known each other for over six years now, from the time before the beginning of the project Safe Haven for Israel. They had remained close friends and had paid each other occasional visits. The Magdevs had never really spent holidays in Israel, other than short working trips, which was how Dani had become such a good friend with Aya.

"They're just fine, and looking forward to the summer holidays. By the way, Sarah and I would like to invite you to come and spend some time with us here in Israel this summer."

"Thanks for the invitation. You'd be surprised but Dani asked us when he'd be able to meet Aya!" Rovine smiled at Dani, who had just entered the kitchen and now blushed. He felt a little embarrassed he was given away.

"Aha, I see. It's interesting because Aya asked me the same question. I suspect they're up to something," Ruben laughed.

"You never know," Rovine laughed, too. "In any case, we will call you for sure about your kind invitation."

"Ruben," Ian spoke up.

"Yes?"

"The reason I am calling you is because I think Dani came across something really interesting yesterday," Ian wasted no time getting to the main point of the call.

"He's right, Ruben," Rovine chimed in.

"I'm eager to hear what it is." Ruben was curious.

"Dani discovered six Cyrillic letters interwoven in David's Star," Ian said and explained to Ruben how Dani had stumbled across the letters. Ian also told Ruben that was not all. "When you arrange the six letters, they miraculously read 'With Huldah.'"

"Huldah? The Old-Testament prophetess?" Ruben was dubious.

"Yes, exactly, no other but her."

"Interwoven in David's Star?"

"Correct..." Ian tried to be calmly reassuring.

"Are you sure?"

"Absolutely. One hundred-and-one percent sure, Ruben."

"But what has Huldah to do with King David? As far as I remember she lived a couple of centuries after he died."

"Just like you, we've got loads of questions and hardly any answers. That's why we need assistance. We need to speak to someone well-versed in the Hebrew Bible..."

"Um, the Tanakh you say. Let me think about it and call you back. All right?"

"Sure!" Ian said. They bid farewell and ended the call, both eager to pursue the subject further.

******

Usually Ian and Rovine drove to work. From time to time, before going up to his office, Ian would first go for a walk downtown. He would pass between the Parliament and the Alexander Nevski Cathedral, the largest of its kind in Bulgaria, and would continue further down to the former palace of the king, now the national gallery. From there he would proceed west to the Sheraton Hotel, swerve down George Washington street, and pass by the magnificent and distinctively decorated building of Sofia Synagogue, a unique landmark for the city. It was the third-largest synagogue in Europe. Today he did the same but this time, just as he headed back to university, his SkyPhone rang. He pulled it out of his handbag, the telephone's screen indicating the caller ID. It was Ruben Openheim.

"Hi, Ruben! Thank you for your quick response."

"Not at all, my friend. Thinking of whom I should call for an expert opinion, I remembered one of Peace Now's collaborators, Professor Nathan Epstein. He teaches Biblical history at Hebrew University. He's an expert in his field."

"Excellent!"

"I've already told him about Dani's discovery. He agreed on taking a look at it. By the way, I think you can contact Rabbi Loew, as well."

"Both ideas are great and I'm getting excited."

"Nathan is genuinely intrigued and I can text you his SkyPhone and email if you wish..."

"That would be superb. Many thanks, Ruben!"

"You're more than welcome, Ian. I'll send you the contact info for Nathan immediately and we look forward to seeing you and your family very soon."

"Again, thank you so much. Until then..."

Ian hung up his SkyPhone. Shortly afterward it vibrated three successive times, indicating he had just received an incoming text message. Ian hurriedly opened it and copied Nathan Epstein's contact information in his address book. He decided to get in touch with the man as soon as he had a chance.

7

DIMONA, ISRAEL
3 MAY 2020
MOSSAD HEADQUARTERS

As one of the leading intelligence services in the world, the Mossad has been endowed with the responsibility of protecting Jewish communities and Israeli citizens not only in Israel but also around the globe. The director of the Mossad reports directly to the Prime Minister of Israel and there is no corner of the planet where its highly trained and respected operatives can't access and protect, if need be.

In fact, the Mossad is a body of different entities, the most extensive of them being the Collections Department. It is responsible for intelligence collection from all over the world as well as for the conducting of covert operations worldwide.

Not a whole lot is known by the public about the Mossad other than the fact that its central building is located in the desert city of Dimona, in Herzliega, a suburb north of Tel Aviv. The offices of this prestigious organization are housed in a nondescript building deliberately constructed to appear insignificant.

Early in the morning, in one of the offices on the third floor, there was a knock on the door. It opened briefly and then closed imperceptibly. A slender dark-haired young operative dressed in a smart black suit squeezed himself through the doorway as quick as a shadow. He stood at attention before a bareheaded man in his late sixties sitting behind a large desk who was none other than the notorious Colonel Zeller from the Mossad's special task force. Aside from the Israeli flag hanging on the wall behind Zeller and a framed photograph of him, as a very young man in military attire, standing proudly next to David Ben-Gurion, one of modern-day Israel's founding fathers, the office lacked any other decoration, its plainness thus perfectly fitting the defense-forces past of its occupant. Only when Zeller looked up did the young operative speak.

"Sir, we've received a report of a curious conversation between Openheim and the couple from Bulgaria this morning."

"I'm listening, Weissman." Zeller raised his eyebrows.

"The conversation was about the discovery of some interwoven symbols and letters in the Star of David. It's all in the report, including a transcript, sir."

"Thank you, agent Weissman. You are dismissed," Zeller said as Weissman handed him a black file. With the same adroit movement as he had used to enter, the young operative slipped from the room, as silent and as unobtrusive as a shadow.

8

SOFIA, BULGARIA
5 MAY 2020
EARLY EVENING

After getting home from Sofia University, Ian and Rovine decided to contact Professor Nathan Epstein before preparing the dinner. The SkyPhone's speaker was on. When the professor answered, both greeted him and Ian told him it was the prophetess Huldah they were calling about. Professor Epstein responded he already knew the reason and said he was greatly intrigued by their son's discovery of the hidden letters and symbols in the Star of David. Then he went on to add a brief synopsis of the biography of the Old Testament prophetess who was related to the prophet Jeremiah. He explained she had lived in Jerusalem during the reign of King Josiah who was admired for his individualism, as was Huldah. During extensive remodeling of the Temple, the high priest, Hilkiah, found the lost copy of the Book of Torah, the Pentateuch. He proudly took his discovery to the king who ordered it revealed to Huldah in order to validate its authenticity. She was the only one able to read the symbols written on the top of each page of the scrolls, a method devised after David became king of Israel.

"Something had to have made her an expert of sorts if she were the only one able to validate the copy, am I right?" Ian suggested.

"Yes, and in modern-day terms she was a kind of expert," Professor Epstein said.

"But then the question would be - an expert in what?" Rovine joined in eagerly.

"Precisely. In her time, she was the only one able to read the symbols written on the top of each copy of the Torah scrolls made after David became king," the professor explained.

"What symbols?" Ian was puzzled.

"David had invented a flexible shield for his army's protection whose structure consisted of interweaving two opposite-pointed triangles, just as you see them on the flag of Israel, and covering them with an iron plate on top. This design is known as Magen David - the Shield of David - and also as the Seal of King Solomon."

"Why were the triangles interwoven?" Ian was curious.

"Good question! King David had at least two reasons for that. The first reason was to give flexibility and strength to the shield. The second one was more sophisticated."

"What do you mean, Professor?" Rovine was in bewildered and so was Ian.

"It was for secrecy, for protecting all communication between his army units. David devised a twenty-two-symbol cipher - each symbol corresponding to one of the twenty-two letters of the Hebrew alphabet - based on simple strokes combined in triangles and other basic geometric forms derived from those triangles. The ingenuity of David's cipher also consisted in the fact that the king's high command could memorize it over time by simply looking at the structure of their shields and sketching out the symbols in their mind."

"So the cipher was only used by David's high-ranking command?" Ian asked.

"Not only. When Solomon built the First Temple in Jerusalem, he ordered the scribe who made the Temple's copy of the Torah to include on top of it a string of symbols from his father's cipher."

"Naturally, the father taught the son," Rovine chimed in.

"Exactly. What's more, it is claimed that the legendary Seal of King Solomon had the two interwoven triangles engraved on it. This way Solomon could constantly rehearse the secret symbols in his mind." Professor Epstein agreed.

"Do you know what the symbols on the temple copy signify?" Ian asked.

"No, I don't know. But people say they served as authenticating marks that ensured the originality of the Torah copy and its belonging to the Temple."

"But how did Huldah know how to read these marks on the lost copy found by Hilkiah?" Ian had started making notes as they talked.

"A reasonable question, Mr. Magdev. As I mentioned earlier, Huldah was exceptional. She had a school in Jerusalem and was one of a long line of descendants of Heldai, David's twelfth captain of the monthly courses for the temple service and one of his high-ranking command. They say Huldah acquired the knowledge of David's cipher from her father who had acquired it from his father and so back in time until Heldai. They also claim that in every generation there are only thirty-six people who are able to read David's cipher. Apparently, in her generation, Huldah was one of those people while in the previous one, it was her father."

"Did anyone born after her know how to read David's cipher?" Rovine asked.

"Sure, as I said, thirty-six people in every generation. I will give you an example. There is a century-old and hardly-known legend told in the annals of the fourth-century Armenian historian Moses of Chorene. The legend tells the story of the kingdom of Osroe founded by the Abgar dynasty. In the 1st century C.E., Osroe was part of the powerful Armenian Empire. The name of the king of Osroe was Abgar whereas that of his queen was Helena. The interesting fact is that the royal family converted to Judaism."

"When did that take place?" Ian was intrigued.

"In about 30 C.E., King Abgar and Queen Helena sent their five sons to Jerusalem to obtain superior knowledge of their ancestral language, customs, and mores. Queen Helena moved to Jerusalem and had a palace built for her in the northern part of *Ir David*. The royal family became prominent in Erez Israel because on a number of difficult occasions they helped the Israelites by sending them food and money. Monobaz, one of their sons, ordered that all the handles of the vessels used in the Second Temple on the Day of Atonement be made of pure gold. Queen Helena did several other important things in Israel as well. She ordered the building of a large booth called *sukkah* in the town of Lod for *Sukkot,* the Feast of the Tabernacles - which was the festival commemorating the *sukkot,* the difficult time in which the Children of Israel lived in the wilderness after the Exodus from Egypt. The *sukkah* ordered by Queen Helena was decorated with short inscriptions in an unknown script people attributed to the queen's homeland and subsequently became the pride of the community of Lod. Then she commissioned a golden candelabrum and set it over the entrance of the Temple. There was, however, one more thing the queen did. She ordered a golden tablet on which the Ten Commandments were written with a special method of shorthand writing known as *notarikon*. This tablet was also placed among the treasures of the Temple. It is said the tablet contained a number of unusual signs for abbreviation. Legend has it these signs were taken from David's cipher as Queen Helena had once seen the original Seal of King Solomon. That latter part of the legend is, of course, highly unlikely."

"It seems however the first part of the legend is very important..." Ian was taking copious notes as the professor spoke.

"Yes, because it ascertains in a way that Queen Helena knew part of David's cipher and incorporated it into her shorthand writing."

"Does anyone know what happened to the tablet?" Rovine wondered aloud.

"It disappeared after the destruction of the Second Temple – also known as the Temple of Herod – by the Romans on the 10th of Av, 70 C.E."

"Logically then, I must ask you, Professor, how is it possible that a Jewish convert – be that person a queen – knew certain parts of the cipher, that most Jews didn't know themselves?" Ian was puzzled.

"She accomplished so much for Israel and saved so many Jewish lives, that she thereby gained the trust of the Jewish sages who enlightened her in some of the most profound secrets and tenets of their faith. What's more, the royal family of Queen Helena and her descendants gained so distinguished a reputation they were buried in a chamber in the Tomb of the Kings in Jerusalem..."

"Do you know what the symbols of the cipher looked like?" Ian asked.

"Legend has it some of them looked very much like the symbols of a simple system of enciphering that schoolchildren use even nowadays to amuse themselves. They call it pigpen writing..." When Ian and Rovine heard this they were shocked.

"Aren't they the same ones Dani uses to write to some of his friends?" Rovine was astonished.

"I believe they are," Ian said. Unable to conceal his amazement, he added, "Professor, our son uses such symbols to write to his friends."

"Ah, there you go. As I told you, schoolchildren find remarkable ways to entertain themselves."

"Who invented the pigpen cipher?" Rovine asked.

"To answer that question, I need to tell you yet another story."

"We are eager to hear it," Rovine said.

"Well, following the destruction of the Second Temple, a small number of Osroenites, related to the converted royal family, remained loyal to Judaism despite the fact that the rest of the Osroenites eventually converted to Christianity. Those few still adhering to Judaism moved to the city of Edessa or modern-day Şanliurfa in southeastern Turkey and settled there. Then, a couple of centuries later, the First Crusade started in August of 1096. It took three years for an army of twelve thousand men to march through Eastern Europe and the Middle East and reach Jerusalem. On the fifteenth of July in 1099, Jerusalem was recaptured. The first head of the newly established 'kingdom of Jerusalem' was Godefroy de Bouillon. However, De Bouillon did not take the title king but chose another one - *Advocatus Sancti Sepulchri* or Defender of the Holy Sepulcher. In this first crusade, his brother Baldwin I and his cousin Baldwin II accompanied him. Shortly after the successful recapture of the Holy City, Godefroy died and was succeeded by his brother. His cousin Baldwin II however, became count of Edessa and reigned there from 1100 to 1118. The fact that he stayed for such a long time in Edessa and was himself a Christian, the count gradually established close connections with some of the more prominent representatives of the small Christian community in the city. Baldwin II showed deep appreciation for the community and was therefore accepted favorably by its members. In him, they saw a figure that could help them improve their living conditions and gain much more advantageous positions for trade among the prevailing Muslims. This way, knowingly or not, Baldwin II managed to gain their trust and hence access to their most sacred secrets. In time, he was slowly but surely initiated in the esoteric knowledge of this small Edessian community. And, I should not forget to mention, their long-preserved secrets."

"What secrets?" Rovine was excited and curious.

"Secrets that the Edessians had been keeping for centuries and were, for the time being, resolved to continue handing down from one generation to another. It was there, in Edessa, where Baldwin II saw for the first time the preserved original of the golden tablet with the Ten Commandments Queen Helena had ordered for the Temple of Solomon. The Christian Edessians told him their Judaism-converted ancestors had managed to save it from the Temple before it was ravished and razed to the ground by the Babylonian King Nebuchadnezzar in 586 B.C.E."

"How is that related to the pigpen cipher?" Ian asked.

"On the 14th of April, 1118, Baldwin II was officially crowned King of the Christian kingdom of Jerusalem. He replaced the deceased Baldwin I. In the same year of Baldwin II's coronation, a curious event took place in Jerusalem. Certain Hugues de Payns founded a religious-military order of knights who pledged to protect Christian pilgrims on their way to Jerusalem. The order became known as the Poor Knights of Christ and of the Temple of Solomon. Initially, the order didn't distinguish itself much from other similar formations. However, once Baldwin II became king, he provided them with quarters in one of the wings of his royal palace on top of Temple Mount. Hence the second part of their name and their rapid gain in prominence! Later on, Baldwin II donated the entire palace to the order. Since then, the order became known as the Knights of the Temple, and that further boosted their reputation and influence. The founder of the order, De Payns, was its Grandmaster from 1118 to 1136. In that period, De Payns and Baldwin devised together a secret Templar cipher to be used for vital communications among the different branches of the order across Europe and the Holy Lands."

"What did this cipher consist of?" Ian was intrigued.

"Triangles and triangle-based symbols. It is also claimed that later on, the Freemasons adopted that very same cipher. Today, they say the pigpen cipher is the closest heir to the Templar cipher," the professor added.

"So are you suggesting that somehow, miraculously, down through the centuries, some part of King David's cipher coincidentally, or not, remained preserved through the efforts of Queen Helena, down to Baldwin II and the Templars and still further to the Freemasons?" Ian was fascinated.

"Not only through their efforts. You probably won't be aware of this fact but the very first Masonic lodges already existed at the time of the construction of the First Temple in Jerusalem. King David had paved the way for their existence well before the beginning of the construction works. You might also be surprised to learn that King Solomon and his brother Nepheg, who supervised the construction, communicated with the lodges' grandmasters using the cipher invented by King David. This way they wanted to make sure all issues remained confidential, especially everything related to the building of the *debir* or the Holy of Holies. You also wouldn't know that the Temple masons secretly incorporated the symbols of this cipher in the architectural designs and ornaments decorating the Temple."

"So, do you think there's any person alive today who would be able to read King David's cipher?" Ian asked.

"Not one, but thirty-six people in this generation."

Ian and Rovine cordially thanked Professor Epstein who reassured them they could contact him anytime if they had any more questions.

After they hung up the SkyPhone, Ian and Rovine stared at each other with a million thoughts racing between them. They knew they were on the brink of a momentous time in their lives.

9

SOFIA, BULGARIA,

6 MAY 2020

BEFORE MIDNIGHT

"Is Dani already in bed, honey?" Ian asked as Rovine emerged from the bathroom and got in bed next to him.

"Yes," she said and hugged him. Then they kissed gently.

"How was today?" he asked, still holding her in his arms.

"Great, met a new colleague...she'll hold some of the extra classes. How was your day?"

"Plenty of work as usual, after a few days' absence."

"Yes, I know what you mean! It was the same in my office."

"Thing is, despite all the work, I couldn't stop thinking about those six Cyrillic letters all day. I've checked out a few ideas..."

"Really? I thought we were through with this, especially after the conversation with Professor Epstein."

"I thought so as well. But something has been tickling my imagination."

"Have you come up with anything?"

"You'd be surprised. You know that ancient alphabets such as the Hebrew, Greek, Latin and others were used as numerals before the advent of the Hindu-Arabic system of numbers."

"Yes, I know that. So?"

"It was the same case with the Cyrillic letters.

A was 1; Д - 4; Л - 30; С - 200; У - 400; and Х was 600."

"Very interesting..."

"Once I got the numbers, a brilliant idea hit me. I decided to translate them into their corresponding Hebrew numerals."

"Now that's something! What did you get?"

"As you can imagine, I got a string of six Hebrew letters:

1 = aleph; 4 = daleth; 30 = lamed; 200 = resh; 400 = taw;

and 600 = final mem."

"It seems your knowledge of Hebrew certainly helped you with that."

"And much more in fact."

"So you instantly began unscrambling the letters, right?"

"Exactly. Not long afterward, I discovered the Hebrew noun *towr* (תור) meaning 'a turtledove', the preposition ל or to and the name Adam (אדם)," Ian showed her a piece of paper he had written the words on.

"*A turtledove to Adam?*"

"Precisely."

"The words make sense as a combination, all right. But do you have any idea what the whole phrase means?"

"The same question kept bugging me as well."

"And?"

"Since Adam is mentioned in the phrase, I gathered it might be somehow related to the Bible but then again I had no clue in what way. Without proper context and despite the grammatical correctness of the phrase, its meaning remains obscure. I think we should call Rabbi Loew for help. What do you think?"

"By the look of it you may be right, we should definitely call him."

"I think he might be the only person we know who would be able to shed some light on the phrase," Ian said.

"First thing in the morning, darling," Rovine said as she kissed him goodnight.

"You bet," he said and kissed her back.

10

SOFIA, BULGARIA,
7 MAY 2020

The next morning at breakfast, Ian shared with Dani what he had discovered the day before by translating the Cyrillic letters into their number equivalents. Dani was thrilled. Rovine reminded Ian about his idea of calling Rabbi Loew. Before they left the house, Ian did just that.

When Rabbi Loew answered the phone, Ian told him everything about the phrase he had come across. He asked him to try to elaborate on it over the SkyPhone's speaker so that the three of them could hear his explanation.

"In antiquity, turtledoves were one of the prescribed species of fowl used for sacrifice," the Rabbi said.

"Hence, *a turtledove to Adam* would mean *one turtledove to Adam to sacrifice*. Am I right?" Ian offered.

"We don't know whether Adam had up to that point offered such sacrifices..." The Rabbi cleared his throat and continued. "What we know from the Torah is that the first bird sacrifice was offered by Noah. After all animals were let out of the ark, Noah built an altar and took a bird from every clean fowl including a turtledove and offered an olah to the Lord. This is described in Genesis eight, verse twenty."

"An olah?" Rovine asked puzzled.

"In Biblical Hebrew, *olah* (עלה) means *'that which goes up'* and denotes a burnt sacrifice. When we speak about *olah*, you should know the person who offers it is called *adam*, that is, a man..."

"Of course," Ian exclaimed, slapping his forehead and turning to Rovine. "In Hebrew, Adam is the name of the first man but as a noun, it means 'a man'."

"Exactly," the Rabbi continued, "So your phrase would read *'a turtledove to a man'* that is, each man, *adam*, offering *a turtle-*

dove. As small fowl, turtledoves were generally offered by poor men because larger birds were too expensive."

"What did an olah consist of?" Rovine asked.

"The burnt offering consisted of *an adam,* a man, who brought an animal, a turtledove in this case, to the north side of the Temple's altar and slaughtered it there. Then the slaughtered bird was handed over to the priest who collected its blood and sprinkled it around the altar. The bird was burned to ashes in the altar's fire thus producing a pleasing odor to the Lord. Hence you have Genesis 8:21: 'And the Lord smelled a sweet savor; and the Lord said in his heart, I will not again curse the ground any more for man's sake...' You should also know that olah was the most common and frequent sacrifice offered in the Temple," the Rabbi explained.

"So the first one to offer an olah was Noah, not Adam?" Ian's tone was very pensive.

"That's right. There is no evidence to suggest that Adam ever offered an olah. Maybe he did, maybe he didn't," the Rabbi replied. "However, do you know who offered the first olah whose place is known for sure?"

"No, or at least I can't remember right away..."

"Abraham. Let me quote Genesis 22:2: 'And he, the Lord, said, Take now thy son, thine only son Isaac, whom thou lovest, and get thee into the land of Moriah; and offer him there for a burnt offering upon one of the mountains which I will tell thee of.' Here the Lord commands Abraham to offer Isaac in an olah," the Rabbi paused for a moment. Then he continued.

"It is interesting to note that the Lord orders Abraham to take Isaac to the land of Moriah – the name itself meaning 'chosen by Yah.'"

"But Moriah is the name of the mount on the eastern edge of Jerusalem," Ian was puzzled.

"Later on known under the name Mount Zion on which Ir David stands to-date and on which Solomon built the First Temple," the Rabbi added.

“So the Land of Moriah was the mount in Jerusalem?” Rovine’s brow was furrowed as she struggled to help clarify the matter.

“To be precise, the Land of Moriah originally designated the mount and the surrounding land, that is, the Kidron Valley…”

“So the phrase ultimately refers to olah and to Moriah, am I right?” Ian made an effort to recap the conversation.

“You see, Ian, it is a general phrase and as such it should be construed in the broadest of terms. The phrase itself doesn’t point to anything in particular except for the name of Adam. So, I’d say yes, to answer your question directly. If you take the traditional use of turtledoves as sacrificial fowl, they were used only in olah. Once you get there, you naturally get to the very first olah whose place is known and was on the hill of Moriah where the City of David has always stood.”

“I see,” Ian said.

“Speaking of Noah who offered the very first olah and also of Abraham and the place where he was preparing the olah of his son, I cannot but think of the most evil Nazi interpretation of the Ancient Greek equivalent of the phrase *burnt offering* – the word *holocaust*. The same word that has come to denote the Catastrophe, the *Shoah,* the largest ever and most abhorrent mass extermination of the Jewish Diaspora in the whole of mankind’s history put into effect by the Nazis. Most of my relatives along with another six million Jews perished in the Catastrophe. The Holocaust was Hitler’s perverted interpretation of a burnt offering,” Rabbi Loew said.

“We are so sorry to hear about your relatives,” Rovine said.

“God blessed them. They are now in the Garden of Eden,” the Rabbi made a short pause and then added enigmatically, “In Gan Yav.”

Both Rovine and Ian didn’t understand that last part. They thanked Rabbi Loew and wished him a good day. Then they sat at the kitchen table and discussed what they had just learned while finishing their coffee.

"I am pleasantly surprised to find your knowledge of Hebrew, more than mine, permits us to work in a refined way with the language," Rovine said.

"What do you mean?" Ian slowly stirred his coffee.

"While talking to Rabbi Loew, my mind was arranging and rearranging all kinds of combinations of the six letters. And then I think I discovered something."

"What?"

"Well, when you take away the name Adam consisting of *aleph, daleth* and *mem,* you are left with three letters. Of those, the combination between *taw* and *lamed* yields the Hebrew word *tell* meaning 'mount'. So, you get something like 'Mount Adam'. But one letter, *resh,* remains unused."

"Let me check something," Ian quickly punched in a search string in his Skyphone's browser and when he got the hits delivered by Uncle Google, he began checking them meticulously. "There it is!" He exclaimed.

"What?" she asked.

"The name of the 20th letter in the Hebrew alphabet is *reysh* (ריש) and it means 'poverty'..."

"So, something to the effect of 'Mount Adam in poverty'?"

"Or the mount of man in poverty," Ian grabbed his SkyPhone and pressed to redial the last called number. Rabbi Loew picked up on the second ring.

"Rabbi, it's us again. We've got one more question to ask you," Ian said.

"Fine, go ahead."

"Could you tell us about Mount Adam?" Ian asked and his question remained hanging in a long moment of silence.

"This is the very first and most primordial name of Mount Moriah, Mount Zion and Ir David or David's City – the southeastern hill of Jerusalem on which Solomon built his temple..."

"Why was it called Adam?" Rovine asked.

"The name should speak for itself," the Rabbi said enigmatically.

"What do you mean?" Ian was bewildered.

"It designates the actual place where Adam was created by God."

******

After hanging up the phone, Dani was even more thrilled than before.

"Dad, what the Rabbi explained is amazing," he exclaimed excitedly.

"It sure is," Rovine said.

"Imagine only what other symbols and letters we might find interwoven in the star," Dani was still keyed up with excitement.

"What is it, darling?" Rovine was concerned about Ian's sudden pensive mood.

"I think it's about time we called Ruben and told him what we've accidentally come across."

11

SOFIA, BULGARIA,
8 MAY 2020

Early in the morning, about an hour before they had to wake Dani up, Rovine and Ian decided they'd call Ruben Openheim. When he picked up, both of them waved at his live-cam image on the screen of the SkyPhone.

Ruben smiled and waved back. "Glad to see you both. What gets you up so early today?"

"We're calling because we've been meaning to talk to you about something," Ian glanced at Rovine who nodded in agreement.

"Thank God there's no time difference between Sofia and Jerusalem," Ruben grinned and his eyes twinkled with good humor. "Go ahead! You have my attention!"

"You remember our last conversation about the amazing discovery Dani made a couple of days ago, right?" Ian was hesitant.

"Of course, I remember," Ruben reassured.

"Well, the six Cyrillic letters interwoven in David's Star led us to more amazing discoveries..."

"What do you mean?"

Ian and Rovine explained how Dani's six Cyrillic letters contained in the graphics of David's Star and their discovery of the phrase *"With Huldah"* had led them to substitute the letters for numbers. Then in turn, they had chanced upon the phrase 'a turtledove to an adam' and hence also to 'olah' and the 'land of Moriah.' They also mentioned the conversations with Professor Epstein and Rabbi Loew who had further clarified their discovery.

"It's really amazing what the three of you have stumbled upon," Ruben said after hearing their story. Then he leaned forward and placed his face closer to the camera. Ian and Rovine could only see a close-up of his face, in the relatively small screen of the SkyPhone. "Did Dani come up with the letters all by himself?"

"Of course he did!" Rovine sounded a bit defensive. "Ask him yourself if you wish."

"Oh, no, that's really not the point... I am genuinely amazed by Dani's intelligence. He's the same age as Aya, you know, and has already come up with something so incredible."

"Yes, he's a bright kid, Ruben, and we are really happy about it..." Ian was almost bragging.

"You know what, give me a couple of days to think this through and then I'll give you a call and tell you what I really think about all this and what we can actually achieve. All right?"

Ian and Rovine looked at each other for a brief moment, then Ian nodded. "All right, Ruben, we'll be waiting for your call."

"Send our love to Sarah and Aya," Rovine smiled at Ruben.

"I will," he smiled back and they hung up.

******

In the evening after dinner, the whole family gathered in the living room. They chatted as usual about their day and what had happened. Ian and Rovine asked Dani about school and the approaching end of the academic year. Then Ian changed the subject.

"Dani, I've been thinking about what you said yesterday..."

"What, Dad?" Dani looked at his father expectantly.

"Do you remember when you said we might possibly find other symbols and letters interwoven in the star?"

"I have a gut feeling there's more but..."

"Well, actually, the discovery of the six Cyrillic letters has paved the way for more breakthroughs," Ian glanced at both Rovine and Dani.

"What do you mean?" Rovine asked.

"I realized it only this morning but if you look closely, you'll see two of the six Cyrillic letters - X and C - are actually Roman numerals."

"Oh, yes, a ten and a hundred..." Dani nodded with delight.

"And all this, my dear, comes as no surprise because Roman numerals were vastly popular throughout the Holy Land and the Levant - The Eastern Mediterranean - as a whole during the times of the Roman Empire. These numerals were primarily used for trade purposes."

"Wait a second," Dani said suddenly. "The pigpen s is written the same way as the Latin letter V."

"So, Dani boy, we've got three Roman numerals: V for five; X for ten and C for one hundred."

"Well, actually, there are two tens because there is an X on each wing of David's Star and also two hundreds because there are two Cs, too," Rovine pointed out.

"I've got an idea," Ian said as he picked up a sheet of paper and a writing pen from a small table beside the sofa. "Now, all in all we have four Roman numerals - V, X, X, and C. To learn how many Roman numerals are actually interwoven, we need to start combining them," he said as he began to write rapidly. Rovine and Dani were looking at him with amazement.

"There we go," Ian said in less then a minute. "We've got altogether twenty-one Roman numerals interwoven in David's Star:

V equals 5; X equals 10; XV equals 15; XX - 20; XXV - 25;
XC - 90; XCV - 95; C - 100; CV - 105; CX - 110; CXV - 115;
CXX - 120; CXXV - 125; CXC - 190; CXCV - 195; CC - 200;
CCV - 205; CCX - 210; CCXV - 215; CCXX - 220; CCXXV - 225."

"I'm surprised there are so many! Rovine said.

"Me too," Dani chimed in.

"If we add them up, we get their total sum of 2595," Ian added, dramatically... Mathematics was by far his strongest passion.

"Twenty-five hundred and ninety-five?" Dani was disappointed. "What does it mean?"

"We don't know just yet. But we should probably ask someone else who would know," Ian said.

"Let's do that. It's getting more and more interesting and now I'm curious!" Dani was inspired once again.

Ian picked up his Skyphone and dialed Ruben. After several rings, Ruben answered the phone. He was glad to hear his friend but explained he was busy and would call the following day.

12

SOFIA, BULGARIA
9 MAY 2020
EVENING TIME

Ian's SkyPhone started ringing. As he picked up to answer it he saw the caller ID. It was Ruben, calling just as he had promised.

"Ian..." Ruben sounded very excited. "I told a few people here about Dani's discoveries."

"And?"

"Look, what the three of you have stumbled upon has great potential. I'm not the only person who thinks that. In fact, everybody here thinks that you've merely cracked open the door to something major. And it's just the beginning of something we don't know anything about yet. We've got to open that door and get inside."

"I agree with you, Ruben. What do you suggest we do?"

"I suggest the three of you come here and we work through this together."

"What do you mean?"

"We have to examine your findings as thoroughly as possible. We have to see whether or not we might make any other discoveries, which could turn out to be very important. We won't be able to grasp their full importance at once, but with a little bit of luck and time, who knows?"

"We've discovered something new..."

"Have you already?" Ruben interrupted.

"Well, we're still not sure what to make of it. We don't seem to know how to interpret it."

"This is the reason why I am telling you, you should come over here. It will be easier to work together because I plan to gather a couple of people in a working group, something like a think-tank. And we ride this through together."

“Do you already have certain people in mind?”

“Yes.”

“Have they agreed to do this?”

“Absolutely. You know Rabbi Loew already. Then, you’ve also spoken with Professor Epstein. The only person you don’t know yet is Uri Zohar. He is an expert in the esoteric sciences and Kabbalah.”

“When do you want us there?”

“The sooner the better is my opinion. This way we’ll have more time to work.”

“Ruben, I have to discuss this with Rovine and Dani.”

“Sure, no problem. Call me when you’ve decided what you’re going to do.”

“I will,” Ian said and bid Ruben goodbye.

After hanging up, Ian went to the kitchen where Rovine and Dani were solving problems, part of Dani’s mathematics homework. Dani had a bit more than a month and a half left until the end of the school year. He interrupted them and told them about Ruben’s invitation to travel to Israel. They were almost too excited to speak. Once they calmed down they began making plans. They decided they’d interrupt Dani’s lessons for a couple of days and stay in Israel.

They all laughed delightedly as Ian Googled EL AL’s website.

******

“There’s an EL AL flight from Sofia to Tel Aviv in two days’ time, on the 11th of May,” Ian said when he called back to inform Ruben of their earliest possible arrival in Israel.

“Great, Ian.”

“I’m just going to book the tickets. It’s going to be Flight Number seven sixty-seven arriving at two thirty-eight in the afternoon…if that’s convenient?”

No problem. I’ll pick you up at the airport,” was Ruben’s reply.

PART TWO

The Alphabets

13

BEN GURION AIRPORT
TEL AVIV, ISRAEL
13 MAY 2020

Ruben was waiting in the huge lobby of the airport. He waved when he saw the Magdevs coming out and rushed out to greet them. Ruben gave a hug to each one of them. He was happy to see them and so were they. "Thank you for coming, my friends."

"Thank you for inviting us," Ian smiled.

"How are Sarah and Aya?" Rovine asked.

"They are fine. Actually Aya has been anticipating your arrival for days now," he said as he turned to Dani. Ruben smiled at the boy. "Let's not waste any more time and hurry home. Sarah has prepared something very delicious especially for your arrival."

******

"How is the situation in the country now?" Ian sat down on the front seat of Ruben's impeccably maintained 1967 Sabra Sussita station wagon – a true relic from the dawn of the Israeli auto industry.

"Things are under control, in general. There has been some occasional shelling every now and then but this is always the case, in a way. Unfortunately we cannot stop it," Ruben went on to update his friend on the latest developments of the situation in the country.

"Where are we staying, Ruben?" Rovine asked as the Sabra Sussita drove slowly down Jaffa Boulevard, one of Jerusalem's main thoroughfares, and she watched the pedestrians on the street and the way they were dressed.

"You are staying with us in our flat. That way we'll be together and we won't have to travel back and forth," Ruben glanced at her reflection in the rear view mirror. The Openheims had a second flat where they usually accommodated their guests.

"You mean we are going to the one in Derekh Hevron, right?"

"Yes, exactly."

"Great. I like that area of Jerusalem. Staying with you will definitely spare us some time but to tell you the truth, I like taking public transportation in Jerusalem. It's all so well organized! One rarely needs a car," Rovine waved back to a toddler waving at everyone from his mother's arms.

"This fact has allowed my father and me to keep our Sussita oldtimer in nearly brand new condition for so many years. It has been rarely used..."

"How's the assembling of the working group going?" Ian shifted in his seat, seemingly anxious to get to work.

"I've already informed each of them and they have confirmed their participation. They're arriving in the office tomorrow morning."

"So we begin right away?"

"The more time we spend on this the better..." Ruben's eyes sparkled with delighted anticipation. Within moments, Ruben pulled by the driveway of a modest apartment house. He took out a small remote control and pressed a button. The metal bar striped in white and red and that was blocking the entrance lifted. Ruben pulled into the driveway, parked the Sussita under the house and shut off its engine. Israeli architects had made excellent use of an ancient but very practical and original feat - pile dwellings. Many apartment houses in Israel were built on concrete pillars, thus leaving the basement floor open and accessible to cars from the street. This feat helped protect cars from the relentless sun of the Levant.

After closing the door, Ruben gestured for his guests to follow him inside. They climbed up to the first floor and Ruben rang the apartment's door bell.

Squeals of joy reached their ears as Aya raced to the door, opened it swiftly and threw herself upon Dani with a smile on her face as wide as the sun and her eyes sparkling with joy. All four parents laughed aloud as the overjoyed teenagers preceded them into the home, everyone talking at once.

"Come, let me show you where you can rest," Sarah extended a hand out to Rovine who grasped it gratefully and smiled back.

"It is so gracious of you both to have us as house guests!"

Ian and Ruben were oblivious to the children and the women as the two families merged with each other and already seemed closely bonded. Sarah guided everyone into the family room, which was adjacent to the kitchen area, beyond which was the dining room.

"Look, Ian!" Rovine was delighted with the food and table Sarah had meticulously prepared in the dinning room.

The table was in the middle of the room and set with six places. There was colorful native pottery on top that Rovine guessed was locally made. The vibrant tints of wine and dark green and sunshine yellow were repeated in the fresh flowers in the center, arranged in an antique brass pot. Next to the flowers, a relatively large menorah with seven lit candles proudly stood on. The aroma of roasting leg of lamb made everyone's mouth water and the anticipated feast was another whisper of the promise of a sumptuous meal.

******

After enjoying a lengthy meal, the two families moved into the living room. Over a glass of Israeli wine, they went on chatting about all kinds of things. At some point, they began speaking about the reason that had brought them together - the discovery of the six Cyrillic letters. Ruben asked questions, Rovine and Ian provided answers. They were methodically shaping their working strategy.

In the meantime, 14-year-old Aya, wearing a tight green dress the exact color of her eyes, took Dani by the hand and led him off into the room where he was going to sleep. The guest room had a single bed and a desk and bureau available for his use.

"Dani, I am so happy to see you..." Aya's eyes sparkled and she tossed her long, straight hair over her shoulder.

"Me, too," he said as they hugged each other. There was an obvious mutual current of magnetic attraction between them.

"I thought it would be another eternity before we met," she said, their arms still locked.

"Unfortunately my parents didn't bring me with them the last time they were here," he said looking into her eyes as if he were spellbound.

"I know and I regretted it so much..."

"It doesn't matter. The important thing is that we are together now," he said. Then they heard Sarah, Aya's mother, calling them for dessert, which turned out to be a homemade cake with several lavish layers of delicious whipped cream. Dani and Aya grabbed their servings and went back to the bedroom.

While savoring the tasty cream, Dani told Aya how he had discovered the hidden Cyrillic letters in the Star of David; how his parents had come up with a meaningful message about the prophetess Huldah; how they had found the reference to olah and Moriah; and finally, how together they had discovered three Roman numerals. Aya was very excited and was surprised her father hadn't told her anything.

"So you're saying your parents have come here to reveal the secret of the embedded letters?" Aya asked.

"This is what they told me. There's more. Your father has summoned several knowledgeable people to help them decipher the meaning of the letters and the symbols," Dani said, a dollop of whipped cream on the tip of his nose.

This made Aya laugh aloud at his appearance. A bit embarrassed, Dani instantly made use of a small napkin. "I am sorry I laughed, Dani, but you looked so sweet with this chunk of cream on your nose," Aya grinned.

"I can imagine!"

"What you're saying about the letters and the symbols is really interesting, Dani. How did you happen to discover them?"

"You know, ever since I got the flag of Israel in my room..."

"The one you showed me on the web cam?"

"Exactly... so ever since we mounted it on the wall in my room, the star in the middle has been calling out to me in a mysterious way, constantly drawing my attention. I can't explain it. It's just that I often catch myself looking at it."

"Looking?"

"Staring, gaping, gazing at it, not just looking. And then, shortly afterward, one by one, four of the pigpen symbols became visible. It was as though, how should I put it, they kind of emerged from the graphics of the star."

"Popped up?"

"Rather materialized, revealed themselves, arose... I don't know how I should put it better. And then, not long afterward, the six Cyrillic letters came up much the same way. It's difficult to explain, Aya. The symbols and letters are there. I just happened to see them."

"It's not so easy to spot them. If that had been the case, surely many would have seen them already."

"Maybe many have."

"Somebody would have caught wind of it, had that been the case."

"Maybe somebody has, but kept quiet."

"You're going conspiracy theory or something, Dani?"

"No, no, no. All I am saying is I am surprised I have come to discover something allegedly nobody else has discovered yet. It's hard for me to believe that, do you understand?"

"Maybe, just maybe, Dani, you were meant to discover them and nobody else was. How about that?"

"Me? Come on, why me?"

"I don't know but the fact is a fact, you've discovered them first."

"Yea, yea, I see, but now who's going conspiratorial on me?" He winked at her.

14

DIMONA, ISRAEL
13 MAY 2020
MOSSAD HEADQUARTERS
EARLIER IN THE DAY

The only noise in the plainly furnished office of Colonel Zeller, the high-ranking Mossad officer, was the discreet sound of the air-conditioning system. He was sitting behind his executive hardwood desk, facing the door with his back to the window and was slowly turning the pages of a typewritten file whose manila folder lay open on the sleek wood-grained surface. A knock on the door caused him to look up expectantly but his expression didn't change. A slender young agent dressed in a designer jet suit slipped inside without making a sound. He stood quietly at attention for a few seconds then cleared his throat before speaking.

"Sir, the Bulgarian family has arrived in Israel today." The agent relaying the message did not blink or look at the seated man. "Openheim met them at Ben Gurion Airport. Then he drove them to his house. Here's the detailed surveillance report." He placed a black file envelope on the officer's desk and turned to leave.

"Thank you, Weissman," said the colonel as he picked up the file. Weissman was just about to slip out as silently as he had slipped in when he heard his superior saying "Wait!"

He immediately froze to attention and remained silent.

"Weissman..." said the superior.

"Yes, sir?"

"You know that Openheim is under surveillance by one of our agents?"

"Yes, sir, I know that."

"The Bulgarian family must surely have been invited by him. I want to know why they are here and what the purpose of their visit is. Understood?"

"Yes, sir," Weissman replied and added, "I assume it is related to their phone conversations, sir."

"This is my gut feeling, too. But we need confirmation. Find our operative and work closely together to collect the information I've requested."

"I will, sir."

"And Weissman, I need your report as soon as possible. We've got to be ahead of events... you are dismissed."

Without further communication of any kind, Weissman slipped unobtrusively from the room.

15

JERUSALEM, ISRAEL
14 MAY 2020
PEACE NOW HEADQUARTERS
MORNING

Sarah got up very early in the morning and prepared a typical Israeli breakfast for her guests: lentil soup, hummus with pita bread, yogurt cheese and the usual vegetable salad. Fresh coffee released a mouth-watering aroma. It wasn't long before Ian and Rovine appeared dressed and ready to go. Ruben arrived last, rubbing the sleep out of his eyes, but cheerful nevertheless. Aya and Dani were still sleeping.

After finishing their meal, Ian and Rovine thanked Sarah for the delicious breakfast and hurried out where Ruben was already waiting for them in the car. Sarah gave her husband one last kiss for the morning and waved at them as they drove off. Jerusalem was waking to another busy day with shop owners making final preparations before opening and people crowding around bus stops.

Ian and Rovine knew the way to the Peace Now office well. They had used it so many times while working on the Safe Haven for Israel project. Once again they passed by the building of the Israeli Parliament - the Knesset - and got to the traffic light where they had to make the usual left turn. A few hundred meters down a wide boulevard and they stopped before the fence entrance of a large compound. Ruben parked the car and they got out. Into the compound they hurried toward a twelve-story building. The office of Peace Now was on the sixth floor. The moment the three of them got out of the elevator and went into the foyer, they discovered that the rest of the people invited by Ruben were already there. Ian and Rovine immediately recognized a familiar face. During their work on Safe Haven for Israel, they had met with Rabbi Loew on numerous occasions. He looked almost like before, with his white hair only having grown longer and his long streaked beard grown greyer. He smiled at them and they greeted one another with visible pleasure. Then Ruben introduced Ian and Rovine to the other two men. The first one was Professor Nathan Epstein, who only days before had already proven very helpful. He looked like he was in his sixties, tall, broad-shouldered, and his eyes alert to every detail around him. The second man was Uri Zohar, a man who, as Ruben's earlier description had put it, had devoted his life to Kabbalah and alchemy and had acquired the reputation of an expert in the esoteric sciences. Uri was a relatively short man in his mid-forties, with short-trimmed black hair sticking up as straight as spring grass, his eyes narrow and looking even narrower behind the immense thickness of his glasses.

"Kabbalchemy. This is what I call my life's passion," Uri Zohar said extending his hand for a handshake with Ian and Rovine who discovered he had a funny voice, too, one that couldn't be mistaken for any other.

"Interesting wording," Rovine remarked.

"You see, I've come to realize it is neither only about Kabbalah nor only about alchemy. They often, if not always, overlap and there are, of course, deep-seated reasons for that going back many centuries. So I'll be the kabbalchemist of the group," Uri said and smiled.

Ruben invited everyone to the conference hall of the office. Inside, there was plenty of light coming through the large windows, their shades half-shut. In the middle of the room, there was a large round table. There were six black-leather chairs with a laptop placed in front each of them. Everyone took their seat. Ruben didn't sit but remained standing. The group grew quiet, looking at him expectantly. "I'd like to thank all of you for responding positively to my request for this meeting," he looked at everyone in turn. "You already know the reason I have asked you to come. We are here because Dani Magdev, the son of Ian and Rovine Magdev, by mere pele, a miracle of God, stumbled upon something extraordinary a few days ago - six Cyrillic letters safely embedded in the graphic structure of David's Star. On the screens in front of you, you are able to see a presentation of Dani's discovery and a summary of its meaning provided by Professor Nathan Epstein, Rabbi Loew, and Ian and Rovine Magdev."

Ruben looked around, then continued. "I've gathered you here with the aim of setting up a special team of some of our closest collaborators. The objective is to figure out the significance of Dani Madgev's discovery and find out whether or not there might be any other interwoven letters and symbols hidden in the Star of David. And indeed, as Ian and Rovine informed me, there are additional symbols..."

"Numerals," Ian corrected.

"Yes, Ian and Dani discovered several Roman numerals interwoven, too. In each case we are here together to put everything in its proper context and interpret it to the best of our abilities."

"What will it mean if we discover even more interwoven letters and symbols in David's Star?" Uri Zohar inquired.

"I don't know yet but, like the rest of the people here, I really want to find out. Let me put it this way, I've got the gut feeling we're going to discover something big, so big we might even change the course of history and the politics of Israel. This is big, really big," Ruben could not keep the excitement out of his voice.

"Not only that," Rabbi Loew added, "but by discovering all these letters and symbols we stand a great chance of finding out what out forefathers put in store for us for the future. I've already begun to regard David's Star as a kind of ark of knowledge. Our task, Mr. Zohar, is to unearth, so to speak, all this knowledge and put it to its best use. And yes, Ruben may prove right, if what we discovered turned out to be such huge significance then we'd really be able to change the course of Israel's modern-day history."

Uri Zohar nodded in agreement. Then Ruben resumed speaking. "First, however, I'd like to hear what you think about all this."

"When Ian Magdev called me a few days ago, I had no idea of the significance of his inquiry. Now I have realized its immense profundity. I am all for bringing this new task to its rightful conclusion," Professor Epstein said.

"Dani Madgev is a very bright kid and I am overjoyed he discovered the letters. I am sure we are at the start of something very portentous. This discovery is a true pele, as you put it Ruben, a genuine sign God has sent us. We have to go for it," said Rabbi Loew.

"I love challenges, Ruben, you know me well. I just need to understand what drives you and the rest of the people here. You can count me in, naturally. Besides, I deeply respect your commitment to this country," Uri Zohar nodded approvingly.

"Is that it, Uri?" Ruben asked, knowing well there was more to what Uri had just said.

"You know me, Ruben. I'm all in for the secret codes, letters, and symbols. You also know how many years I have devoted on them. I am glad to be able to provide my services and learn something new in the meantime," Uri looked around the room at his friends, nodding his head affirmatively.

"Now, then, we will be working in this very room. Food, coffee, water and beverages are readily available," Ruben explained.

"Where do we start?" Professor Epstein asked.

"Following the simple principle discovered by young Dani Magdev, Ian will explain it to you briefly. I will ask you to apply the same method and try to sketch out other possible letters, numbers and symbols interwoven in the graphics of David's Star. If we find any, our next task will be to place them in their proper context and interpret them to the best of our knowledge and abilities," Ruben said.

"When do we start?" Uri asked.

"Right now," Ruben said.

A surge of subdued laughter wafted across the room. The answer was self-evident after all.

16

JERUSALEM, ISRAEL

14 MAY 2020

LATE MORNING

Aya and Dani hurried into the kitchen where Sarah was preparing lunch. They had spent most of the morning in Aya's room reading some of her latest poems she had published on her blog. They had become inseparable.

"Mom, I'm taking Dani out. We're going to pick up groceries for Rapha, all right?" Aya looked up at her mother.

"All right, honey, but make sure you are not late for lunch," Sarah glanced at both of them.

"Yes, mom, we'll be back early. Do you need anything from the grocery?"

"No, I've got everything I need right here."

"OK then, we're off."

******

Once they got out of the building, the hot dry air hit their faces but they got used to it quickly. Walking down the street, Dani asked, "Where are we going, Aya?"

"I want to show you around the neighborhood. Besides, I have to pick up some groceries for Rapha. I'll introduce you to him."

"Who's he?"

"Raphael Luria is his name. He is the grandpa I've always dreamed of having and never actually had."

"What do you mean?"

"Rapha is ninety-two and is one of the very few remaining Holocaust survivors. My maternal and paternal grandparents survived the Holocaust but because of deep-rooted injuries they sustained during their imprisonment in Treblinka and Auschwitz they died early and never made it to such a ripe old age as Rapha. So I never got to meet them."

"That is really sad, Aya, I'm sorry. Listening to this, I feel guilty for having maternal and paternal grandparents and for having spent my childhood with them."

"You shouldn't feel guilty, Dani, but happy. In a way, I am happy, too. I have Rapha. My parents are really glad I spend time with him."

"You're lucky he survived the Holocaust and has reached the age of ninety-two to be your grandfather. Destiny has its ways, hasn't it?"

"Yes, this is true. Rapha was only twelve when he was sent to the Buchenwald concentration camp with his parents. They perished tragically but he miraculously survived. After the war, he went to Israel and stayed with some relatives of his."

"Do you often visit him?"

"Yes, almost every day. He really enjoys fresh food so I buy small quantities for him regularly. He's old, Dani, and he cannot do things like that by himself anymore."

"I understand. This is in fact very nice of you..."

"What?"

"What you do for him."

"It's no big deal for me," she said modestly. "Besides, he's really nice to me, you know, really nice. Often when I visit him he tells me tales or legends about the distant past of our ancestors and land. I love to listen to him."

"Are we going to the grocer's or to his place first?"

"To his place. He has to give me a small list of things he wants me to buy."

"Is his place far?"

"Actually, it's just around the corner," Aya said as they made a right turn down a narrower street. When they reached a six-storey apartment building, Aya opened a small wooden gate and they got inside a tidy little garden. They walked down a short paved alley to get to the building's main entrance. Aya pressed the doorbell carrying the nameplate *Luria*.

"Is this you, Aya?" They heard the frail voice of an old man. It was the usual time of her visits to him. That was how he could guess it was her.

"Yes, Rapha, it's me," she said, her words followed by a buzz coming from the massive entrance door. They opened it and walked inside. The elevator was at the opposite end of the entrance corridor. They took it to the sixth floor, where Rapha's apartment was. When they got out of it, a very old-looking man with shoulder-long white hair was already waiting for them at the open door of his flat. His face was beaming – his smile curving his wrinkles upward and thus only further emphasizing his emotions. It was obvious he was very happy to see Aya. Her visits were in reality the high points of his days. For him, she was the granddaughter he never had. He loved her immensely. When she came to him, he hugged her and kissed her forehead.

"Rapha, this is Dani," Aya said introducing one to the other. They shook hands and Rapha motioned them in. In the meantime, Aya was telling him who Dani and his parents were and where they came from.

"So your parents worked with the parents of Aya on the same project?" Rapha asked Dani.

"Yes, Safe Haven for Israel!"

"A remarkable project this is, I admit. A brilliant idea!" Rapha commented. Then he asked. "Have you been here before, Dani?"

"Yes, several times."

"Do you like Israel?"

"Yes, very much. It is a beautiful country and you don't have to travel long to get to all kinds of interesting and magnificent places."

"This is true, our country is small but full of history," Rapha said.

Aya, impatient to tell Rapha more about the Magdevs, explained to him about Dani's discovery of the six Cyrillic letters interwoven in David's Star. She told him about the message they yielded about Huldah. He was in awe. He found this discovery miraculous.

"And the message read exactly *With Huldah?* These very words?" he asked as though still seeking to confirm the discovery.

"Yes," Dani said. He asked for a sheet of paper and a pencil. Once Rapha gave them to him he drew a Star of David on the paper and began sketching the six Cyrillic letters out of the star, one by one. Then he recited them as they were read in Bulgarian and told Rapha that the phrase translated as 'with Huldah.' Rapha was deeply impressed.

“The problem is,” Dani said and continued, “We don’t really know what this phrase means.”

“Yes, Rapha, we don’t know but perhaps you may help us because you know so many stories. Do you by any chance know a story about Huldah?” Aya asked him. He looked at them pensively.

“I do know a few stories about Huldah,” he said, Aya and Dani’s faces beamed.

“Can you tell one of them to us now?” Aya asked, her curiosity aroused.

“First, go to the grocer’s,” Rapha said as he handed her a small sheet of paper on which he had written the list of goods he wanted her to buy. “When you come back, I’ll tell you a story,” he said and smiled.

Dani and Aya raced out of Rapha’s flat and hurried to the grocery store, finished Rapha’s shopping and rushed back where the elderly man was waiting for them to return.

******

Rapha was glad the teenagers had bought everything he had asked for. While they were gone, he had time to prepare tea. The three of them sat around the kitchen table, standing under a large window and next to a glass door opening to a small terrace. The tablecloth was white and a small fine-crafted bronze menorah stood in the middle of the table.

“What’s the story about Huldah, Rapha?” Aya asked eagerly.

Rapha smiled and began. “One day, Huldah took her students for a stroll down to the Water Tower and to the source of the spring of Gihon. Huldah sat on a large stone by the source while her students drank as much water as they wanted. Then they all sat around her and she told them the following story.” Rapha made a short pause and continued by slightly altering the tone of his voice to resemble that of the elderly woman Huldah was.

"As you all know, dear students, we are commanded to visit Jerusalem on three festivals each year. Once, a group of pious Jews set out from Jericho to attend one of those festivals. On their way to Jerusalem, marauders attacked the group and stole the money of all its members. Because of the divinely-imposed command upon them, they had no choice but to continue their journey. Upon arriving in Jerusalem, the pious Jews from Jericho were exhausted, hungry and thirsty. In that year, the summer was very dry and the few wells in Jerusalem had all dried up. There was only one place where they could quench their thirst - at the spring of Gihon, below the City of David and the Temple.

"All of them headed for the spring. When they got there, they were told the owner of the well was the avaricious Mayimzahav because he was able to turn water into golden coins from the citizens of Jerusalem who came to draw water from his well. Mayimzahav unemotionally told them they had to pay if they wanted to drink from the well. Eleazar, one of the pious Jews, came forward and begged Mayimzahav to give them water and save them. He told them they were only visitors to Jerusalem and they had to be exempt from paying for the water. However, Mayimzahav, who constantly sought to increase his wealth, paid no heed to the pleas of Eleazer. Showing no compassion he told them they had to pay first. If they paid they could use as much water as they needed.

"Seeing no way out, Eleazar hurried up the Water Tower. When he came out of it, he scurried uphill to the Temple. He entered the Temple and began praying to God to help him and his townsmen out of this dire predicament. Eleazar's prayer was answered. When he got out of the Temple after prayer, he started downhill and back to the Water Tower from which he could descend to the well near the spring of Gihon. He began climbing down when, lo, a weasel came out before him and looked at him. Eleazar immediately stopped not wanting to hurt the animal and at the same time surprised how the little creature was looking at him as if trying to tell him something. Then the weasel hurried down the steps and Eleazar decided to follow it. Just before one of the curves of the winding staircase, the weasel slipped into a hole in the rock. Eleazar bent over and tried to look inside the dark hole. Just then, the weasel suddenly stuck out its head, a golden coin in its mouth. It dropped the coin before Eleazer, who took it in his palm. Then Eleazar thrust his hand into the hole and, behold, when he drew it out, he held a small bag full of golden coins. He rejoiced and hurried down the staircase to the spring and his fellow townspeople suffering from thirst. When he came to the well, he paid Mayimzahav and his fellow townsmen and women could quench their thirst. Afterward, they all sat around the spring of Gihon to ask Eleazar what had happened. He told them about his prayer and the story with the miraculous appearance of the weasel that led him to the bag of golden coins. At that moment, the weasel came out of the opening of the Water Tower and it looked at Eleazar once again. Then it darted forth and disappeared into *Gannah Pele* - the Garden of Miracles," and Huldah, now Rapha switched to his tone of voice, pointed down the valley between Mount Zion to the left and the Mount of Olives to the right. Then he continued with his imitation of the voice of Huldah.

"The weasel had conveyed the will of God and Eleazar and his townspeople's strong faith had been rewarded. This is why from that moment on, it was decided that all pious Israelites from all corners of the Jewish kingdom who visited Jerusalem for any of the religiously required festivities were to be exempt from any taxes on water. And this is the end of the story," Rapha said.

"Rapha, what is Gannah Pele?" Dani asked.

"This is the name of the garden that stretches between the foothill of Mount Zion, on whose top the City of David stands, to the foothill of the Mount of Olives. Legend holds it that many centuries before David's conquest of the Jebusite stronghold, Gannah Pele was a beautiful garden in which God performed miracles to those faithful to Him," he explained.

"You mean the Kidron Valley?" Aya asked.

"Kidron is the name that came much later in time. After David became king, another name - 'The King's Valley' - came to prominently designate the Kidron Valley. In ancient times the name of that valley was simply Gannah Pele," Rapha smiled at his mesmerized audience.

Aya and Dani had drunk their tea. It was already noon and they had to hurry back home. They bid Rapha goodbye and left.

17

JERUSALEM, ISRAEL
14 MAY 2020
PEACE NOW HEADQUARTERS
EARLY AFTERNOON

"Before we continue any further, I'd like to dwell a bit on the phrase 'With Huldah' initially discovered by the Magdevs," Rabbi Loew said and looked at everyone in the room. "I will tell you the most important story I know related to Huldah," he said and then continued. "There was once a stone placed right next to the northern gate leading to the Temple. The name of that stone was Yahalom - the stone of faith. No one was allowed to either touch it or sit on it except Huldah, the prophetess. It was said that God conveyed his will through her when she was sitting on it." Rabbi Loew paused a moment and took a deep breath. "So, as the story goes, one afternoon Huldah was sitting on Yahalom as she was wont to do. At that time, she was already very old. A multitude of students had gathered, sitting on the ground around her, and some passers-by had also joined the group. The people were quiet, waiting for her to speak up. They all wanted to hear what she was going to prophesy. They wanted to know the will of God. And she spoke to them in this manner: 'When the time comes, the Messiah shall enter the Temple Mount through this very gate on my side.' Few know nowadays why the gate she was sitting by later became known as Huldah's Gate but the reason actually was her last still unfulfilled prophecy. However, like all her other prophecies, that one too is bound to come true at the right moment in time."

"How can you possibly know all that?" Ian asked surprised.

"The rich aggadah (meaning 'narrative', 'story', and 'legend' and referring to sections of the Talmud and Midrash that contain legends and stories of the Bible and folklore) tradition of the Children of Israel is full of accounts of events of olden times. And despite the fact that we were scattered all over the known world, we succeeded in preserving this tradition as every generation made it richer."

"Rabbi, doesn't the name yahalom mean 'a precious stone renown for its exceptional hardness'?" Ruben inquired, in a way to make it clear for Ian and Rovine rather than for the rest of the people who were native Hebrew speakers.

"Yahalom is the Hebrew for 'diamond', so you are right," the Rabbi replied.

"But then it must have been a very large diamond and that seems impossible. It's hard to believe. Where could anyone find such a large precious stone?" Rovine was curious.

"Let me tell you another story. Once, a young man asked Rabbi Menachem Mendel Schneerson what a rabbi was good for. The rabbi was not at all surprised at the young man's question. He wasn't offended by it either. On the contrary, he even welcomed it. He told him the earth actually contained all kinds of treasures. All these were created by God and scattered all over the place. But the most important thing was to know where to dig for them. If a man didn't know where to dig, he couldn't find anything except dust and broken rocks. However, if a man asked the right person – the so-called geologist of the spirit and soul – the one who knew where the treasures were to be found, he could find silver, which is love of God; or gold, which is awe before God; or even a diamond, which is faith in God. A rabbi was that geologist of the spirit and soul who could show a man where to dig. However, the actual digging had to be done by each person on his own."

"A very thoughtful story. So, in a way, Huldah sitting on Yahalom was symbolically equivalent to Huldah being one with her faith in God," Rovine commented pensively.

"You could put it that way," Uri Zohar chimed in.

"The name Yahalom is written in Hebrew with four letters: יהלם. It is an ingenuous combination of two other words: יה referring to one of the names of God, namely, Yah and halom (הלם) meaning 'to smite' and 'strike down'. This way, the Hebrew word for diamond actually says 'Yah smites'," the Rabbi explained further.

"How interesting!" Ian exclaimed. "Now, suddenly, it all makes sense to me. The diamond is the hardest stone known to man and hence it is also an unbreakable weapon with which God is able to smite."

"Or, alternatively, the toughness of God's smite resembles the hardness of a diamond. So allegorically speaking, Yahalom could have been any large stone with exceptional hardness," Rovine offered.

"The relation between the stone Yahalom and Huldah as transmitter of God's will also implies that Yah's will is unbreakable, hard and precious as a diamond. And diamond implying faith means that if one's faith in Yahweh is as hard as a diamond, it too is unbreakable," the Rabbi said and suddenly things started to make sense.

******

“How interesting,” Uri Zohar exclaimed after everyone had been silent for a short while.

“What is it?” Ruben asked.

“If one slightly rearranged the four Hebrew letters of Yahalom, one would get Imlah (ימלה), the name of the father of the prophet Micaiah.”

“So we come across yet another prophet. This is indeed really interesting,” Ruben said.

“Who was Imlah?” Rovine asked.

“Nothing is known of him except the fact that he was the father of the prophet Micaiah,” Rabbi Loew explained.

“Well, then who was Micaiah?” Rovine asked.

“He was the prophet who went to King Ahab of the Kingdom of Samaria, a.k.a. the Northern kingdom of Israel or the House of Omri, who was married to the idolatrous Jezebel,” Rabbi Loew said and continued. “Micaiah, known for his unbreakable faith in God, that is, as unbreakable as a diamond, told the king that his army would suffer a defeat at the battle of Rimoth-Gilead and that the king himself would be killed in it. As you can imagine, Ahab went berserk. He was furious with the man who had dared to face him predicting such a gruesome fate to his great military campaign. The king hurried to the house of the false prophet Zedekiah ben Chenaanah. Zedekiah calmed down the king by telling him that not very long ago, the prophet Elijah had prophesized that the king would be slain but nothing like that had happened. Reassured Ahab went to battle. The interesting thing was that the prophecies of Micaiah and Elijah both came true. In the battle of Rimoth-Gilead, Ahab's army was defeated whereas he was seriously wounded but he didn't die on the battlefield. Lying wounded in his bed, King Ahab was slain by Jehu who overthrew him and ascended the throne of the Kingdom of Samaria. The slaying also put an end to the idolatrous practices embraced and practiced by Ahab and his wife Jezebel.”

18

JERUSALEM, ISRAEL

14 MAY 2020

OUTSIDE PEACE NOW HEADQUARTERS

LATE AFTERNOON

"Agent Schwartz?" Agent Weissman knocked on the window of an inconspicuous sedan and looked inside at a stunningly beautiful brunette wearing a designer black silk suit. She appeared to be in her early thirties. Her eyes were dark brown, her eyelashes long, her raven-black hair tied neatly behind her nape in a well-shaped chignon.

"Yes, it is me, Agent Weissman. Get in," she said as she rolled down the window. Weissman walked around the car to the other side, opened the door with a flourish and sat on the seat beside the driver.

"How long has Openheim been inside?" he asked.

"All day long," she replied while quickly sizing him up. He looked to be in his late thirties, had a neat tall figure and already had a few streaks of grey hair.

"Do we have any idea what he's up to?"

"He's been having a meeting of sorts. I saw a number of people arriving in the morning."

"Isn't it odd that the meeting has been going on all day long?"

"Well, it is but he hasn't made any phone calls yet, so we don't know what it's all about."

"Why is Openheim under surveillance in the first place?"

"You know that the Big Brother view incorporates interest in the good and the bad guys alike. Openheim is of course one of our good guys. Yet, we still have to keep track of what he is doing."

"I've got to write a report and submit it ASAP."

"My point, exactly. I'll provide you with all the intelligence I've got."

"I'll appreciate the input." Agent Weissman took the opportunity to scrutinize the gorgeous woman next to him in the car. He had never seen a woman more beautiful than her.

19

JERUSALEM, ISRAEL
15 MAY 2020
PEACE NOW HEADQUARTERS
MORNING

It was a hot morning in Jerusalem and the city's daily hustle and bustle only contributed to the sensation of heat. Inside Peace Now's headquarters the drone of the relatively large air-conditioners mounted on the exterior could hardly be heard but the temperatures they maintained created the feeling of comfort.

"As we further examined the graphics of the star back home," Ian Magdev said when the morning session of the team gathered by Ruben Openheim began, "Rovine and I discovered some of the Cyrillic letters were in fact orthographically full-fledged Roman numerals."

"Do you mean X and C?" Professor Epstein asked, never taking his eyes off the screen before him.

"Yes, in fact there are two Xs, one on each wing of the star," Ian explained.

"But then there's also a Roman V undoubtedly embedded in the geometrical structure of the star," Rovine clarified, lifting a sheet of paper with David's Star on it and pointing with her slender finger at the two numerals.

"That makes it three Roman numerals - a ten, a five and a hundred," Professor Epstein said pensively.

"Actually, one five, two tens and two one hundreds," Ian pointed out.

"Yes, yes, you are right," the professor agreed.

"What do we do with these five numerals?" Ruben asked, looking at Rovine's sheet of paper.

"We play by combining them in all possible combinations," Uri said victoriously.

"Well, let's do it then," Ruben urged everyone.

In a very short time, with everyone typing on their laptops, their combined efforts produced a list of Roman numerals which appeared simultaneously on everyone's screen:

V = 5; X = 10; XV = 15; XX = 20; XXV = 25; XC = 90; XCV = 95; C = 100; CV = 105; CX = 110; CXV = 115; CXX = 120; CXXV = 125; CXC = 190; CXCV = 195; CC=200; CCV=205; CCX=210; CCXV=215; CCXX=220; CCXXV=225

"So, we've got 21 Roman numerals," Ruben concluded.

"When we add up their numerical values we get the sum total of 2595," Uri said.

"Whose single digits add up to 21," Ian observed.

"What do you mean?" Rabbi Loew asked, his eyes intently on the screen before him.

"Two + five + nine + five gives exactly twenty-one," Ian explained.

"Oh, yes, you're right," the rabbi exclaimed.

"This gives us two times twenty-one," Uri joined in.

"Which is forty-two," Ian said.

"No, it is two times shin - the twenty-first letter of the Hebrew alphabet," Uri clarified and continued. "In Hebrew two shins put together - שש - yield the word *shesh* meaning six."

"How curious!" Ian exclaimed. "You'd be surprised, Uri, but coincidentally enough, I should tell you that number six in Bulgarian is *shest*."

"Shesh as the six rays of David's Star," Uri pointed out.

"Yes, exactly," Ruben said, glad with the first quick exchange of brainstorm passes between Ian and Uri. At the same time, he couldn't shake off the feeling they had somehow arrived at a dead-end.

Silence fell upon everyone in the room. All six of them were looking at the screens before them and either reading or typing something, trying to fathom the meaning of the numerals.

Suddenly Rabbi Loew broke the silence.

"I think I made an interesting observation," he said as everyone looked up.

"What is it?" Ruben asked, suddenly animated.

"Well, we all know Roman numerals were widely used in our lands during the times of the Roman Empire. Now we've got all those twenty-one Roman numerals and we seem a bit lost as to what to do with them," he said and looked at everyone in turn. He was right about the confusion and the tinge of despondency that had fallen upon everyone. But Rabbi Loew was determined to change this. Most importantly, he knew how. He knew they hadn't ended up in a dead-end street. He spoke further.

"What do we have?" he asked and paused.

"A sum total of 2595," Ruben pointed out.

"Exactly," the rabbi smiled.

"But what should we do with this number? This is what we don't know," Ruben said, a shade of despair in his voice.

"I've discovered what I think we should do with it. We should take it as a Strong's concordance number," the rabbi said firmly.

"A Strong's concordance number?" Rovine asked, not comprehending.

"Yes, a Strong's concordance number. In the late eighteen-hundreds, Dr. James Strong was a biblical scholar, professor of Biblical Literature at Troy University in Alabama and creator of the Strong's Exhaustive Concordance of the Bible," Rabbi Loew explained.

"Can you be a bit more specific?" Rovine asked.

"Of course, Rovine," he said respectfully and smiled. Then he continued. "James Strong's is the most comprehensive index of words and their immediate contexts in the Hebrew and Greek Old Testaments. Basically, each word in the Hebrew Old Testament has a number assigned to it. This way it is easier to find it and compare it to other words and passages. Strong discovered eight thousand six hundred seventy-three Hebrew roots used in the Old Testament hence we have a range of numbers from 1 to 8673."

"This is very interesting," Rovine commented.

"Surely, a remarkable way to encode the entire Bible," Uri chimed in.

"Why not," Professor Epstein nodded in agreement.

"Luckily, our work is made easier by an Internet tool. If all of us surf together to blueletterbible.org, click on the site's search engine in the upper left corner under the site's logo, select Strong's Search from the search tools, type 2595 in its search box, we will get to the root in question. In our case, we get to the Biblical Hebrew noun *chaniyth* - חנית - meaning 'a spear' or 'a spear-head'," Rabbi Loew explained.

"Now what do we do once we got *chaniyth*?" Ruben asked puzzled.

"I would assume we have to put it in a proper context," Rovine added.

"King David and his shield are our context as well as all the symbols and stories related to them," the Rabbi said.

"So how do we fit in *chaniyth*?" Ruben spoke still not comprehending.

"For a starter, I'll quote you 1 Samuel 17:7: *'And the staff of his [Goliath's] spear [was] like a weaver's bean; and his spear's head [weighed] six hundred shekels of iron: and one bearing a shield went before him.'"*

"This is the description of Goliath before the battle with David," Professor Epstein pointed out.

"Exactly," the Rabbi agreed.

"But how does this quote fit in?" Ruben asked, still puzzled.

"I am just about to tell you how," the Rabbi said and smiled calmly. "Abishai was a nephew of King David and also one of his most loyal military officers –"

"As far as I remember, he was a very good friend of Heldai – one of David's high-ranking warriors and it was the prophetess Huldah who stood in a long line of his descendants. You'd surely recall Heldai, too," Professor Epstein glanced at both Ian and Rovine. They nodded in agreement. Then the professor excused himself for the interruption. Rabbi Loew resumed.

"There are many legends about the warrior Abishai. He is said to have killed three hundred people and to have been the head of a group of thirty of David's mightiest warriors. In each case, Abishai was exceptionally strong," the Rabbi explained.

"What does Abishai have to do with the spear?" Ruben asked.

"I've just come to the story I'd like to relate to you. In the aggadah, there is a legend that has survived to-date. One night, while David was in his palace in the City of David, the one below the Temple, and was sleeping, he received a bewitching vision. Belial – the very prince of evil – appeared in David's sleep disguised as a poor fellow-countryman asking for help. David woke up in the night and rode off to the place he had seen in his vision. This place was on the border of the Philistines' land. By dawn, David was standing on the border and looking around for the poor fellow-countryman he had seen in his vision. The bushes near David shuffled violently and, lo, suddenly Ishbibenob – the giant brother of the slain Goliath – jumped out carrying in his hand Goliath's spear whose head weighed six hundred shekels of iron. Caught by surprise David was easily captured by the fierce Philistine who was looking for revenge.

"At the same moment, Abishai, who was still in Jerusalem, was taking a bath and was preparing for the Sabbath. Then, out of nowhere, a turtledove miraculously landed on the windowsill of his bathroom. There was a message tied on its foot. Abishai untied it and let the turtledove fly away. He read the message, which informed him of the precarious predicament David was facing. Since the message was written in the military code invented by King David, Abishai knew his king was in grave danger. Immediately Abishai mounted his horse and hurried to the place where David had been captured. When Ishbibenob saw Abishai, he planted the heavy spear in the ground, tossed David up in the air and said: 'Let the one who killed my brother fall on his spear and perish instantly.' Upon seeing this, Abishai immediately pronounced ha-Shem, the Tetragrammaton, the four-letter name of God, and, lo, miracle, David remained suspended in mid-air. As an answer to Abishai's prayer, David slowly descended to the ground, away from the danger of the planted spear and its heavy and sharp spearhead. Then the two mighty warriors launched one last attack on Ishbibenod who was slow-witted albeit a giant and unaware of David's amazing intelligence. They assaulted him on both sides and managed to injure him. Soon, Ishbibenod fell on the ground and David dealt him a final blow by piercing him with the heavy spear of Goliath. Ishbibenod perished at once. David and Abishai returned victoriously to Jerusalem!" Rabbi Loew concluded the story. Everyone was captivated by the passion with which he had related it.

"So, this was the meaning of encoding *chaniyth* in the graphics of David's Star," Ruben wrapped it up.

"Yes, this is a story that demonstrates what strong faith can do," the Rabbi clarified. Then the meeting was disbanded and everyone left for lunch.

******

"I was really intrigued by the discovery of the Roman numerals," Uri Zohar said after everyone had returned from lunch. "I was contemplating David's Star while you were speaking and I think I came to a startling discovery."

"We are eager to hear it," Ruben said.

"You see, there is an X on each of the two wings of the star, right?" Uri asked making sure everyone was attentive.

"Yes," Ruben replied.

"Put together they yield 20. In their midst, there's also a V or five," Uri continued.

"Correct," Ruben confirmed, following Uri's point.

"Now when we put twenty and five in succession, we get something like twenty point five or twenty slash five."

"Wait a second, you mean as a date of the calendar - the twentieth of May?" Ruben inquired, guessing the direction Uri was taking.

"Yes, I mean precisely that," Uri beamed.

"Good but which year then?" Professor Epstein inquired pensively. Then he added. "If we had a year, we would have been able to define the meaning of this date more accurately."

"I'd imagine that if we, for instance, put the two Xs together we'd get 1010."

"Clever but not correct in terms of Roman numerals, Mr. Zohar," Professor Epstein said. "By the way, 1010 B.C.E. marked the beginning of the reign of David as a king of the kingdom of Judah."

"We will have to do some additional calculations before we are able to determine any year with credible exactitude," Ruben clarified.

"How about if we read the pair of Xs from left to right and then from right to left?" Uri suddenly said, seemingly enlightened by an idea.

"What do you mean?" Ruben asked, an expression of puzzlement on his face.

"I mean the following. When we read the xs on the wings of David's Star as a pair from left to right, as Ian and Rovine do, we get the Roman numeral for twenty. If we do the same from right to left, as we do here in Israel, we get another pair of Xs -"

"- and this is another Roman twenty," Ruben interrupted.

"Now put the two twenties one after the other -"

"And you get 2020," Ruben said, bewilderment on his face.

"So this might be the encoded version of the year for of the date we've already deciphered," Uri explained.

"20th of May, 2020?" Professor Epstein asked.

"Yes," Uri Zohar confirmed.

"Despite the incorrect arrangement of the numerals of the year, not following the Roman configuration, it sounds sort of credible," Ruben said.

"Credible?" Professor Epstein asked in disbelief, a hint of palpable irritation in his voice. "It's lay, unprofessional and even amateurish to make such sloppy claims. I mean putting two pairs of Xs together and claiming they yield 2020. This is not a game."

"Precisely, professor," Uri Zohar said. "With all due respect, no one here claims we are playing games. We are conjecturing on possible interpretations of letters and numerals we discover and don't know how to assimilate. I've just made a conjecture."

"Oh really? Would you please tell us on what grounds you've made your assumption?"

"Well, for a start... On Kabbalah –"

"– Ah, yes, Mr. Zohar, in Kabbalah everything is possible," the professor interrupted heatedly. "I'm aware of that. I've heard it from lay people at least a million times. In Kabbalah you jumble and mumble all kinds of numbers and permutations. You do what you like or what fits your claims to get what you want. But in science, Mr. Zohar, we cannot do such things. So, I'd much prefer to stick to what we've got and work with the facts."

"And yet, jumbling and mumbling I can say two pairs of Xs that give us 2020," Uri pressed on.

"Today is the 13th of May 2020, Mr. Zohar. You seem to suggest we are speaking about the 20th of May of this very year. Provided I accept your blatantly slipshod claim, tell me, please, what do you think this encoded date conceals?" the professor asked retaining his composure.

"I don't know. I'd imagine some event of great importance for us, the Jews," Uri offered, a shade of uncertainty in his voice.

"What event, Mr. Zohar? Employ the skills of your imagination, the ones you make so good use of in your exercises in Kabbalah," Professor Epstein charged on, leaving the rest of the people in the room with the impression he had made the remark with a touch of mordancy.

"The final settling of scores between Jacob and Esau, I'd imagine," Uri said, these words clearly allowing him to regain the upper hand in the discussion.

Surprisingly, Uri Zohar's words seemed to have struck a resonating chord with the professor.

In fact, it was not about the accuracy of the date and the year. Professor Epstein clearly thought Uri Zohar had it wrong with those. However, the professor had expected to hear something about the advent of the Messiah. Yet, the kabbalchemist, as Uri Zohar had introduced himself at the beginning, had touched a nerve. It was about settling scores, not about any advent. Professor Epstein might have thought Uri was up in the clouds initially but he'd just come to realize the kabbalchemist had been down on the ground for he wasn't dreaming or preaching the arrival of the son of David. Uri Zohar seemed to know before any such arrival could ever take place, the century-old scores between Jacob and Esau had to be settled first and foremost.

"So, the 20th of May 2020, this is our presumed date?" Professor Epstein said, traces of resentful resignation in his voice, not because he had accepted the date and the year but because he had always thought the same way as Uri – first there would be settling of scores and only afterward, the Messiah, the rebuilding of the Third Temple and the age of God would come.

"Yes, it seems so," Uri Zohar said calmly.

"So, it means we don't have much time," Ruben chimed in excitedly.

"No, we only have a couple of days left," Uri Zohar said.

"Which means we have to work hard and play for time," Ruben said.

******

"I think I've noticed something," Uri said after a period of silence. "Ten corresponds to *yod* (י) - the tenth letter in the Hebrew alphabet while five to *he* (ה) - the fifth letter. If we put them together -"

"We get *Yah* (יה), one of the abbreviated names of God," Rabbi Loew said interrupting Uri Zohar.

"O, yes, you are right," Ruben exclaimed, his facial expression one of pure awe.

"But then, there's another X, on the right wing of the star," Rovine said.

"This means yet another *yod*," Ian clarified.

"No problem, X-V-X or *yod-he-yod* gives you the Modern Hebrew word *yahi* (יהי) which means *Long Live*!" said Professor Epstein.

"Do I understand correctly that in this case, we've got a phrase to the effect of *Long Live, Yah!*?" Ian asked no one in particular.

"Absolutely," Uri Zohar confirmed.

It seemed another moment of silence had settled in. Just then Rabbi Loew who had been quiet for some time joined the conversation, "I think I've noticed something interesting as well."

"What is it?" Rovine asked, turning to him.

"You see, when you place all five Roman numerals in succession such as CCXXV, they yield 225. Now if you want to express this number through the Hebrew numerical system, you'll have to use Hebrew letters. Two hundred twenty-five is equal to a string of the following letters: *resh* - *kaph* - *he* or רכה. Put together, however, the three Hebrew letters yield *Rekah* - the name of a Rechabite settlement some five kilometers south of the City of David," the Rabbi offered.

"Indeed, a very creative method of approaching the Roman numerals," Professor Epstein commented.

"Who are the Rechabites?" Rovine inquired.

"They were members of a small and very religious tribe which wandered the wilderness beyond the Dead Sea, where they lived in tents. They were one of the staunchest followers of Yahweh known in history. They claimed descent from Jonadab son of Rechab who was a contemporary of King Jehu - the one who overthrew the idolatrous King Ahab and his wife Jezebel," Professor Epstein explained.

"The first one to speak about the Rechabites was Jeremiah. One day, God commanded him to take the Rechabites to one of the chambers of the Temple and to serve them wine there. He did as he was commanded. He took them there and handed them glasses. Then Jeremiah filled the glasses with wine and invited the Rechabites to drink it but they refused. When he asked them why they wouldn't drink from the Temple wine, one of them explained that their forefather Jonadab, son of Rechab, had once forbidden them to drink wine, cultivate land, possess fields, vineyards or orchards and even build houses. They were commanded to live in tents and wander the wilderness. Jeremiah didn't insist because he saw God's wisdom in this act. Jeremiah knew he had been sent to test the purity and the resilience of faith of the Rechabites," Rabbi Loew said.

"But then, when Nebuchadnezzar invaded the land of Israel, the Rechabites became unable to roam the wilderness any longer. As a result, they moved to Jerusalem and pitched their tents below the City of David and near the spring of Gihon. In their view, this was how they were able to best protect the purity of faith of their fellow Israelites. Not long afterward, they were asked to move and settle a bit further south from the tip of the City of David in the Kidron Valley. The Rechabites did so and settled on top of a hill overlooking the City of David and the Temple. They gave the name Rekah to their settlement," Professor Epstein explained.

It was late and everyone in the room looked tired. Ruben stood up and announced the end of the day's session. Everyone packed their things and left. At that point, none of them suspected how important those seemingly random intellectual exercises were.

20

JERUSALEM, ISRAEL
15 MAY 2020
OUTSIDE PEACE NOW HEADQUARTERS
LATE MORNING

"Good job, Chasin. I can hear them quite well. I didn't know you could handle wiring so well," Agent Adah Schwartz said to Agent Weissman while they were sitting in her inconspicuous black sedan and listening to what the people gathered in the office of Peace Now on the other side of the street and several floors up above them were discussing.

"It wasn't particularly difficult to bug the room," he said modestly and smiled. In the small hours of the night, Agent Weissman - masked, carrying task gear and using state-of-the-art devices - had gained access to the office of Peace Now and had successfully wiretapped the conference hall where the team assembled by Ruben Openheim held its daily meetings. This way, the two agents would not just sit in the dark, unknowing and waiting to see what happens next but would be in the whirlwind of events as they unfolded on the sixth floor of the building across the street. In fact, they would be a step ahead and anticipate the action, rather than just guess what would happen next.

"I bet it wasn't that easy to plant the bugs. Where did you learn to do it so well?" she complimented him, never taking eyes off his face. For him it felt as though she were cross-examining him. They had only met the day before but it wasn't easy to be confronted by such a stunningly beautiful woman.

"Well, a couple of top-secret missions, I guess," he said unpretentiously.

"Oh, stop playing the shy guy, will you?" an ounce of mischievousness in her voice.

"I'm not playing anything. Okay, how about you, what are you good at?" he asked in a move of unacknowledged defiance. She looked at him just as she had done an instant ago. This time her eyes felt penetrating, nay, piercing, as if a legion of unthinkably thin and mind-numbingly sharp blades. Then, all of a sudden, the blades disappeared replaced by the warmth of a genuine feminine smile. She realized the effect of her look had on him. That's why she had opted for a smile, to ease the tension. Only after all that did she speak to him.

"I am good at reading minds," she said calmly and confidently. Still under the hypnosis of the legion of blades, he had absolutely nothing to say. Apparently, her smile hadn't finished mending the aftermath of the attack of the blade legion. His thoughts seemed still paralyzed like amputated limbs. Then she burst into a genuine laughter, "I am kidding, you know," she winked mischievously.

Chasin didn't know what to say and laughed it out awkwardly.

"There they go again," she said all of a sudden when a baritone cracked into their headphones. "This is the professor. A very smart guy," she said, not expecting any comment from her fellow agent.

21

JERUSALEM, ISRAEL,
15 MAY 2020
PEACE NOW HEADQUARTERS
AFTERNOON

After lunch, everyone returned to the conference hall of Peace Now's office. Uri had spoken excitedly about the discoveries during the meal and now he was the first one to address the gathering.

"I was impressed by the discovery of the Cyrillic letters. I was even more astounded by the fact that they were used as numerals which, ingeniously, Ian and Rovine translated into Hebrew letters. I agree with their discovery of the phrase 'a turtledove to a man' but I've come to discover these same six Hebrew letters: 1 = *aleph;* 4 = *daleth;* 30 = *lamed;* 200 = *resh;* 400 = *taw;* and 600 = final *mem,* yield something additional, as well."

"What is it?" Professor Epstein was intrigued.

"Well, Professor, you can see it for yourself. All we need to do is arrange the letters in a specific order," Uri explained.

"And which is the order you have in mind?" Rabbi Loew asked.

"The first word I've arranged is deleth (דלת) meaning 'door' while the second one is reem (ראם) meaning 'wild ox'. Once put together, the two words yield something like *deleth reem* or '[the] door [of the] wild ox'."

"I see. How interesting, indeed," the Rabbi exclaimed.

"Perhaps you explain for the rest of us, rabbi?" Rovine asked.

"I think I can. I should begin by saying that the wild ox was embroidered on the flag of the tribe of Manasseh. It was the tribe's symbol."

"How did this come to be?" Ian inquired.

"The aggadah explains this with the following narrative: In ancient times, before the *galut* (exile) from Egypt, the phrase 'the door of the wild ox' designated the door of the house of Manasseh – the elder son of Joseph and his wife Asenath, grandson of Jacob, and begetter of the tribe of Manasseh. There was something very peculiar written under the wild ox's emblem. It was a non-existent Hebrew word," the Rabbi said calmly.

"A non-existent word? What do you mean, Rabbe?" Ruben was puzzled.

"Yes, indeed, a very peculiar word. It read *elefpeh* and was written as אלפה in Hebrew."

"But what did it mean?" Ian asked, now utterly stunned on his part.

"You probably know the Hebrew letter *aleph* (אלף) originated from the Early Semitic pictograph of a wild ox," the Rabbi told Ian.

"Yes, I do know that. In fact *eleph* means 'an ox'," Ian said, trying to keep up with the rabbi.

"That's right."

"In ancient times, the ox was a symbol of immense strength and power."

"And that's precisely where the ingenuity of Manasseh lies. *Elefpeh* did not read as *eleph* and *peh* –"

"– The mouth of the ox," Ruben translated by joining in.

"– But as *El* and *peh,*" the Rabbi continued undisturbed.

"– The mouth of God."

"Exactly," Rabbi Loew nodded.

"So, the ox pictograph was a kind of allegorical representation of the mouth of God, right?" Rovine inquired.

"Yes, that's right," the Rabbi confirmed. Then he continued. "But this is not all. You know that *aleph* (אלף) also means 'thousand'. On the other hand, the numerical value of *aleph* as letter in the alphabet is 'one'. In one and the same word, you have something very small and very big – 1 and 1000."

"Very small and very large value," Rovine chimed in.

"You can also put it as one extreme and its opposite, a metaphorical figure of God in a way," the Rabbi explained.

"Something like 'the beginning and the end' of things?" Ian asked trying to make certain that he and Rovine were following correctly.

"Yes, but where the end is, a new beginning starts off," the Rabbi said.

"Like at the end of days and after Judgment Day, a new beginning would follow for those who passed the judgment levy," Uri added.

"You cannot be more right, Mr. Zohar. That's the day when the Messiah will arrive in Bozrah," again the Rabbi.

"Absolutely," Uri exclaimed. He was glad he had contributed something important.

"It is Isaiah 40:5 that clearly speaks about the Mouth of God," the Rabbi said and began quoting by heart: *'And the glory of the God shall be revealed, and all the flesh shall see it together: for the mouth of God hath spoken it.'*"

"Here, Ian, Rovine, Isaiah's prophecy speaks about the time when the road shall be prepared and so will be people's hearts for the revelation of God's glory. That will happen at Judgment Day in Bozrah, at the end of the present age, for after it the perfect age of God will come."

"Bozrah?" Rovine asked, unable to comprehend.

"Yes, the ancient capital city of Edom, the kingdom of the descendants of Esau, the twin brother of Jacob," the Rabbi clarified while Rovine just nodded. She wasn't sure she got the point. The Rabbi continued.

"In a way, by placing a pictograph of a wild ox on its door, Manasseh sought to demonstrate his strong faith - as strong as an ox - but also wanted to imply that when the end of days came and when according to the prophesy the mouth of God would speak, it would be before Manasseh's very door. Then and there."

"And after that will come *El dowr tam* or '[the] perfect age [of] El', that is, of God," Professor Epstein suddenly said. All of them turned their eyes on him. He continued.

"While the reverend Rabbi Loew was speaking, I kept on rearranging the six Hebrew letters and three new words emerged. I couldn't help noticing the first one - *El* (אל) - one of the names of God. With only four letters remaining from the string, I arranged another word - *tam* (תם) meaning 'perfect'. Left with only two letters, *daleth* and *resh,* I discovered they yielded the word *dowr* (דר) meaning 'age'. Once I put them together, I got the phrase '[the] perfect age [of] El'," Professor Epstein explained.

"O, great, this is really another great discovery," Ruben couldn't conceal his joy. "You've discovered several ingeniously interwoven phrases in the very heart of the Star of David. Isn't that amazing?"

"It is," Uri beamed.

Shortly afterward, everyone packed up and left. It was the end of the working day. There was this prevailing sense of achievement in the air. The joint efforts of everyone had led to specific accomplishments.

Later in the car, Ruben shared with Ian and Rovine how glad he was that people would take time off from their work and families and devote it to deciphering the arcane knowledge deeply hidden in David's Star. He also said he truly appreciated their determination and commitment to finding a lasting solution for peace in Israel. He said he didn't know what would come out from all this but he believed that the group was on the right track.

In the evening during dinner and afterward, sitting in the living room enjoying drinks, Ruben, Ian and Rovine discussed in great detail what the group had discovered during the day. Sarah, Aya and Dani listened and often joined in with a question or a remark. It was a good way of summing up how far they had progressed keeping everyone up-to-date.

22

JERUSALEM, ISRAEL
16 MAY 2020
PEACE NOW HEADQUARTERS
MORNING

On the way to the office, Ian and Rovine marveled at Jerusalem which had woken up to yet another beautiful and invigorating morning, one full of anticipation too.

After the group had gathered and everyone took their seats, Uri Zohar stood up and gestured for everyone to pay attention.

"I'd like to show you something I've been working on since yesterday evening," he said noticeably excited and then opened up a symbol on his computer screen so everyone else could see it on theirs.

"What is this?" Rovine asked.

"It is a watermark, or more precisely, a translucent imprint. One of the earliest documented uses of this particular watermark comes from paper manufacturers in Europe in the Middle Ages. It is said its original use dates back to the times after the Greek and Roman conquests and before the destruction of the Second Temple," Uri explained. Then he continued, "If you take a very good look at the lines of the symbol, you will see it has been sketched out of the graphics of David's Star. In fact, this symbol stands right in the heart of the star," Uri looked at everyone present, checking their reactions. He saw amazement. "What does it look like to you?"

"It looks like an A of sorts," Rovine offered and Ian nodded in agreement.

"Yes, definitely an A but one written in some archaic way," Ruben clarified.

"You are right in a way, but this is not the whole story. Undeniably, there's an interwoven A in this symbol but there's one more letter in it as well. Take a good look at the lines and tell me whether there's anything else you see," Uri waited patiently while the rest of the people in the room stared at their computer screens.

"I am not sure but I think I vaguely discern the Greek letter *pi,*" Professor Epstein offered.

"Looking at the horizontal bar, I cannot help thinking of some kind of T," Ian suggested.

"You are on the right track, Ian. The A you all spotted is most certainly there. However, the second letter is not the Greek π but a schematized version of the Hebrew *tau,*" Uri said.

"*Taw?*" Ian exclaimed in surprise.

"Yes, why?" Uri asked and then looked around, surprised at the interest he had generated. "In this watermark, *A* and *Tau* were meant to stand for the *Aleph* and *Tau,* that is, the Hebrew expression which, later on, gave rise to the Greek phrase *Alpha* and *Omega* with its meaning 'the First and the Last' or 'from beginning to end'. In some way, it is the exact equivalent of what we discovered yesterday - 1 and 1000. And that's not all. One of the scholars who studies and writes on these watermarks has suggested that the French word *auteur* originated precisely from the merging of *a* and *tau*. The author is always the first and last of what he creates," Uri Zohar explained.

"We should also bear in mind that once put together, the Hebrew letters *aleph* and *taw* yield the word *ath* (את) meaning 'a (miraculous) sign', 'a wonder' and 'a portent'," Rabbi Loew said. Then he added, "Ath is used altogether only three times in the Hebrew Bible and all of them in the Book of Daniel. I shall quote from Daniel 4:3: *'How great [are] His signs! And how mighty [are] His wonders! His kingdom [is] an everlasting kingdom, and His dominion [is] from generation to generation.'*"

"So, the Book of Daniel says it right - God's signs are truly great," Professor Epstein said.

"What's more," Ruben joined in, "The sign of God - *ath* - is interwoven right in the heart of David's Star."

"This, I think, is the most amazing discovery we've made so far," Rabbi Loew too was excited. "I mean just think about it, David's Star has been known to Jews and non-Jews for millennia."

"To be more precise, since the times of King David, when he invented the exceptionally strong shield for himself and his army in the form of two superimposed and interwoven opposite-pointed triangles - the Magen David, the Shield of David," Professor Epstein responded.

"Yes, exactly. And as a symbol, David's Star has always been related to Jews and Jewry. But we can equally well ask ourselves where did David get the inspiration and knowledge to construct such an exceptional shield? I think we know the answer. It's Him. It was He who helped David in the battle against the bastard of Geth, Goliath the Philistine. It was He who also inspired and taught David how to construct the extraordinary shield. To phrase it in your terms, Uri," Rabbi Loew looked at his friend. "God is the first and the last author of everything in the universe. And how do we know this for sure? Because God left an imprint, a kind of signature, a stamp, on his creation of the shield, right in the heart of its structure and in the form of the symbol you see before yourselves."

"So, Rabbe, you're saying that God sort of autographed his creation, am I right?" Rovine inquired.

"Yes, this is correct. Literally speaking, He put His stamp on His creation for a special few to see. Whenever people contemplate David's Star they see the star but it is only an enlightened minority that also recognizes God's stamp as interwoven in the star's heart," the rabbi explained.

23

JERUSALEM, ISRAEL
16 OCTOBER 2020
MOSSAD HEADQUARTERS
NOON

After knocking on the Mossad colonel's office door only twice, Agent Weissman slipped through the doorway as silently as a shadow.

"Colonel Zeller, sir," Weissman said, and waited.

"Yes, what is it Weissman?" Zeller asked, finally looking up.

"We know what Ruben Openheim is doing. He's gathered a group of people, six in total, together with the two Bulgarians. From what I've perceived, they've been trying to work out some puzzle or riddle."

"Any details?" Zeller asked, raising his eyebrows.

"It's all in this report," Weissman handed Zeller a file.

"I'll read it through and contact you if anything else is necessary."

"Thank you, sir," Weissman turned to leave the room.

"By the way, Weissman, how are you getting along with our surveillance operative Schwartz?"

"Perfectly, sir."

"Good. Successful cooperation is vital for our operations."

"That's right, sir."

24

JERUSALEM, ISRAEL
16 MAY 2020
PEACE NOW HEADQUARTERS
AFTERNOON

When everyone returned to the conference hall after lunch, Ruben took the floor. He began by explaining he had had a marvelous idea originating from his field of expertise – the Semitic languages. His idea was to translate the Cyrillic letters into their Hebrew equivalents. To Ian's surprise, Ruben explained most of the alphabets in the Levant and Europe owed their origin to the Phoenician alphabet. He said he had traced the Cyrillic letters back to their Latin and Greek equivalents which, in turn, he had then relayed back to their Phoenician originals. Once he had obtained the string of Phoenician letters it was easy to translate them to their corresponding Hebrew letters.

"In the end, I had a string of six Hebrew letters," Ruben said and posted the string in the communication window so everyone could see it on their screens.

"Did you arrange them to result in anything meaningful?" Ian was curious.

"I did, but I want you to look at them first…"

"So, you are saying, Ruben," Professor Epstein spoke up, "the six Cyrillic letters АДΛСУХ corresponded to *aleph, daleth, lamed, samech, vav,* and *shin,* right?"

"Absolutely. What is more, we need these letter-to-letter transmutations in order to perceive what the resulting Hebrew letters would yield," Ruben explained.

"This is a brilliant idea," Uri heartily approved. Then everyone stared at their screens, trying to combine the six letters into commonly used words.

"Now that I am looking at these letters," Professor Epstein mused, "I see the name *Lud* (לוד) – one of the sons of Shem and grandson of Noah. As some of you know, Lud was considered the progenitor of the Lydians whose kingdom Lydia was in Asia Minor between the kingdoms of Phrygia and Ionia. Curiously enough, one of the kings of Lydia who reigned over the kingdom at the time of the fall of Troy was Lydus. His brother – Tyrrhenus – sailed off westward with a group of people – called the Tyrrhenians – and reached the shores of present-day Italy. There they settled down and became known as the Etruscans."

"This is interesting but there are three letters remaining which don't yield anything," Ruben said.

"This is also true," Professor Epstein agreed.

"What else have you discovered, Ruben?" Ian inquired...

"Well, after a thorough examination of all possible combinations, I did come up with a message. It consists of two words: *eshel* (אשל) meaning 'a tamarisk tree' and *coud* (סוד) meaning 'an assembly' of 'a company' of people. At first, as you can imagine, I was puzzled because it seemed the meaning of the message was unclear. However, when I proceeded by checking on which occasions the word *eshel* had been used in the Bible, I came across 1 Samuel 22:6," Ruben began reading a quote:

When Saul heard that David was discovered, and the men that [were] with him, (now Saul abode in Gibeah under a tree in Ramah, having his spear in his hand, and all his servants [were] standing about him;)

"What this passage describes is the moment when Saul got to know the whereabouts of the constantly fleeing David. At that time, David had fled to the forest of Hareth as 1 Samuel 22:5 reports. What is interesting in this verse is that the Hebrew word *eshel,* i.e., *tamarisk* has been used in the phrase *'a tree in Ramah'.* In other words, Saul *abode under* a tamarisk tree together with *all his servants* who *were standing about him*. The people around Saul constituted a kind of company, that is, an assembly gathered with a particular reason, namely, to decide upon the capture of David. So then, the whole phrase would read something to the effect of *'the assembly under the tamarisk tree'* and would refer to Saul and his servants resolved to capture David," Ruben explained.

"There is another instance in which the word *eshel* has been used in the Bible. This is in Genesis 21:33," Rabbi Loew began quoting by heart: *'And [Abraham] planted a grove in Beersheba, and called there on the name of the LORD, the everlasting God.'*

"And as all of you probably know or remember, especially our two Bulgarian guests to whom I explained this some days earlier, this is where the first olah was offered," the Rabbi said.

"It was Abraham offering his son Isaac on Mount Moriah, here in Jerusalem," Rovine said.

"In the City of David," Ian clarified.

"Precisely," looking at them the rabbi smiled. "Well, after the angel of God stopped Abraham from offering Isaac on the altar he built for the occasion on top of Mount Moriah, Abraham offered a ram. After that, followed by Isaac, Abraham climbed down the mount and reached the garden situated amidst the Kidron Valley. There he planted a tamarisk-tree, an *eshel*, from then on considered sacred among Israelites. He also called on Ha-Shem, the sacred and unpronounceable name of God. And it was under this tree that Abraham worshipped El Olam, the everlasting God."

"Abraham was a good man and he sought to propagate his goodness and faithfulness to God through his own deeds," Professor Epstein added.

"So what Abraham did in Beersheba was a reiteration of what he had done in the garden below Mount Moriah," Rabbi Loew added thoughtfully.

Not long afterwards, the meeting ended and everyone left, full of thoughts. David's star seemed to hold much more than any of them had anticipated at the beginning of their quest.

25

JERUSALEM, ISRAEL
17 MAY 2020
MORNING

The call of duty took Aya and Dani to Rapha's apartment. It was time they stocked up on his food supplies.

When Rapha answered the door and saw Aya and Dani in front of him, he beamed with delight. He invited them in and took them straight to his kitchen. There he offered them a cup of te tsmakhim, herbal tea, he had steamed for them. After he took a sip, Dani said he thought it tasted like spearmint and Aya wanted to know how to prepare it, she liked it so much.

"Oh, dear child, I have some very old recipes. Following them, I know the exact amount of each herb or dried plant I have to use. Once I've prepared the mixture, I put it in this large jug and pour boiling water over it, very slowly so as not to bruise the herbs. Then I place a small lid on top and wait for the tea to steep."

"But where do you get the herbs from?" Dani took another sip from his cup.

"Usually I purchase the rarest herbs – the ones we cannot find in Israel – from the herb shop across the street. A neighbor of mine buys them for me. For those herbs that can be picked in our land, I usually ask an old friend of mine to pick some for me during his long walks in the fields and meadows."

"I can also buy the herbs for you, Rapha," Aya said eagerly.

"I know you can but you already have another important duty – to buy groceries for me. What you do is more than enough and I am sincerely grateful to you for that," Rapha said and smiled. Then Rapha seemed to drift away, and his eyes were clouded and their expression distant.

"Will you tell us a story?" Aya asked, interrupting the brief moment of silence and bringing Rapha back from the involuntary mental journey he seemed to have embarked on. Startled as if awakened from a light nap, Rapha looked at her.

"What kind of story do you want to hear?"

"Any kind. Whichever one you choose," she said, stirring her tea to melt the cube of sugar.

Rapha sat down and leaned back on the thick cushion of the settee. "Once, a very long time ago, in the wilderness beyond the Dead Sea, there lived a nomadic tribe. They were known as the Rechabites, the descendants of Jonadab, the son of Rechab. Jonadab had commanded them to live in tents as nomads and never to drink wine. They became goat-breeders to abide by the command of God, and on account of that, they constantly moved from place to place, to provide fresh pasture for their many goats. They had no permanent settlement. Their life was primitive and simple but pure and contented, as they explained to strangers when they were asked about their way of life. But they were known to be very strong physically and exceptionally faithful. They were fervent, loyal, uncorrupted people and staunch believers in their God."

"What was the name of their God?" Dani asked interested.

"YHWH."

"So it means they were Israelites, right?" Aya asked.

"Yes, they were related to the Israelites through their kinship to the Kenites - a tribe of wandering metalsmiths who lived in the same wilderness. It's significant for you to know that none other than Moses himself took on a Kenite wife," Rapha paused briefly and then continued.

"The Rechabites were a curious people. They had no possessions, except for their goats which provided them with food and drink and some income from sales. The only thing the Rechabites said they had was their God."

"But they didn't have him the same way as we have a book or a house or a computer or as they had goats," Aya cut in.

"No, of course not. They didn't have him in the sense of possessing him. No one can possess God. What they meant by expressing themselves in this way is that they had faith. And not just any kind of faith but the strongest kind there was on the face of the earth. When the Rechabites passed through villages in the wilderness on their way to yet another pastureland, the locals would hurry inside their houses to hide and from within they looked at them through small apertures in the walls and window panes with a mixture of awe and fear."

"Why fear?" Dani asked.

"By wandering throughout the land and having no permanent settlement and no lasting place of worship unlike the rest of the Israelites, the Rechabites had assumed the role of guardians of the faith and its purity. Whenever they passed by an altar or high place erected in veneration of one pagan deity or another, they crushed it to the ground. Circulating rumors warned everyone the Rechabites would often raid the settlements of the idolatrous worshippers of Baal –"

"Who's Baal?" Aya interrupted surprised.

"The word *bal* meant 'master' and it was the name of a deity, a weather-god worshipped throughout the land of ancient Israel. For the pious Rechabites and Israelites, Baal was an abomination, drawing many into senseless and wicked rituals and heinous idolatry."

"So what happened during the raids of the Rechabites?" Dani asked intrigued.

"Whenever they'd raid a stronghold of Baal worshippers, they'd usually slay every last one of them. The Rechabites wanted to exterminate sinful practices. They were known to be fierce combatants showing no mercy to the wicked worshippers of pagan deities.

"Although the Rechabites were nomads, one of them left the wandering group in the desert east of Jordan and settled down in a cave in search of ascetic seclusion and communion with his God. This man was Elijah, whose name meant 'God is Yahweh' and who has remained in history as a major prophet. Indeed, during his stay in a cave, Elijah received many visions from God which helped him predict a number of events that were to unfold later. Unlike the case with Moses who saw a burning bush that remained unconsumed by the flames that burnt it, Elijah heard a powerful voice, and he knew God spoke to him calmly and of pure faith..."

"Was he someone like Nostradamus?" Dani's question brought a smile to Rapha's face.

"To answer your question, Dani, I will tell you the following story. At the time of Elijah, the king of Samaria was Ahab, son of Omri, the founder of the House of Omri. King Ahab, under the influence of his Phoenician wife Queen Jezebel, sank into numerous idolatrous practices worshipping all kinds of abominations brought to the land of Israel by the queen. The Israelites too followed their king and fell into idolatry. This fact greatly angered God who revealed his anger through a prophecy he sent to Elijah, the cave dweller. Commanded by God, the prophet went to the palace of King Ahab to warn him against a three-and-a-half-year-long drought that he foresaw coming. Elijah was himself a destitute man and he spoke out on behalf of the poor and oppressed whom he sought to protect by alerting the king to the drought and giving him chance to prepare for it by increasing the kingdom's food reserves. After delivering his prophecy and under the command of God, Elijah fled the kingdom because the king had already become furious with him," Rapha said and stood up. He went to a shelf by the kitchen door and chose a book, which was the Bible. He returned to the table and sat down, opening the book and leafing through its pages. When he found what he was looking for, he said. "In 1 Kings 17:3-4 it is written how God spoke to the prophet Elijah:

Get thee hence, and turn thee eastward, and hide thyself by the brook Cherith that is before Jordan.
And it shall be, that thou shall drink of the brook; and I have commanded the ravens to feed thee there.

"What happened afterward?" Dani asked eagerly.

"While hiding from the king's pursuers, Elijah remained by the brook of Cherith. In the meantime the drought he had prophesied hit the Kingdom of Samaria. There was no rain. Wells dried up and so did brooks. The crops withered. People began starving. Everyday many of them would awaken to search the morning skies for signs of rain but there were none.

"Then Elijah received another command by God - to leave the brook of Cherith. He did so and began traveling alone on the road. While wondering, Elijah walked past Scythopolis and climbed up Mount Tabor. When he descended the mount on the other side, he reached the Plain of Esdraelon where accidentally he met yet again with his wandering fellow-Rechabites. He joined them and they passed the Valley of Iphtael together. Soon they reached the city of Achshaph in the foot of Mount Carmel. There, suddenly, Elijah had a vision. He received an owth, a sign, from God who commanded him to travel south, to the foot of Mount Carmel. Elijah told his fellow Rechabites about the vision and, sensing they were a formidable group, they marched on south. Soon they reached the boundaries of the Kingdom of Samaria and the foot of Mount Carmel. When they got to the place seen in the vision, they saw a despicable scene. There was a large booth with a large table at which King Ahab and Queen Jezebel of Samaria and their sons were sitting. They were preparing for a special rain-invoking ceremony with their Baal-priests. The ceremony was to be carried out at the highest place on Mount Carmel. On the left as well as on the right, the booth was surrounded by a huge number of tables whose seats were occupied by a hitherto unseen crowd of Baal priests," Rapha said and leafed through the Bible. Then he read from it (1 Kings 18:19): '*... and the prophets of Baal four hundred and fifty, and the prophets of the groves four hundred, which eat at Jezebel's table.*'"

"Were the prophets of Baal really so many?" Dani asked in disbelief.

"Yes, 850 altogether," Rapha replied.

"Wow," Dani exclaimed.

"All tables were lavishly laden with food," Rapha continued relating the story. "The king and the queen, their sons and the 850 priests were in the middle of a shameless exercise of public gluttony. The ravenous priests could be seen stuffing themselves with meat and other treats. A voracious appetite was visible on their faces and in their insatiable eyes."

"Were the priests so hungry?" Aya asked.

"No, but they were greedy and wanted to consume as much food as possible. To Elijah's surprise, however, a bit farther away from the lavish tables, he could see another crowd gathering, yet they had sullen faces, starving eyes, skinny bodies covered in rags. They were the poor peasants of the kingdom who were waiting for the rain-invoking ceremonies to begin. While waiting, they had involuntarily turned into witnesses of this pompous, self-gratifying event. Elijah was outraged. He was furious. The ferocious Rechabites - the combatants of their one and only Yahweh - were instantly ready to slay all priests and the royal family. But by raising his hand, wise Elijah stopped them just on time. He had something else in mind."

"What was it, Rapha?" Dani was impatient to get the answer.

"Elijah split from the multitude and started climbing the mount. Once he had reached the damaged altar of Yahweh at the top, he shouted out the following words: *'Have faith in Him or hide!'* All eyes suddenly were focused on him. He continued to speak loudly and addressing the Baal priests, he challenged to a rain-invoking contest. He told them that if they succeeded in summoning their god Baal to bring rain, then all gathered were obliged to follow Baal. If the reverse were true, and it was Elijah's God Yahweh that brought rain, then all people were to follow Him and not Baal. Surprised by the challenge, the priests of Baal had no other choice but to engage in the proposed contest. They laughed at the wild-looking, hairy man who had confronted them and mocked him for wearing only his girdle of leather about his loins. Elijah just stood there firmly and paid no attention to the ridicule because he knew he had much more important mission – to take people out of idolatrous worship and bring them back to the one and only true God.

"And so, the priests of Baal began performing their rituals for rain-making. Some of them kneeled and recited magical invocations. Others took knives and began making cuts into their own skin until blood gushed from their upper and lower limbs. Still others cried out, loudly begging god Baal for rain. But nothing happened."

"Absolutely nothing? Like no sign of rain at all?" Aya asked with astonishment.

"Yes, absolutely nothing. From above, Elijah began mocking the multitude of crying and self-mutilating priests of Baal. Here the Bible describes it (1 Kings 18:27): '*And it came to pass at noon, that Elijah mocked them [the prophets of Baal], and said, Cry aloud: for he [is] a god; either he is talking, or he is pursuing, or he is in a journey [or] peradventure he sleepeth, and must be awaked.*'"

"So Elijah was suggesting that their god may be asleep and unable to hear their cries because he was indifferent to their pleas," Aya surmised.

"Yes, Elijah wanted to show that if their god was a real one, he would have responded to the summon of his priests. But he didn't reply because most probably he was busy with something else, something more important. So, seeing the futility of all actions of the prophets of Baal, Elijah gathered up twelve large stones."

"Why twelve?" Dani inquired.

"To match the number of tribes of Israel. With the stones he repaired the damaged altar of Yahweh. Elijah dutifully placed offerings on top of the repaired altar and began praying to Yahweh asking Him to show that He was the one and only true God of Israel. Instantly, God's fire descended from the heavens and consumed the offerings. Upon seeing that, the people who had gathered at Mount Carmel fell on their faces and acknowledged unanimously the singularity of YHWH – the only God of Israel. At this point, Elijah called on the crowd of poor people to round up all of the priests of Baal and not to let anyone of them escape. The people vehemently attacked the priests and captured them. They were then dragged to the brook of Kishon where Elijah and his fierce Rechabites slew them all."

"All of them?" Dani exclaimed in disbelief.

"Yes, all 850 of them."

"That's a lot of people!" Dani remarked.

"Who had, mind you, inflicted much damage to the veneration of Yahweh in the lands of Israel."

"What happened to Elijah afterward?" Aya asked.

"As you can imagine, Jezebel the queen, being of Phoenician stock and a potent sorceress swore bitter vengeance to Elijah for slaying her priests. But Elijah remained unconcerned about Jezebel's oath of revenge."

"Why?" Aya inquired.

"Because he knew what would happen to her."

"How?" again Aya.

"God had already revealed it to him while he was still residing in the cave," Rapha replied.

"What was supposed to happen to the queen?" Dani asked.

"Her corpse would be chewed up by stray dogs."

"Ugh," Aya grimaced.

"Shortly after slaying the 850 prophets of Baal, Elijah met his attendant and disciple Elisha. God commanded Elijah to anoint Elisha as his successor. As they were walking in the wilderness, a whirlwind suddenly appeared and swept Elijah off his feet who then mounted a chariot of fire drawn by horses that were themselves ablaze and they all ascended to heaven. Elisha was left holding Elijah's snow-white mantle which he carried with him all the way to the capital Samaria where he met Jehu. Together they planned how to deal with the idolatrous king and queen. First Jehu went to the chambers of King Ahab who was lying in bed, wounded very seriously in the battle of Ramoth-Gilead and slew him then and there. Then Jehu went to the queen and threw her out of the window. Stray dogs immediately gathered and began to tear into her mutilated body just as Elijah had prophesized. Jehu went on to slaughter all remaining prophets of Baal in a campaign to exterminate pagan practices in Israel. Once he accomplished this and gained the popular support of the people who had returned to their faith in Yahweh, Jehu became king," Rapha smiled as he finished the story.

"It was a bloody episode in our history," Aya commented thoughtfully.

"There was a reason for that, dear Aya. If we hadn't succeeded in maintaining belief in our one and only God, we would not have been able to preserve ourselves as community. This belief kept us together and intact throughout the centuries and prevented others from assimilating us.

"As you pointed out, this was but an episode of our ancient history. In later centuries we had other similar problems with the invasion and introduction of pagan, idolatrous, and non-Jewish religious practices. It was for this reason that a century after the death of the prophet Elijah, some of the wandering Rechabites were asked to settle near Jerusalem."

"Why?" Aya inquired.

"To help maintain the purity of our faith. They were among the most fervent followers of Yahweh."

"Did they agree? Because you said they were nomads for the most part," Dani asked.

"Surprisingly, some of them did agree. They chose a site some five kilometers south of the City of David and built their settlement there," Rapha explained.

"What did they name it?" Aya asked.

"Rekah."

26

JERUSALEM, ISRAEL
17 MAY 2020
PEACE NOW HEADQUARTERS
MORNING

The team put together by Ruben Openheim reconvened early the next day, all of them driven by zeal to uncover additional symbols and meaning. They were enjoying a second cup of coffee, when Ruben tapped his water glass with his spoon and everyone grew silent and attentive as he began speaking.

"Yesterday's conversation really got me thinking," Ruben said and looked at everyone in turn. "Yesterday we spoke about Elijah and Ahab's kingdom with its capital, the city of Samaria. This particular city features prominently in history as the place of origin of the Samaritans and their language," Ruben paused for a moment.

"As you know I am a linguist in Semitic languages by education and formerly by vocation, too. This is the reason why I want to make a clarification related to this field. The Semitic languages divide into two major branches - East and West Semitic. The West Semitic branch then opens into two divisions - Northwest and Southwest Semitic languages. The Northwest division breaks into two subdivisions - Aramaic and Canaanitic languages. On its part, the Aramaic subdivision splits in the Eastern and Western Aramaic subgroups. The Samaritan language belongs to the second subgroup."

"Is there any linguistic connection between Samaritan and Hebrew?" Rovine asked.

"In fact there is. They belong to the Northwest Semitic languages, but while Hebrew belongs to the Canaanitic languages, Samaritan to the Aramaic ones."

"This is really interesting," Rovine remarked.

"Indeed it is. However, there's something even more compelling. We spoke about the Kingdom of Samaria yesterday and that made me think of the Samaritans, their language and most importantly their alphabet. I resolved to check whether any of the Samaritan letters had been interwoven in the graphics of David's Star. I worked late last night and I got a result. There are three interwoven Samaritan letters."

"This is exciting, indeed," Rovine exclaimed. The others also looked at him with curiosity.

"Which letters?" Uri Zohar drummed on the table impatiently. Everyone had already noticed that he had a habit of fidgeting when he was excited.

"The Samaritan *gimel, lamed,* and *taw,*" Ruben replied and uploaded a visual diagram of the three letters to everyone's screen.

"Amazing," Ian exclaimed in his turn.

"The truly astounding find is that we don't have only three letters. We've got six of them. What you see on the diagram in front of you are three letters each on the left wing of the star. But it has a right wing as well," Ruben pointed out.

"So, we've got two *gimel*s, two *lamed*s and two *taw*s," Uri concluded, his legs now vibrating rhythmically with excitement.

"Exactly," Ruben confirmed. "The question about their meaning, however, remains largely unresolved."

"What do you mean by largely?" Professor Epstein asked.

"You will see for yourselves shortly that it is quite difficult to arrange a pangram out of this set of letters," Ruben explained.

"Have you come up with any results, Ruben?" the professor inquired.

"The nearest thing to a pangram I got was two times the Aramaic noun *telag* (תלג) meaning 'snow'."

"This is why we are here after all, to try to solve the riddles we come across," Rabbi Loew said.

"So we need to do our best to retrieve the meaning of these six letters," Uri chimed in. All of them concentrated on the screens in front of them.

******

"There are plenty of single words I can perceive," Uri Zohar said after awhile.

"Yes, I also discovered a lot last night," Ruben agreed.

"The thing is, we have to find one pangram message with all letters used only once," Ian said.

"If possible," Professor Epstein pointed out.

"The longest word I've unscrambled so far is *gulgoleth* (גלגלת) meaning 'a skull'," Uri said.

"One *taw* remains unused," Ruben observed.

"Yes, I know but I don't know what to do with it," Uri said.

"I think I've got it," Rabbi Loew said after contemplatively re-arranging the letters.

"What do you have, Rabbe?" Ruben asked, his curiosity now aroused because he knew the learned rabbi wouldn't speak if he hadn't come up with something important.

"When the two *gimel*s and *lamed*s are put together, they yield the Hebrew *gilgal* (גלגל) meaning 'a circle of standing stones'. Gilgal was the first site at which the exiled and wandering Israelites camped after they crossed the River Jordan," the Rabbi explained.

"The place was east of Jericho," Professor Epstein added.

"Exactly," the Rabbi confirmed.

"But the two *taw*s remain unused," Uri Zohar remarked.

"Not true," Rabbi Loew disagreed. "When placed next to each other, the two *taw*s don't yield anything, which is true. However, if they are taken as their numerical values, that is, two times 400, we'll get the sum total of 800."

“What do we do with 800 then?” Uri inquired.

“We take it as one of Strong’s numbers and as such it corresponds to the noun *eshshah* (אשה) meaning ‘fire’. Hence the entire phrase reads ‘The Fire of Gilgal’,” the Rabbi explained.

“What could it possibly mean?” Ian asked.

“Good question ... Now that I come to think of it and based on what I know, I believe there’s an interesting interpretation of ‘The Fire of Gilgal’,” the rabbi paused for a moment.

“You see, Elijah was known as the fiery one. When he was born his father had a dream. In it, the father saw his son being born and then wrapped in sheets of fire. Not only this, the new born was given not milk but fire to eat. The father woke up sweating and stressed. The next day he bid his wife good-bye and set out on the road to Jerusalem. When he got there, he went to the Temple, towering above the City of David, to consult the priests about his vision. Upon hearing about his dream, the priests told him not to be afraid because his son was going to be like fire and his words were going to be like fire as well, burning wrongdoers for their evil.

“Later in life, following the tradition established by the prophet Samuel, Elijah the fiery gathered a group of young men around him and founded a school of the prophets in Gilgal, in the Kingdom of Samaria. Long before Elijah, Samuel had founded similar schools in Bethel, Gibeah and Jericho. You might ask why exactly Elijah founded the school nowhere else but in Gilgal. The answer follows. One day, when Elisha, later the most fervent pupil of Elijah, was born, a miracle took place. Just after Elisha’s birth, a mighty bull in Gilgal lowed so loudly his low was heard in Jerusalem. Upon hearing the powerful low, the chief priests in the Temple said a mighty prophet had been born, one who would destroy all idolatrous images of pagan deities worshipped across the land of Israel,” the rabbi concluded.

“So the phrase ‘The Fire of Gilgal’ could be taken as a metaphor for the prophet Elijah the fiery and his most zealous pupil Elisha, is that right?” Rovine inquired.

“Absolutely,” the Rabbi agreed.

“But then why would Elijah feature so prominently in the context of David’s Star?” she asked further.

“Because it is said the advent of the Messiah will be announced by no other than Elijah the fiery himself who would return to earth shortly before it takes place. And, even more importantly, the Messiah will be a descendant of the House of David,” the rabbi explained. There was this moment of silence during which the assembled tried to assimilate what the rabbi had just said. In a way, it all made perfect sense. The rabbi spoke again.

“I also have an explanation for Ruben’s double encounter of the Aramaic word *telag* which is used only once in the Tanakh. In Daniel 7:9 the Ancient of the Days was described as being dressed in ‘garments white as snow’. In his last day, Elijah, accompanied by his loyal pupil Elisha, set off on the road in the wilderness beyond Gilgal. They were both dressed in garments as white as snow to exemplify their purity and devotion to Yahweh – hence two times *telag*. Then the whirlwind appeared and with it the fiery chariot which took Elijah to heaven. During Elijah’s ascent, his garment fell. Elisha picked it up and kept it because he knew it was a symbol of prophetic inspiration,” the Rabbi said.

“So it all somehow falls into place,” Ian said.

“Thanks to this series of amazing discoveries and interpretations we seem to have accommodated it all,” Ruben added.

27

JERUSALEM, ISRAEL

17 MAY 2020

RAPHA'S APARTMENT

NOON

"Here are your groceries, Rapha," Aya said as Dani lifted two full paper bags on the table in the kitchen. "I saw the red apples were really fresh today, so I bought a kilo. I know how much you like apples!" She smiled proudly at her old friend when she saw how pleased he was.

"Ah, this is good of you, Aya. They really have a wonderful smell."

"The woman at the pharmacy told me to say hello to you."

"Toda raba (thank you very much). Deborah is a very kind and caring woman. Everybody in the neighborhood likes her and shops at her store."

"Yes, I saw with how much care she packed all your herbs. She is very nice –"

"– And talkative," Dani added.

"He's right. The moment she found out Dani was from Bulgaria she literally overwhelmed him with questions. She told us her grandparents had been born there."

"Yes, I know!" Rapha almost laughed out loud, as he remembered Deborah's talkative manner.

"She said she was so grateful to the Bulgarian people for sparing their fellow Jewish countrymen from the Nazi concentration camps. I didn't know much about that episode of history."

"It's a long and very painful story," Rapha said, "but the important thing is to recognize is that due to the concerted and selfless efforts of a number of prominent politicians and the Bulgarian people as a whole, not a single Bulgarian Jew from the 49,000-strong Jewish community was sent to the Nazi death camps during the Second World War."

"I know about it, too," Dani said. "I've studied it at school."

"At that time, there were a few selfless politicians who risked their lives and political status to make that happen. I think this is a great heroic act in itself," Rapha said.

"Deborah thinks the same. She said she really wanted to visit Bulgaria one day. She had heard a lot about it from her grandparents before they died. But she said she had a lot of work and was needed here," Aya said.

"One day I know she will visit Bulgaria, when she has more spare time. She is right because many people in the neighborhood rely on her for their herbal preparations and medicaments. They know they can trust her. Are you able to stay a little longer with me?" Rapha raised his bushy eyebrows with a hopeful look in his eyes.

"Yes, we are," Aya replied.

"Let's have tea and I'll tell you another interesting story!" He had already put the tea kettle full of water on the stove to bring to a boil for the tea.

"What is the story?" Dani asked eagerly.

"It's an old one," Rapha said as he lifted mugs down out of the cupboard and put three spoons on the table along with the sugar bowl. "It happened long time ago, somewhere in distant Hesperia..."

"Hesperia?" Aya interrupted, puzzled.

"Yes, Hesperia or Western Lands as opposed to Levant or Eastern Lands," Rapha clarified as he folded three paper napkins very precisely into triangles.

"This is too general. Where was Hesperia?" Dani inquired.

"All lands west of Greece to the end of the known world," Rapha answered.

"This means to westernmost Portugal," Dani again.

"No, the westernmost parts of the Albion Islands," Rapha turned off the gas flame under the tea kettle.

"What was meant by the Levant then?" Dani asked, impatiently.

"The Easternmost Mediterranean," Rapha answered quietly as he poured boiling water over the tea bags in all three mugs. He looked at the two teenagers staring at him with fascinated expectation, and then continued telling his story.

"So once, somewhere in Hesperia, in a town overlooked by a castle, there was a separate quarter surrounded by walls and hosting a relatively large Jewish community. All of its members were good citizens paying their levies regularly and strictly abiding by all local rules and regulations. The monarch who lived in the castle was neither ill-disposed nor particularly approving of the Jews. They received his protection as did everybody else. For him, they were equal to all other citizens and were treated the same way. However, the local population, mainly poor peasants, hated the Jews because the latter worked hard, earned well and lived a prosperous life.

"One day, in the morning, the town-crier announced the monarch was going to visit the Jewish community in three days' time. The Jews immediately began preparing. Their tidy homes were swept twice a day instead of only once. Most façades were given a new coat of paint. Roofs, balconies, windows were repaired where needed. Pots of blooming flowers were put everywhere. On the morning of the third day, the Jewish Quarter shone in meticulous, spotless splendor. Even the locals stared in disbelief. Their own miserable huts couldn't compare to those wonderfully clean houses of the Jews. Naturally, bitter envy wedged itself into the poor peasants' hearts. One of them went so far as to swear vengeance to restore justice in the face of what he conceived as gross disparity..." Rapha sipped from his mug of tea.

"Was there really such a huge rift between the Jews and the local peasants?" Dani asked.

"Most of the peasants were just unskilled workers whereas among the Jews there were many craftsmen and tradesmen.

They earned well and they donated to their community. That was why even the poor Jews had a relatively good life.

"So when the monarch arrived, all Jews had lined up along the main street of their quarter. They were holding flowers in their hands and were cheering him as he slowly rode by in his open carriage. The monarch was really pleased with the hearty reception and was smiling joyfully. Then, all of a sudden, a large brick landed on the floor of the carriage, right next to the standing monarch. The coachman whipped the horse and they lunged forward. The monarch sped out of the Jewish Quarter and into his castle. The following day, the town-crier arrived. He announced the monarch demanded the wrongdoer to be brought to justice the following day. Otherwise, the whole community would be bitterly punished. Naturally, panic and fear quickly overwhelmed the entire community. They didn't know who the perpetrator of the heinous act was. The rabbi hastened to the castle to try to appease the monarch and settle the matter. Upon his return, he looked grim. All the Jews knew they were doomed. They began praying all through the remainder of the day and well into the evening. Some of them continued throughout the night. In the morning of the following day, a cart arrived from the castle to carry the wrongdoer to face justice. All Jews were out in the square, standing and shivering in fearful anticipation. As the cart was about to leave empty, a man stepped out from the crowd. His name was Eshiyah and he and his wife had six children. He bid his wife farewell by hugging and kissing her. She started crying bitterly, her body shaking as though in fever. He kissed each one of his children. The older ones began crying as well. The three youngest didn't know what was going on but they saw their mother and siblings bitterly weeping so they wept too. The rest of the crowd stared at Eshiyah in disbelief and pain. No one could believe the humility and courage of Eshiyah who had been known as a very quiet man. His selfless act shook everyone to the core. No one had expected something like this from Eshiyah."

"How awfully terrible and sad! Rapha this is a horrific story," Aya interrupted, her eyes welled up.

"Our people know many such stories of suffering, dear child," Rapha said and stroked her head. Then he resumed the story.

"And so, Eshiyah mounted the cart and off it went up to the castle. The whole day the entire community prayed for the salvation of Eshiyah. The next day, at the town's central square, a stake in the middle of a pyre was hastily erected and Eshiyah was brought out in chains and tied to it. Then the monarch arrived with his entourage to watch the punishment. He took his place under a large booth. Then one of the executioners lit the thick pile of kindling around Eshiyah's feet.

"Just at that moment, the sky got dark and a rain storm hit the square, its deluge instantly putting out the fire around the stake. The crowd scattered into nearby houses and under roofs to wait for the storm to end. The monarch was under the shelter of his booth. Only poor Eshiyah stayed out in the rain, alone and chained to the stake. Soon, the storm ended as suddenly as it had started. The sun broke out. People emerged from their shelters and a crowd formed once again around the stake. The wet wood was replaced with dry and the executioner once again lit the fire at the stake.

"For a second time, clouds instantly rolled up above the square and the gates of a second downpour flew open. All people ran away to their previous shelters. The monarch was furious. He cursed the bad weather. Soon the sun broke out for a second time. Again the executioners set about fixing the fire at the stake. This time some of the peasants joined in to help them. When all was ready the fire was lit for a third time. And for a third time, the mysterious heavy shower broke out and extinguished the fire. Only then did the monarch realize that this was no ordinary happening. He knew it was impossible for three cloudbursts to take place in such a short succession. He saw Divine Providence in this act. Then he also realized God was telling him poor Eshiyah was not guilty of the crime he had been accused of. Thus the monarch ordered Eshiyah to be released and set free. The crowd of Jews which had gathered on the other side of the square rejoiced in loud voices. Eshiyah started off in their direction. Just in that moment, a large brick was thrown at the poor man. He only moved his head to the left and the brick flew by his ear and fell on the ground before him. Eshiyah didn't turn back."

"Why?" Aya asked excitedly.

"Because there was no need. The monarch, his entourage and all the poor peasants saw who threw the brick. It was one of the wickedest men in town. He was instantly captured and brought before the monarch who began questioning him. The wicked man confessed his desire to set up the Jews for the attempted murder of the monarch. Without any further delay, he was burnt at the stake and justice was served and peace restored."

It was already time for lunch and Aya and Dani bid Rapha good-bye and hurried back home. On the way back, they discussed the story they had just heard. It turned out they both liked its message about envy being the wickedest mentor.

28

JERUSALEM, ISRAEL
17 MAY 2020
PEACE NOW HEADQUARTERS
AFTERNOON

After the lunch break, Uri Zohar was kind of agitated, the way one is when one really wants to do something right away. In his case, Uri was eager to speak. It was obvious. He had been quiet and pensive all throughout the lunch.

"After a careful examination of our Hebrew alphabet," Uri began, "I found a curious fact. There's only one Hebrew letter interwoven in the graphics of David's Star."

"Which one?" Ruben was intrigued.

"Tsade," Uri said and instantly uploaded a schematized picture of the graphic on his computer and transmitted it to everyone's screen.

"Excellent work, Uri!" Ruben was impressed.

"It means we've got two *tsade*s, one on each of the star's two wings," Ian observed.

"Yes, that's true," Uri agreed.

"Any suggestions as to what to do with them?" Ruben asked looking around at everyone in turn.

"To me, the two *tsade*s put together are like an abbreviation. For instance, two *koph*s written together stand for an abbreviation of *Kahal Kadosh* or Holy Congregation," Rabbi Loew pointed out.

"What could two *tsade*s stand for in our case and in the context of David's Star?" Ruben asked puzzled.

"Think of words beginning with the letter *tsade*," the Rabbi urged everyone. Once again, silence fell over the room.

"How about *Tsedeq Tsion* (צדק ציון)?" Uri Zohar suggested after a while.

"The Righteousness of Zion," Ruben translated. "It could be."

"Alternatively, *Tsadi Tsion* (צדי ציון)," Uri further suggested.

"Righteous Zion," Ruben, translated again.

"How about *Tsiyr Tsion* (ציר ציון)?" Uri proposed.

"The Messenger of Zion," Ruben said.

"The Star as a Messenger of Zion and at the same time standing for a symbol of the Righteousness of Zion," Uri pressed further.

"You are striking a chord there, Uri, but let's hear a few more suggestions," Ruben said in a move to mediate the situation. He wanted to hear what the Rabbi and the professor would say.

"You see, I tend to agree partially with Mr. Zohar," Professor Epstein said and continued. "I think he definitely struck a chord with his interpretation. I will tell you why. Take David's Star. What is it? Before all, it's a symbol. It has always been one for that matter. We should bear that in mind at all times. This way it will not be difficult to take the star as a symbol standing for, say, the 'Righteousness of Zion'. Why not? It sounds perfectly credible. But most of us know the other name of David's Star is *Magen David* (מגן דוד). Herein lies the key for me. In our Jewish tradition we don't see the two-interwoven triangles as a star but as a shield. It is a symbol of protection of what is dear and holy to us. Hence, for me there is only one reason why anyone would interweave two tsades in Magen David and the reason is *Tsinnah Tsion,* (צנה ציון), the Shield of Zion, or, if you prefer, *Tsinnah Tsedeq* (צנה צדק), that is, the Shield of Righteousness," Professor Epstein said and looked around to see how his opinion had been taken.

"Very interesting interpretation," Ruben added thoughtfully.

"*Tsinnah Tsion* sounds credible to me as well," Ian agreed and added. "I mean, the Shield of David is the Shield of Zion since David's residence was the stronghold of Zion."

"Precisely," Professor Epstein vigorously confirmed. "After all it was David who conquered the Jebusite stronghold which was on top of Mount Zion. Since that moment, David and his shield had been protecting Zion.

"I'd like to clarify something here," Rabbi Loew suddenly interrupted everyone. "I cannot agree more with what you are saying, gentlemen. Either *Tsinnah Tsion* or *Tsinnah Tsedeq,* they both fit well into our context and make sense. For me, however, the discovery of the two tsades is ominous enough and its meaning is absolutely clear. There's only one interpretation of this discovery we've made. The answer lies once again with the Tanakh, our most venerated book. Allow me to quote for you from the Book of Jeremiah, chapter 23, verse 5:

Behold, the days come, saith the LORD, that I will raise unto David a righteous Branch, and a King shall reign and prosper, and shall execute judgment and justice in the earth.

"This is a very portentous verse. It speaks about the end of days, judgment day. Then, God says, he will 'raise unto David a righteous Branch'. The words Righteous Branch stand in Hebrew for *Tsaddiyk Tsemach* (צדיק צמח). These are two *tsades* together – *Tsaddiyk Tsemach* or the sprout of David, that is, the Messiah, the future king. The second confirmation of my claim lies again with Jeremiah. This time it is chapter 33, verse 15:

In those days, and at that time, will I cause the Branch of righteousness to grow up unto David; and he shall execute judgment and righteousness in the land.

"Here again, the Messiah, the future sprout of David, is referred to as the Branch of Righteousness or *Tsemach Tsedeqah* (צמח צדקה). It is about David and it lies interwoven in his star or shield, if you prefer," the Rabbi said. And everyone knew he had indisputably made a sound point.

"So, we could deduce David's Star stands for the Shield of Zion, the one protecting the land of the Jews and as the Branch of Righteousness who is the future Messiah, one of the House of David. Right?" Ian proudly summarized the conversation.

"Yes, you are right, we could deduce what you've just summed up because both interpretations are equally credible," Professor Epstein said.

"I agree," Rabbi Loew announced.

"It means we've reached an important point. We've just discovered what lies interwoven in David's Star through the two *tsade*s expresses the essence of what the star stands for as a symbol," Ruben recapped.

"I think this discovery of ours also adds to the understanding why we Jews have chosen precisely this star to be our national symbol – it stands for David as much as it does for Zion," Professor Epstein clarified.

"True," Uri Zohar agreed.

"But it just occurred to me that there is one more aspect to the two letters. *Tsade* is the 18th letter in the Hebrew alphabet, its name צדי is the Hebrew word for 'righteous'," Professor Epstein said as though thinking aloud.

"The adjective *tsadi* shares the same root as the noun *tsadik* or צדוק meaning 'a righteous person'," Ruben explained.

"I am thinking here of the *tsadikim,*" the professor said pensively.

"Who are they?" Rovine inquired.

"In Jewish tradition, it is believed there are 36 righteous men in every generation, the so-called *lamedvav tsadikim* or *lamedvavniks,*" the professor clarified.

"*Lamedvav?*" Rovine didn't understand totally.

"The number 36 is expressed in Hebrew with the letters *lamed* which equals 30 and *vav,* 6. Hence *lamedvav* or number 36. The origin of the *lamedvavnik* tradition could be traced as far back as the Babylonian Talmud where it was first found. Since then, the belief in their unselfish and miraculous work had been handed down from generation to generation," the professor said.

"The *lamedvav tsadikim* are completely anonymous. They help sustain the world and it is for their sake the World is spared, that is, not destroyed by God. Figuratively speaking, we owe our existence to them," Rabbi Loew added.

"So 36 in every generation?" Ian asked thoughtfully.

"Just like the Talmud and later on the Kabbalah taught," Uri explained.

"Just like the two *tsade*s on each wing of the star. 18 plus 18 equals 36," Ruben chimed in.

"Openly hidden amongst us, nobody actually knows who they are," Professor Epstein began. "What is more, they themselves don't know who they really are. They don't know they belong to the *lamedvavniks*. They are hidden, yet right among us. They are one of us, yet unknown to anyone of us. With their selfless acts, they constantly bring about goodness to the world."

"There's one thing I don't understand. Why would there be reference to those *lamedvavniks* in David's Star?" Rovine asked, puzzled.

"Because the Messiah will be one of them – the thirty-sixth, the *Tsaddiyk Tsemach,*" Rabbi Loew said.

29

JERUSALEM, ISRAEL

17 MAY 2020

OUTSIDE PEACE NOW HEADQUARTERS

LATE AFTERNOON

The two Mossad agents were sitting side-by-side in the black inconspicuous Chevrolet sedan, trying to be as unobtrusive as possible. They had been parked there watching the headquarters of Peace Now for the most part of the day. To Agent Schwartz the shift seemed to drag on indefinitely. She felt exhausted. Then as she was listening to what the people upstairs were talking about she said.

"Have you ever heard about those lamedvavniks, Chasin?"

"Yes, I have. My grandfather used to tell me stories about the anonymous 36 men who maintain the balance in our world…"

"It sounds like bedtime stories for little kids to me. Besides what's the relevance of all this?" Agent Schwartz looked straight ahead.

"What do you mean?"

"They've been discussing some letters and symbols for days. What's the point? I don't get it."

"I guess they want to make sense of their initial discoveries and reach some conclusions, if possible..."

"And so what if they find more? It's only letters and numbers that they find anyway."

"It's not so simple, Adah. Look at what they have achieved recently. True, they have discerned some letters and numbers embedded in our Star of David. And when they put them together, amazing things have come out."

"Most of the things we already know."

"But not all of them... Besides, you never know what they may come up with if they keep digging in that direction."

"And why are we assigned to do all this sitting and watching! It's so uninspiring," she said with a facial expression indicating her boredom.

"I guess you signed up for the job expecting it to be like James Bond excitement twenty-four-seven..."

"I guess I did," she said and smiled, looking at him.

"Imagine, what we're going now is the part we never get to see in the James Bond movies."

30

JERUSALEM, ISRAEL

17 MAY 2020

EVENING

In the evening, the two families decided to go out before dinner. It was very warm outside and quite pleasant for taking a stroll. There were many other families out in the streets of the neighborhood. It was springtime in Jerusalem, one of the loveliest times of the year. While walking, the parents discussed their work while Sarah listened closely and asked questions from time to time. Dani and Aya were listening as well. They learned much about the lamedvavniks through the discussions of their parents.

After a few blocks, they came to a bar with an open-air terrace overlooking part of the city. They sat down at a large table with a beautiful mosaic-tile surface and ordered aperitifs. Dani told his parents about his and Aya's visits to Rapha and about the interesting stories the old man told them. When Ian inquired about the nature of the stories, Dani began relating the story about the selfless act of Eshiyah. Aya joined in occasionally by adding some details.

The parents were impressed with the story, especially Ian who went pensive for awhile.

After everyone had finished their drinks, all of them strolled back home for dinner. Once again Sarah had prepared a delicious, nourishing dish of rice, meat and vegetables. In the meantime, more discussions about the Star of David followed. After dinner, Aya told Sarah she was going to take Dani out for an evening walk.

"Don't be gone too long, sweetheart!" Sarah watched the two young people walk out into the sunset of the evening.

Outside, it was the magic hour of fading light in the skies merging slowly and gracefully into thick darkness. Dani and Aya hurried along the street, walking silently, each looking around. Dani's hand inadvertently brushed into Aya's. They looked at each other, still walking.

"Let's cross the street," Aya said. In the middle, they could see the downtown lights ahead. On the other side, they kept walking. Soon they reached a small city garden to the left. It had a low fence running along the street side. In the middle, a white wrought iron gate stood ajar. Aya walked into the garden and Dani followed. Inside the area, narrow cobbled alleys wound in stylish parabolas through the gardens ahead. Bushes and low trees grew in disciplined groupings and the grass was meticulously mown. The strong and pleasant aroma of gardenias and roses filled the air around the teenagers as they inhaled the spring air together.

"Aya, can you see anything?"

Without saying a word, she gently took Dani's hand and made him stride behind her. The branches of the low trees were enlaced above their heads, shielding the city's lights reflected by the sky above. Suddenly, they found themselves in a clearing. Aya sat down on a small bench surrounded by evergreen shrubs. Dani sat by her side. She leaned back and slowly rested her head on the back of the bench. He did the same. This way they were looking straight up at the night sky and were still holding hands. After awhile, Dani turned his head and looked at her. She did the same. Their eyes locked on each other as if they had always meant to be as close as they were right here and right now. A burning light shined forth from her eyes, untamed, untamable. A glow of teenage fever echoed in his, erupting, gushing upward. Her lips, so full but soft, delicate, graceful and tender, all at the same time. His nose, protruding boldly in an ever so masculine manner, sturdy, dignified. Her chin so fine, small and elegant. His lips were irresistible. His mouth moved an inch closer and stopped. Breathing time. Then it moved another inch closer. More breathing time. Then another inch forward. Still more breathing time. The last inches separating them were covered imperceptibly and soon there were no inches left keeping them apart. Their lips, propelled by a forthcoming eruption of ardor, touched ever so gently and then the persistent longing took over and they kissed tenderly, as if they had always known they would. Their shared intense breathing felt like a potent drift of hot air spurting through smooth alcoves and apexes, soft nooks and crevasses.

Both pairs of lips instinctively parted, ever so slightly. Then they brushed together most tenderly. A first and most gentle kiss. Then, the overwhelming sudden gush of excitement, and Aya and Dani were caught up in an ardent whirlwind of kisses.

The night had fallen fast. Only the moon above was witness to the birth of a sweet love.

31

JERUSALEM, ISRAEL
18 MAY 2020
PEACE NOW HEADQUARTERS
MORNING

Two days left until the 20th of May.

"Today, I'd like to share a new discovery with you," Ruben began. "Since yesterday's uncovering of the three pairs of Samaritan letters, I've had the idea of checking whether, by chance, any other Semitic letters might have been interwoven in the graphics of David's Star. Yesterday evening we had a lengthy discussion with Ian and Rovine about the Phoenician alphabet – the one that made the bridge between the Semitic and the Greek and through the latter to the Latin and most of the other European alphabets."

"We did come up with a startling finding," Ian said.

"No less than six individual Phoenician letters are interwoven in David's Star," Ruben said, a tinge of triumph in his voice.

"An entire set?" Uri was surprised.

"Yes, very originally interwoven letters: *'alef, gimel, dālet, wāw, lāmed,* and *taw,*" Ruben pasted a scanned hand-drawn illustration of six stars, each depicting one of the letters in bold script.

"All of these letters are harmoniously interwoven into the graphics of David's Star," Rovine noted with excitement.

"As most of you know, we Jews have derived our Hebrew alphabet from the Phoenician one," Ruben said, the rest nodding in agreement.

"It's interesting to note we've only discovered a single pair of Hebrew letters, the *tsades*, directly interwoven in the graphics of the star. No other Hebrew letters. Otherwise, we've discovered entire strings of letters belonging to other languages. This is odd," Uri cocked his head to the side as he pondered the enigma.

"Or is it?" Ruben countered. "Look at the illustration. Six full-fledged Phoenician letters. Look at them. What do you see?" Ruben looked at everyone in turn.

"I'd say simplicity of calligraphy," Rabbi Loew chimed in.

"Thank you, Rabbe. This is the point," Ruben picked up excitedly. Imagine now, how could it have been possible to interweave the Hebrew alef, gimel, dalet, vav, lamed, and taw? Our letters are more curved and sophisticated. But this is not the case with the ancestral Phoenician alphabet and its plain letters. They are way more pointed and containing mainly straight lines. Just what is needed to easily incorporate them in the graphics of David's Star. This sounds like the most logical explanation to me."

"It does sound logical, I must admit," Professor Epstein said pensively.

"I absolutely agree with you. I'd even go as far as to claim the immense wealth of possibilities provided by the interweaving of the two opposite-pointed triangles of David's Star was the main reason why it was chosen as our symbol. The star's wealth lies with the host of letters of several alphabets we've so far uncovered. And this isn't the whole story. In all cases of letters of other alphabets we've managed to link them to Hebrew through their Phoenician correspondences. So, the Phoenician alphabet is the key link," Ruben said.

"Once again, very logical reasoning," Professor Epstein pointed out.

"Then," Ruben continued, "Something very important dawned on me. If these more angular and square Phoenician letters were the precursors of the Hebrew alphabet then they were only used as links to other alphabets and also as vehicles to encode the Hebrew letters to which they corresponded. This being so, any letters we discover have to be traced back to the Phoenician ones and subsequently translated to their Hebrew equivalents. The latter have to be combined together to yield adequate Hebrew words and hence meaning. Something we already know how to do."

"So, we've got six Hebrew letters to arrange," Rabbi Loew said.

"It definitely feels good to be back on the right track, doesn't it?" Uri chimed in.

"Indeed. Let's get down to work. Aleph-gimel-daleth-vav-lamed-taw is our string for unscrambling. Remember we are looking for pangrams - combinations which use all six letters without repetition," Ruben said, inviting everyone to begin.

"In other words, we assume we are looking for a meaningful message that has to be only six-letters long and surely written by a combination of any of the six letters without any of them being repeated," Rovine clarified.

"Exactly," Ruben confirmed.

"I am thinking something like the perfect Hebrew pangram שפן אכל קצת גזר בטעם חסה, ודי," Professor Epstein explained.

"A rabbit ate some lettuce-flavored carrot and that's it! You are right, this is a 22-letter anagram in Hebrew," Ruben exclaimed. "No repetition of letters and each letter used only once."

"There are such perfect 26-letter pangrams in English as well," Ian joined in, "But most of them, actually all of them, in fact, make hardly any sense. Think only of *Glum Schwartzkopf vex'd by NJ IQ*. It is a perfect pangram but it makes no sense except, perhaps, immortalizing the name of the famously unknown character of *Glum Schwartzkopf*," Ian said, his comment evoking a few smiles.

People grew quiet as they concentrated on working their way through the six letters. Not long afterward, scores of single words began to pop up on everyone's screen. Then, the very first string emerged. Ruben discovered it. The string consisted of the following three words:

אל or *El* referring to one of the names of God
ות or *ot* meaning a sign; omen; token
גד or *gad* meaning good fortune; happiness

"If we put these three words together, they'd yield a coherent and meaningful message reading something like '*El* (is) a sign (of) good fortune'," Ruben said.

"This definitely makes sense," Uri agreed.

"God (is) a sign (of) good fortune," Rabbi Loew repeated the phrase, obviously enjoying how it sounds aloud. He continued. "Yes, it makes perfect sense. All the more because the Hebrew word *ot* (ות) is frequently used in the most ancient Biblical texts to denote the omen or token by which *El* (God, YHWH) gives a sign to His people that a prophecy about a future event is true and genuine; or that He will participate with all His might in an important undertaking of theirs; or that He has entrusted one of His chosen people with a special mission. In the Torah, each *ot* always comes from *El*, from God Himself. He thus guarantees the validity of all prophecies, important events, undertakings and missions. I have a good example for you. It is how *ot* is used in Exodus 3:11-12:

At this, Moses said to God, Ah, who am I, that thou shouldst sent me to Pharaoh? Who am I that I should lead the sons of Israel out of Egypt? I will be with thee, God said to him. And here is a sign (ot) for thee, that thy mission comes from me; when thou hast brought my people out of Egypt, thou wilt find thyself offering sacrifice to God on this mountain.

"A sign for thee that thy mission comes from me, beautifully said, indeed. The *ot* of *El* guaranteeing Moses' mission is divine," Rovine said and added. "Wish we had such *ots*."

"And what makes you think we don't have them?" The Rabbi said in a somber tone of voice.

******

A second string appeared on the screens. Ian and Rovine sent it. It consisted of two simple words:

דגל or *degel* denoting banner or flag; and
תאו or *teow* denoting wild ox

"We believe when putting these two words together, we get a phrase that would read 'A banner (with) a wild ox'," Ian explained.

"This message is a straightforward reference to the tribe of Manasseh. In olden times, all tribes of Israel had their own banners. Each depicted something. On the banner of Manasseh there was the depiction of a wild ox. Do you remember the story I told you?" Rabbi Loew turned to Ian and Rovine.

"Oh, yes, of course," Rovine exclaimed. "I remember about the door of the house of Manasseh before the exile from Egypt. On it a wild ox was depicted."

"This is correct," the Rabbi confirmed and went on to tell the others what he had told Ian and Rovine only a few weeks ago.

"But Rabbe, we now come across a second reference to the tribe of Manasseh. Why do you think that is?" Ian inquired.

"I might put forward a few credible conjectures. Only time will show which one is right. First I think coming across Manasseh twice underscores the importance of the enigmatic and non-existent word *elefpeh* - אלפה. Second, the Early Semitic pictograph of the wild ox -𓃾- stood for *aleph* - the first letter in the Hebrew alphabet. From this pictograph, simpler forms emerged later - 𐤀 and 𐤀 - until they evolved into its Late Hebrew form of א. From that, the Modern Hebrew letter *aleph* a developed. It is said that from *aleph* all other letters sprang. However, I think the main reason we stumble upon one and the same reference twice is hidden in the name Manasseh or *Menashsheh* - מנשה - meaning 'one who forgets'. We've got it twice in order not to forget."

"Not to forget what?" Ian asked, puzzled by the explanation.

"I can only guess but I'd say not to forget how it all began," the Rabbe said enigmatically.

"How what began?" more puzzlement on Ian's part. The Rabbi just looked at him, a look full of suggestion. Then he spoke.

"Sometime in the 2nd century C.E., the great Rabbi Akiva lived. He wrote *The Sepher Yetzirah* or 'The Book of Creation'. Mr. Zohar knows this book well. It is claimed to be the earliest known kabalistic text ever written. So, *Sepher Yetzirah* explains how God created the world by means of the twenty-two letters of the Hebrew alphabet. There is one sentence in the book which says it all and sums it up simply but brilliantly:

And this is the impress of the whole, twenty-one letters, all from one, the Aleph.

"So, Rabbe, with all due respect, it seems the Kabbalah tradition holds some water for you, too," Uri Zohar said, contentment in his voice. The rabbi didn't say anything in return.

Emboldened, Uri continued.

"I cannot agree more with the explanation offered by Rabbi Loew. Indeed, *Sepher Yetzirah,* the seminal book in Kabbalah, purports it clearly. It all began from *aleph*. But I have one additional answer to your question, Ian," Uri said and turned to him.

"You just asked how life began. I think that coming across Manasseh on two occasions is no mere accident. If the first letter of the name Menashsheh - the *mem* - is moved two positions forward and placed between the *shin* and the *he* - another Hebrew word is thus formed. It is *neshamah* or נשמה meaning 'the breath/spirit of God that imparts life'. Hence Genesis 2:7:

And the LORD God formed man [of] the dust of the ground,
And breathed into his nostrils the breath of life; and man became a living soul."

"Very interesting, Mr. Zohar, and a very good point," the rabbi said. "Indeed, this was how it all began... for us."

******

"I've come up with a phrase," Ruben said suddenly and posted it on everyone's screen. This third string also consisted of two words:

גאות or *geuwth* meaning pride; and
לד or *lod* designating the town of Lod

"The entire phrase simply reads 'The pride (of) Lod'," Ruben explained. At that moment the light of recognition went on in the minds of Ian and Rovine. They had already heard that phrase before.

"I have no idea what this phrase could mean," Ruben continued. "I only remember that after the fall of the Second Temple, the town of Lod was the seat of a number of Jewish sages and a prominent center of Jewish learning. It had its own academy in which the outstanding scholar Akiva studied."

"This is true," Professor Epstein joined in. "Of course, there is more in this line of thought. We shouldn't forget another important figure in the academy in Lod. His name was Tarfon - a rabbinic teacher and a celebrated scholar who worked closely with Akiva. Then there is a much lesser known fact. The important book *Sifrei Zuta* – a halakhic Midrash to the Book of Numbers – was compiled precisely in the academy of Lod. The compiler was certain Bar Kappara who was a disciple of Judah ha-Nasi – the head of another eminent academy, located in Bet Shearim."

"Hence, as I get the picture, the pride of Lod may refer to all of the above-mentioned, right?" Ruben inquired.

"It depends on the point of view. If you ask Ian and Rovine about what the pride of Lod was, they'll tell you a completely different story," the professor said while Ruben turned to his Bulgarian friends.

"This is so, Ruben. The pride of Lod were the Sukkot, the booths, ordered by Queen Helena from the Osroenite royal family for the Feast of the Tabernacles – the festival commemorating the booths in which the Children of Israel lived in the wilderness after the Exodus from Egypt," Ian explained. Then he went on to tell the whole story as he had heard it from Professor Epstein. He didn't forget the strange and unknown script with which each booth had been decorated.

******

Surprisingly, the possible combinations hadn't been exhausted. This time, the fourth string came from Rabbi Loew. He posted it to everyone:

גדול or *gadowl* signifying great; and
תא or *ta* meaning chamber

"'(The) Great Chamber'," the Rabbi said. "In Judaism there has always been one most significant chamber – the Temple's devir or the Holy of Holies. That is, the chamber used as a tabernacle for the Ark of the Covenant."

******

The fifth phrase came from Uri Zohar. It was a string consisting of the following two words:

אות or *owth* meaning sign, symbol; and
גדל or *godel* denoting magnificence and greatness

"I read it as 'A Symbol of Magnificence.' Since *godel* was used as a description of God - most notably in the 5th Book of the Pentateuch, Devarim, or Deuteronomy, 3:24 and 5:12 - the phrase could be interpreted as another epithet describing God as a symbol of greatness and magnificence."

"Your explanation is what logic invariably dictates, Mr. Zohar," Rabbi Loew said, looking at him. "But we have here the word *owth* and this makes a huge difference."

"What do you mean, Rabbe?" Uri was intrigued.

"You see, in my arranging and rearranging of the letters I also came across *owth*. But I paired it with another Hebrew word דגל or *dagal* denoting 'to behold'. So for me, the phrase basically reads as an imperative 'Behold the Sign', understand?"

"Yes, I do," Uri blurted, his curiosity now sky-rocketing.

"Naturally when taken as an imperative - Behold the Sign - you immediately ask yourself which sign there is to behold."

"David's Star, of course. We've discovered this imperative enciphered in the graphics of the star itself. So I wouldn't dwell too long on the question as to which sign. I'd instantly know the imperative refers to David's Star. It's that simple."

"Brilliant display of logical deduction, Mr. Zohar, I must admit that. You are absolutely right. But I will tell you this - you base your conclusion on logic and logic alone. I am not saying you have no right to do so. On the contrary, I admire your logical mind. But, Mr. Zohar, there are things beyond the scope of logic. I am personally surprised that you, as such a huge devotee of Kabbalah, haven't yet noticed the key to this phrase."

"What do you mean?" Uri was puzzled.

"I mean the phrase itself contains a second confirmation that the symbol at stake is David's Star."

"How so?" Uri was still puzzled.

"I'll parse the Hebrew word *owth* for you, in a Kabbalah-friendly manner. You see, owth consists of three letters - *aleph-vav-taw* / א-ו-ת. You will notice the middle letter is *vav* - the sixth one in the Hebrew alphabet. We know that in Hebrew grammar, *vav* has the very important function of connector and as such it means 'and' and is called in Hebrew *vav hachibur*. You will notice the *vav* in question connects an *aleph* and a *taw*. Only two days ago, Mr. Zohar, we stumbled upon a watermark interwoven right in the heart of David's Star."

"I remember that, of course," Uri nodded.

"Then you'd also remember what we said about that watermark. It was the A and Tau that gave rise to the word auteur, the Aleph and Tau, the Greek the Alpha and the Omega, the expression 'the First and the Last' or 'from beginning to end'. *Owth* is the alphabetical expression of this watermark but it goes beyond that with its meaning of sign and symbol. And, to further make things ever more enigmatic and wondrous, when *vav*, the connector, is taken away, we see *owth* contains the Hebrew word *ath* (את) meaning 'a (miraculous) sign', 'a wonder' and 'a portent'," Rabbi Loew said triumphantly. Everyone was astonished. Most so was Uri Zohar. As if reading his thoughts, Rabbi Loew added.

"This is how I understand Kabbalah, Mr. Zohar, to discover the enigmatic connections between words because our Hebrew language is a whole, vast universe. It's endless. It provides limitless connections and permutations. And we should never forget our language comes from our *Auteur*. Our language is divine, divinely beautiful, and even more than that, divinely infinite. This is its beauty and Kabbalah needs only reflect it," Rabbi Loew said, while Uri's expression was one of defeat. The self-confident and self-proclaimed kabbalchemist had been beaten on his own home ground. He hadn't seen what was there in front of his eyes. He had slipped down the safe path of conventional logic, no harm, true, but nothing original either. The Rabbi had penetrated the divine logic of language. He had seen the concealed connection through the hidden word within another word. This was the essence of genuine Kabbalah and Uri had failed on this particular score. The Rabbi had just given him the greatest lesson in Kabbalah.

"Speaking of permutations, Mr. Zohar, there's one more thing. If you had calculated the numerical value of the word *owth*, you'd have gotten 407 (*aleph* = 1 + *vav* = 6 + *taw* = 400 = 407). If you had taken 407 as a Strong's number, you would have realized it referred to Achshaph – the city where the prophet Elijah received an *owth* from God to go to Mount Carmel and exterminate all idolatrous practices conducted there. But I guess you already know that," Rabbi Loew said, which was the last straw. Uri's mouth gaped open in speechless astonishment.

32

JERUSALEM, ISRAEL
18 MAY 2020
OUTSIDE PEACE NOW HEADQUARTERS
BEFORE NOON

The two Mossad agents who had been patiently staked outside Peace Now headquarters with their sensitive listening devices were fanning themselves with maps to relieve some of the heat inside the sedan.

"Are you hungry, Adah? It's been a long time since we had breakfast … I'd be happy to run across the street to that sandwich shop and get something …" Agent Chasin Weissman smiled at the sophisticated beauty next to him in the front seat. The days spent together had provided him with enough time to begin to get to know her better and also to start nurturing some feelings for her. He only hoped it was mutual although she hadn't given him any sign of such possibility. Adah was a self-reliant and self-contained woman and that fact made her a hard bite for any man.

"That's very thoughtful of you, Chasin. I think I would enjoy a stuffed pita in a little while, along with a large plastic cup of very cold iced tea!" Adah Schwartz stretched her neck from side to side to relieve the tension. Chasin felt she possessed the gracefulness of some superior feline animal and enjoyed watching her stretch.

"Good. I'll wait about a few minutes till the lunch crowd has thinned down and then I'll get us some food…" He adjusted his position to get more comfortable. "You know we are sitting here and listening to the guys upstairs and their conversation got me thinking," he spoke softly.

Adah Schwartz looked at him expectantly.

"I'm talking about this…searching for hidden words they are working on. So far none of them has spotted one very obvious combination."

"Which is?" she asked him.

"Combining *gimel-vav-aleph-lamed* gives you the word 'savior' while the combination of *dalet-taw* gives you 'faith'. So at the end you get a phrase like 'Faith (in the) Savior'."

"Very observant, Chasin, and a nice phrase. Straight to the heart of their context. But you've apparently missed one tiny detail."

"Which is?"

"All morning they have been working with Biblical Hebrew, not the Modern one."

"Oh, damn! You are right," Chasin slapped his forehead.

"Nice try, though," she chuckled.

"Yeah, just next time give me the right rifle," he laughed aloud.

"If you take Modern Hebrew into account, you can get other combinations as well. I've spotted something myself while listening. *Daleth-gimel-lamed* gives you 'flag' while *aleph-vav-taw* gives you 'omen'. Hence a phrase that connotes 'a flag of omen'," Adah said looking at Chasin and smiling.

"You definitely have a point, Adah. Now I'm going across the street to get us some lunch..." he jumped out of the car and ran across the street. All throughout, Adah's eyes followed him.

33

JERUSALEM, ISRAEL
18 MAY 2020
PEACE NOW HEADQUARTERS
AFTERNOON

"Professor Epstein, you really made me think about my approach to letters and words and my ways in Kabbalah," Uri Zohar began after all of them had come back from lunch. Nathan Epstein looked at him patiently.

"While having lunch I decided to calculate the numerical value of the six Phoenician letters and I got the following," Uri said, uploading what he had written onto everyone's screen.

(Aleph) 1 + (gimel) 3 + (daleth) 4 + (vav) 6 + (lamed) 30 + (tav) 400 = 444

"An admirable exercise," Rabbi Loew studied his screen.

"A very symmetrical sum, isn't it?" Ruben asked rhetorically.

"Then, I decided to translate 444 into its corresponding Hebrew letter-number and I got the following string," Uri said and pasted another note.

Tav-mem-daleth, that is, תמד (Tav = 400; mem = 40; and daleth = 4)

"Hmm, a non-existent combination of letters," Professor Epstein exclaimed.

"True," Uri agreed, "But if you take a better look at the three letters, you'll discover a different story."

"What do you mean?" Ruben asked.

"The three letters should be read as a combination of two Hebrew words: *tam* (תם) and *mad* (מד)."

"What do these two mean?" Rovine inquired.

"Tam is an adjective that means 'perfect'. Mad is a noun meaning 'measure'. Thus together the two words would yield 'perfect measure'," Uri Zohar explained.

"Perfect measure," Rabbi Loew said pensively as though talking to himself. Then he added, "Now you got me thinking, Uri."

Silence prevailed until Rabbi Loew interrupted after a few moments.

"I can think of one explanation of the phrase 'perfect measure'. It is in Job 11:7-9..." He began reciting from memory:

'Canst thou by searching find out God? Canst thou find out the Almighty unto perfection?

[It is] as high as heaven; what canst thou do? Deeper than hell; what canst thou know?

The measure thereof [is] longer than the earth, and broader than the sea.'

"Good observation, Rabbe," Uri Zohar smiled and added, "But I think you are slightly off the mark." The Rabbi looked surprised.

"You see," Uri continued, "In Kabbalah, when somebody says 'perfect measure' the expression can only refer to one thing, and one thing only - *Shi'ur Komah* or 'the measure of the body'."

"I get your point," the Rabbi smiled knowingly. He was glad that this time Uri had hit the target, right on the bulls' eye.

"I will finish my explanation for the others," Uri said looking at the Rabbi. Then he turned to everyone else and continued:

"Merkabah mysticism - *merkabah* meaning chariot - is a Jewish mystical teaching related to Ezekiel's vision of the divine chariot. This teaching was studied and developed further in the academy in Lod by Akiva of whom Ruben spoke in the morning. Merkabah deals with the most secret and esoteric doctrine regarding the measure of the body of God. The calculations of God's body were awakened by the following words found in Psalm 147:5: "Great is Our Lord, and mighty in power." What became so important was the expression 'and mighty in power.' The expression consists of the Hebrew words *ve-rav ko'ah*. According to gematria, which is a way to calculate the numerical values of each Hebrew word and then explain its meaning accordingly, the numerical value of *ve-rav ko'ah* turns out to be 236. Now, to get the most approximate measurement of the body of God, 236 was multiplied by 10,000 celestial leagues and the result served at the basic reference point of further calculations and extrapolations."

"In other words, a size of 236,000 celestial leagues," Ian said.

"Exactly, but the perfect measure of God is 236," Uri confirmed. "It is believed, however, that the value of this perfect measure had been received by Adam, while he was still in *Ginnah Pele* -"

"Ginnah Pele?" Rovine interrupted.

"The Garden of Wonder, that is, the other name of the Garden of Eden. So, tradition tells us while Adam was still in *Ginnah Pele* he was visited by an angel of God who revealed to him the perfect measure of God's body. Much later, David, a direct descendant of Adam, encoded the value of this measure in Psalm 147. In still later centuries, Merkabah students decoded the value of 236 and therefore, thanks to their scholarship, we have it and we know it to this day."

34

JERUSALEM, ISRAEL

19 MAY 2020

PEACE NOW HEADQUARTERS

MORNING

In the morning, Ian was the first to speak after the group finished a hearty breakfast in the meeting hall of Peace Now's headquarters. They were lingering over their second and third cups of coffee when he stood up and smiled at his friends.

"You all remember the three Roman letter-numerals that we've discovered – C, V and X…Yesterday evening, Rovine, Ruben and I had the unorthodox idea of trying to find any other possible Latin letters in the graphic structure of David's Star. We all know the Land of Israel had been part of the Roman Empire for quite some time. And at that period of history, Roman letter-numerals and the Latin alphabet were readily available for communication and trade between Jews and Romans," he paused and glanced at his attentive audience. "We had good reasons to go forward in our search, and our best guess was that other Latin letters could be found interlaced. Well, to tell you the truth, it wasn't very hard to find the rest. We've already discovered the Cyrillic A – written the same way as the Latin one. The Cyrillic U is У which writes the same as the Roman Y. Last but not least, we spotted the Roman letter Z. At the end we got a string of six Latin letters – A, C, V, X, Y, and Z," Ian explained and uploaded the string on his laptop so everyone could see it.

"As you can see," Ian picked up, "There is much to be unscrambled here with only two vowels and such rare consonants."

"Of course, we instantly recognized YAV – the three-letter Latin transliteration of the Hebrew name for God (יו)," Rovine explained. "By taking away the only two vowels we got stuck in a dead-end street."

"Hence we opted for a different approach. First and foremost, we translated the Latin letters back to their Phoenician equivalents. From there it was easy to make the connection to Hebrew," Ian said and opened a small chart of correspondences for everyone to view.

A - *aleph;* C - *gimel;* V - *vav;* X - *samekh;* Y - *vav;* Z - *zayin*

"Once we got to the Hebrew letters, we could arrange and rearrange them all we wanted until we got something meaningful. Before I give you the solution the three of us have discovered, I invite you to try and rearrange the letters a bit and see what will come out," Ian said and smiled. There was very brief silence this time.

"I see the adjective *ge* (גא) meaning 'proud'," Uri Zohar spoke first.

"There is the noun *vav* (וו) meaning 'a hook'," Rabbi Loew joined in.

"Taking separate words into account, there's *ziv* (זו) meaning 'brightness'," Professor Epstein said.

"There's also the noun *gav* (גו) meaning 'back' as the back of a person," Uri added.

"In this sense, there's also the noun *ow* (או) meaning 'desire'," the professor again.

"As you can see, many single Hebrew words can be arranged with a combination of any of the six letters but nothing really meaningful comes out," Ian said and then continued.

"The solution we've come up with is rather unconventional to what we've dealt with so far. The string of six Latin letters A-C-V-X-Y-Z contains three Roman letter-numerals: C-X-V which is 115. We take these three numerals out. There are three Latin letters remaining: A-Y-Z. They correspond to *aleph, vav,* and *zayin*. Once put together, *aleph* and *zayin* yield the Hebrew adverb *az* (אז) meaning 'at that time'. The remaining letter *vav* is the adverb 'so'. Put together they form the expression 'so at that time'. What is left for us is to understand what 115 means or refers to. Rovine suggested yesterday we translated it into Hebrew letter-numerals. Since we were testing all hypotheses we agreed on doing so. We got the letter *qoph* standing for 100, *yod* for 10 and *he* for 5. It didn't take Ruben long to arrange the letters and get one meaningful combination - *Jakeh* (יקה) meaning 'blameless' and referring to the name of the father of Agur the sage.

"And then we had it all - the entire expression therefore reading 'so at that time Jakeh'. Of course, we came to an expression but we had absolutely no idea what it meant. So we left the solving to your immense expertise," Ian said looking at Professor Epstein, Rabbi Loew and Uri Zohar in turn.

"An admirable endeavor, I must admit, and an even more admirable result," Professor Epstein said.

"I can't agree less with you, Nathan!" Rabbi Loew said and added, "Ian, Rovine, Ruben, I think all of you have done a great job. What's more, I think by having already arrived at the expression you have also nearly arrived at the answer as to what its meaning really is. Little extra explanation is needed, believe me."

"We are really happy to hear that," Rovine chimed in.

"Nothing is known of Jakeh except that he was the father of Agur the sage. The only thing we know of Agur is that he was one of the authors in the Book of Proverbs also known as *Mishle Shlomoh* or the Proverbs of Solomon. Actually Agur is believed to be the author of Proverbs 30:1. Since nothing extra is mentioned in the Bible about Jakeh and Agur, most people take them as just another set of names. The truth about who exactly Jakeh and Agur were is to be found in our rich aggadah tradition. There it is said that Jakeh was a pseudonym for King David, while Agur was a pseudonym for his son Solomon, himself the author of the Book of Proverbs."

"Straight to the point, Rabbe," Professor Epstein commented.

"You can naturally ask why the need of pseudonyms when the authorship of the Book of Proverbs is well known. After all, in Hebrew, the title of the book carries the name of its author Shlomo, that is, Solomon. To answer such a question, I must say that the key is in the text of Proverb 30. The tone of speaking is different, concealed under an alias of an ordinary man albeit a sage, Solomon was able to say some things that otherwise would have been more proper to have come from a king. Even without the rich aggadah tradition, the author of Proverb 30 has signed it and we know for certain that it is Solomon. You only need to read Proverbs 30:5:

Every word of God [is] pure: he [is] a shield unto them that put their trust in him.

"The word for shield used in this verse is *magen* (מגן). You know that the Hebrew name of David's Star is Magen David or the Shield of David. And what is that trust? The answer is simple. It is the trust in God, a man putting his trust in God. We have a fine example of that in 1 Samuel 17:45-46:

Then said David to the Philistine, Thou comest to me with a sword, and with a spear, and with a shield: but I come to thee in the name of the LORD of hosts, the God of the armies of Israel, whom thou hast defied.

This day will the LORD deliver thee into mine hand; and I will smite thee, and take thine head from thee; and I will give the carcasses of the host of the Philistines this day unto the fowls of the air, and to the wild beasts of the earth; that all the earth may know that there is a God in Israel.

"This is one of the finest examples in the entire Bible of a simple man, David, a shepherd, putting all his trust in God and defeating, against all odds, the giant Goliath. This is it, people. This is pure faith. The ancient sages have encoded a reference to an example of pure faith and trust in God. And they have done so with an expression full of meaning – 'so at that time Jakeh'. You are probably wondering about what time the expression refers to. That time? And which is that time? It is again very simple. It refers to the time when the descendant of David, a.k.a Jakeh, will arrive – the time at the end of times. This is what we are expecting tomorrow, aren't we?" Rabbi Loew said and looked slowly at everyone in turn, his eyes probing their hearts as if he sought to know how they felt about all those revelations they had been coming up with in the days before. Everyone was silent. The rabbi had made a point. His explanation was seamless.

35

JERUSALEM, ISRAEL
19 MAY 2020
PEACE NOW HEADQUARTERS
EARLY AFTERNOON

Ruben stood up before the gathering of his closest friends and collaborators and detected a slight wave of unrest but attributed it to the sense of anticipation that had overrun most of them. He cleared his throat and his audience became very attentive and unusually solemn,

"Dear friends," Ruben began. "Today is the last day before the ominous 20th of May that Uri Zohar has deciphered and the rest of us have been expecting. If he calculated it right, tomorrow would be the big day, not only for us here but also for everybody elsewhere. Just in the very last moment, this morning, we seem to have uncovered a confirmation of what we might expect to take place tomorrow. It cannot be denied that we've put immense efforts into finding it out and I want to personally thank each and every one of you for devoting time, zeal and energy into this rather unusual exercise. In those few days we spent together we discovered amazing things interwoven in the graphics of David's Star, right in front of our eyes, everyone's eyes, yet fully and securely concealed.

"Now is the time to tell you I kept one of our high-ranking government liaisons informed about our work. I wanted to make sure our government would be prepared and kept ahead of events. So now they know tomorrow is the big day and they are ready to act if need be. Thank you once again," Ruben said and was about to shake hands with everyone in turn when Rabbi Loew suddenly arose from his seat.

"Dear Ruben, just to say it once again as I have already done before, I do not accept Mr. Zohar's calculations. You've accepted them so easily and so readily but you shouldn't have. You should have put them under more questioning and sought more verification. I think Mr. Zohar got it wrong. Tomorrow is not the big day. You will see that fairly soon. In this sense, you shouldn't have bothered the government. They have enough problems to deal with."

"I agree with you, Rabbe," Professor Epstein said. "Mr. Zohar made his conclusion too hastily. Worse, his conclusion didn't follow any of the established rules for composing Roman letter-numerals. I simply cannot accept the date he came up with."

Then Professor Epstein and Rabbi Loew shook hands with everyone in turn, expressing their appreciation for having been chosen to participate in this small project, and took their leave.

Uri Zohar hadn't dared to speak up. He was palpably indignant.

"I know I am right," he said turning to Ruben who didn't say anything. Then Uri stood up, bid them farewell and left.

36

JERUSALEM, ISRAEL

19 MAY 2020

OUTSIDE PEACE NOW HEADQUARTERS

EARLY AFTERNOON

The two Mossad agents had been listening quietly for over an hour when suddenly Chasin Weissman sat bolt upright. "'High-ranking government liaison,' what is Openheim talking about?"

"Surely, some Peace Now lobbyist in the government," Adah Schwartz replied calmly. "You know in our politics it is all about lobbies and lobbyists. They have theirs as surely as we have ours."

"We?" Chasin's voice was sarcastically doubtful.

"Well, our organization," Adah said glancing at him.

"Listen, listen, they've just finished. Openheim is disbanding them."

"They've done their job and this means we're through with our surveillance as well."

"Do you believe in what they've discovered about tomorrow?"

"You mean the day at the end of times?" her tone of voice indicated her incredulity.

"Yes."

"Do I *sound* like a person who believes in such idle talk?"

"But –"

"There are no buts here, Chasin. This self-proclaimed kabbalchemist Uri Zohar threw a monkey wrench into the works. For this reason I strongly advise you to rethink your position on this issue before you show up at the office of your chief!" Adah's lips were a thin line of assertive authority as she dipped her chin in a firm nod.

37

JERUSALEM, ISRAEL
20 MAY 2020

Ian woke up just before sunrise, got out of bed and stretched. Then he went out on the balcony and inhaled deeply the crisp, clean air of the receding night. The crimson sun was just emerging from the tops of the hills to the east, separating Jerusalem from the Dead Sea. It was the dawn of an anxiously anticipated day.

It was Wednesday. Urban life was seemingly waking to another day of its unending daily grind, or was it so? No. It wasn't so. Ian and the others knew otherwise.

On the way to the bathroom, Ian saw Ruben slouched down in an overstuffed armchair. He told Ian he hadn't been able to sleep much during the night.

"I'm not surprised!" Ian shook his head in sympathy.

Later in the morning the two families gathered around the table in the kitchen. Sarah and Rovine had prepared a delicious breakfast. Cornflakes, hot milk, toast, butter, jam, pancakes. It was a lavish meal before a very important day.

The adults didn't speak much. The anxiety of anticipation had already preoccupied their conscious minds. They didn't tell Aya and Dani because they didn't want to upset them. They were still kids, in a way. Besides, no one knew exactly what was going to happen.

"Are you going to the office today?" Aya turned to her father.

"No, today we're not going there. Instead we are all going for a walk downtown," Ruben replied.

"How cool!" Dani beamed and cast a glance at Aya who returned it boldly. They exchanged smiles. None of the adults noticed their flirtatious games.

Then Aya picked up, "So where are we going?"

"Downtown, sweetheart, your father said it," Sarah chimed in.

"The Old City, the Wailing Wall, the City of David, Dani has to see them all," Ruben said looking at Aya.

******

It was past midnight, the first hours of Thursday. It was quiet in the neighborhood. Occasionally a car would pass in the street. A few stars could be discerned in the sky, but the rest remained obscured because of the light pollution. The air was still as was the spirit of everyone on the table. The four adults were sitting and quietly sipping their drinks. Dani and Aya had gone to bed. Nothing of what was expected to happen actually happened. Uri Zohar had it all wrong while Rabbi Loew and Professor Epstein had it right.

"Dear Ruben, we had a wonderful day out in the city but nothing really came to pass today," Ian spoke grimly.

"Our endeavor has been compromised, Ian," Ruben said, the expression in his eyes one of despair.

"The government liaison?"

"Oh, don't mention it. I don't know what I will have to explain in the morning," Ruben said, massaging his scalp. He was worried. Sarah stroked his tense shoulders. She was worried about him.

"Ruben, look at this positively. Nothing bad happened and that's good," Rovine tried to cheer him up.

"Still we got it wrong and I believed in the information we came up with, Rovine," he said looking at her. "It's about respect. You know I am a well-respected man in the government circles. Now I've lost most if not all of my trustworthiness."

"Yes, sure, we got it wrong but we are human, Ruben. We are prone to make mistakes sometimes. I am telling you, the good thing here is that no one is hurt and no one suffers. You will regain your respect. This is possible unlike bringing the dead to life. No one died today. We have to celebrate that fact," Rovine said passionately and in a very convincing way. Her words seemed to have struck a chord with Ruben and he relaxed in his chair. Then he proposed a toast and glasses clinked.

"Well, I guess you have a point," he finally said.

"At least we've tried, Ruben, and I still believe we did a good job. I mean judging by the results only. No one has ever come up with anything like this. We should be grateful we've discovered the interwoven letters. Who knows what will come out of them one day. But this is not for us to worry about now, you know." Ian too tried to sound positive.

"I agree, the discovery of the letters is what we should be happy with and celebrate now," Rovine chimed in.

"She is right, Ruben," Sarah said looking at her husband. He looked back at her, a shade of gloominess on his face. She leaned forward and kissed him.

"Now that the job has been done, we can go back home," Rovine said. Ian looked at her and spoke.

"Yes, we can. Tomorrow?"

"If there's a flight, why not," she said and smiled at him.

38

JERUSALEM, ISRAEL
24 JULY 2020
THE HEADQUARTERS OF THE TEMPLE MOUNT
AND LAND OF ISRAEL FAITHFUL MOVEMENT
MORNING

The meeting room was like a schoolroom, only the tables and chairs were not child-sized. There were many computer-operators working on their machines, each of them occasionally leaning forward to study their computer screens more intensely. The atmosphere was tense with the combined mental energies of all the dedicated people in the room.

"Has everything been prepared?" asked Caleb Medan, crew-cut middle-aged head of the movement. He rubbed the distinctive scar on his left cheek nervously.

"Yes, sir," the young computer specialist answered.

"Then publish the announcement right now! We've got no time to waste."

In seconds, the following announcement appeared on the official website of the Temple Mount and Land of Israel Faithful Movement:

You are invited to march with The Temple Mount and Land of Israel Faithful Movement to the Temple Mount and take part in the ceremony of the anointing of the cornerstone for the Third Temple. We shall march from the Temple Mount to the City of David where the ceremony of the anointing will take place. Then we shall march to the Shiloah Pool where the ceremony of the Pouring of the Water will take place as it was done in Biblical times. The marble cornerstone, untouched by iron, weighing four and a half tons, will be carried on a flatbed truck, covered with Israeli flags together with the reconstructed vessels for the Third Temple, a priest in the original garments, and Levites who will play music. This historical and fateful event will take place in exactly 15 days' time on Friday 31st July 2020, at 9:00 a.m. We shall meet at the Western Wall plaza close to the western (Mugabi) gate of the Temple Mount. The event has the approval of the Israeli authorities and will be protected by the Israeli security forces and army. No foreign powers and alliances will be allowed to interfere in order to prevent the event from taking place. Israel, the Chosen People of God, is now living in the most invigorating time in their history. These are the godly and prophetic days at the end of times in which God is going to redeem the people of Israel at last. The biggest dream and vision of the God and people of Israel – the rebuilding of the Temple – is becoming a reality in the great time in which we are living. All this shall happen in sight of all nations of the world and in their face we shall erase the stain of the moral blemish inflicted upon us many centuries ago.

39

SOFIA, BULGARIA
24 JULY 2020
EVENING

Rovine had a delightful summer meal ready by the time Ian got home in the evening. She had prepared an assortment of salads accompanied by a large pitcher of aromatic green tea and her famous homemade cheese pastry known in Bulgaria under the name of banitsa. Dani arrived for dinner as well. While they were enjoying the repast, they discussed what had happened during the day. Dani said he was well-prepared for an end-of-the-school-year test in mathematics. He had spent the afternoon studying and had later gone out with his friends only for a couple of hours. He had a lot of pressure and deadlines at school but he was all right with it because he knew the summer vacation was just around the corner. After he finished his dinner, Dani went outside for another hour with his friends, in the city garden across the street.

Rovine and Ian went into the living room and as they were taking their seats before the large flat TV screen, Ian said 'On' as a voice command. The TV set sprang to life, switching itself on. Then Ian said 'CNN' and the news channel was on. Both of them had been following the news for the past few days since the peace negotiations in Sofia had begun. Ten years earlier, in 2010, the then Israeli President and Nobel-Peace-prize-winner Shimon Peres had visited Bulgaria. During his visit, he had hinted at the possibility of Sofia becoming the place where peace talks between Israel and Palestine could be held. The initiative for the renewal of the peace talks in 2020 belonged, as expected, to Hillary Rodham Clinton, the first woman to be elected as the 45th President of the United States running her second term in office in the White House. In 2012, only months before the president elections, the then U.S. President Barack Obama had made an utterly surprising move by declining to run for office. Caught off guard, the camp of the Democrats had quickly managed to regain positions by launching the candidacy of the well-respected country's Secretary of State. The elections had been a total triumph for Clinton.

In 2010, still serving as the 67th United States Secretary of State, Hillary Clinton had embarked on a risky move by starting negotiations between Israeli and Palestinian leaders. Sadly, the negotiations had failed bitterly with PLO and Hamas diehard militants shelling at Israeli settlements for days on end. Then the Israeli Army quickly restored order by crossing into Gaza and the West Bank and destroying the nests of Palestinian militants.

Spending her whole first term in office as U.S. President on preparations, Hillary Clinton had come out strong in her second term and absolutely resolute in dealing with the problem in the Middle East. When she was ready she announced the renewal of, as she put it, the final negotiations between Israel and Palestine. The Bulgarian government had responded positively to her announcement reminding the global community of Shimon Peres' idea. And so, after careful preparations, the peace talks had been launched in Camp Boyana in the foothills of the Vitosha Mountain, to the south of downtown Sofia. The whole world was watching the events unfolding in tiny Sofia.

In the meantime, Hillary Clinton had reassured the general public there would be no more setbacks. She had said America had always supported Israel because this small state had been a solitary outpost of democracy, maintaining the rule of law, justice and civilized conduct in a region where a blind eye had been largely ignoring such important global values. She had also said the Middle-Eastern peace process had always topped her agenda and the moment had at last arrived for it to be settled, once and for all.

Across the TV screen was CNN's wide yellow banner announcing breaking news. On screen was CNN's Becky Anderson, still maintaining her short hair, now dark brown, a streak still over her right eye-brow, her eyes and gestures as brisk and vivacious as ever. She had been born for the vocation of TV journalist and throughout the years she had fashioned that vocation after her own personality and temperament rather than the other way round. On the other side, from CNN's temporary Larry King Live studio in Sofia was no other than Richard Quest, the man who had replaced the retired Larry King, the very king himself. In the regiment of CNN, Quest had been the only logical and expected substitute for Larry, although he had always had a constant tone of sensationalism in his raspy voice when on screen. For that matter, Richard lacked the tone of coolness so typical of the great Larry King that had made him an icon able to talk anyone into pouring their heart and soul out on TV. Interestingly, Richard's wide-beamed smile and his thin-rimmed glasses seemed to have a similar effect.

Becky Anderson was speaking as Ian and Rovine watched: *As you can see in the distance behind me, Richard, there are mass protests of Palestinians and clashes with the Palestinian security forces. As I speak, tires and effigies clad in the Israeli flag are being burnt everywhere across Gaza and the West Bank.*

Richard Quest with a question shot in his rasping voice from the studio: *Becky, what has provoked those protests? We hear all kinds of rumors here.*

Becky: *The protests were sparked by an announcement published this morning on the website of The Temple Mount and Land of Israel Faithful Movement. The announcement invites everyone to attend a ceremony organized by the movement of anointing the rebuilding of the Third Temple on Temple Mount.*

Richard: *What kind of ceremony is this?*

Becky: *The movement plans a march from the Temple Mount to the City of David where a four-and-half-ton marble cornerstone will be anointed. This event is supposed to lay the foundations of the rebuilding of the Third Temple on top of Temple Mount.*

Richard: *Is this announcement serious, for real? I mean in light of the ongoing peace negotiations?*

Becky: *Very much so. The Temple Mount and Land of Israel Faithful Movement have been known for decades for their extreme right-wing activities. So, yes, everyone here believes it is for real. What is more, Richard, the announcement claims the support of the Israeli authorities, security forces and army. This, of course, is still to be verified. I've been trying to reach the Israeli Prime Minister for comments or confirmation but, as you know, he is currently attending the peace talks in Sofia and seems to be out of reach for journalists.*

Richard: *When is the ceremony scheduled to take place?*

Becky: *It is scheduled for Friday 31st July 2020. You know, Richard, what is most striking is the tone of the announcement. It speaks with great pathos of no foreign powers and alliances being allowed to interfere in order to prevent the event from taking place; of these, and I am quoting here, 'being the godly and prophetic days at the end of times in which God is going to redeem the people of Israel at last. The biggest dream and vision of the God and people of Israel – the rebuilding of the Temple – is becoming a reality in the great time in which we are living. All this shall happen in the sight of all nations of the world and in their face we shall erase the stain of the moral blemish inflicted upon us many centuries ago.' End of quote, Richard, now back to you in the studio.*

"I've got to call the Openheims," Ian said with great concern turning to Rovine.

******

Ian greeted Ruben when he picked up on the other side. The loudspeaker was on. Rovine also greeted him. Ruben greeted them back, distress obvious in his tone of voice.

"Are you all right? You don't sound particularly good, you know."

"Well, how can I sound good?" Ruben mumbled.

"We're just watching the breaking news on CNN."

"So you know."

"Yes, we do."

"This statement of The Temple Mount and Land of Israel Faithful Movement has brought havoc just in a matter of hours of its online publication. Unbelievable, yet we know how quickly social-networking operates! Just now we have the Americans hundred-and-one-per-cent committed to peace and we have the Palestinians, too, unswerving and cooperating, and, on top of all this we have you, too, the Bulgarians, taking an active role in the peace process and, suddenly, some of our own camp will now mess it all up. This is so unfair, Ian, so unfair."

"We've heard about the statement. They've read parts of it live but what we don't understand is the claim that the entire event is backed up by the Israeli state and army. Is this really true?" Ian asked, his tone of disbelief.

"Unfortunately this particular piece of information hasn't been verified here yet. You know our President and Prime Minister are in Sofia."

"It seems they can't get to them here, either," Ian said. "CNN has been trying to get in contact with any high-ranking Israeli representative but there seems to be a total information blackout imposed on the peace talks in the Boyana Camp."

"Since noon Palestinians from the Gaza and the West Bank have been staging mass anti-Israeli rallies with burning of effigies and chanting anti-Semitic slogans. So also has been the case in Lebanon, Syria, Jordan, Egypt, Iran, Iraq, and across the

Arab world – everywhere mass anti-Israeli demonstrations of people in a state of fanatical rage."

"We're watching just that."

"PLO and Hamas militants have been shelling occasionally and indiscriminately at Israeli settlements for a couple of hours on end. This is crazy, Ian. They are harassing the beast and the beast will get really pissed off and will obliterate them with one sweep of its mighty paw. This should not be allowed to happen. Israel should not be plunged into a fresh wave of terror. I think if all goes the way it's headed, the army will retaliate full scale very soon."

"It seems so."

"You have no idea about the state of frenzy we are in at the moment."

"In fact we are getting the picture from CNN."

"A weird mixture of restlessness, despondency and extreme anxiety are felt all over the place, in every street and settlement across Israel. This is so odd, Ian, so odd," Ruben said with sadness in his voice.

"Ruben," Ian suddenly said, determination in his voice. "It's about time you packed up your staff, got Sarah and Aya and came here, immediately."

"I've thought about it but what about the rest of our people?"

"If the situation deteriorates rapidly, you can coordinate the entire humanitarian mission from here and with our help. In each case we will need you here to set the entire Safe Haven for Israel in motion. Do you understand? You must come here, Ruben, all three of you."

"Ian is right, Ruben. Don't take any unnecessary risks," Rovine joined in. "You've got nothing to lose by coming here first. This way you'd be able to respond quickly and most adequately to the situation should any need arise."

"Dear friends, don't you think I haven't realized that already? Peace Now has been bracing for such a moment since its very inception. I cannot run away now. I have to give my due share. You and Rovine have been with us for over six years now. You've given your fair share and have no obligations, no strings attached."

"Don't say that Ruben, don't! I just don't want to hear you saying that. Of course there are strings attached – strings attached so strong you can't detach them with any amount of force applied."

"For you, it's all a matter of good will, Ian."

"Well then, consider this, there's plenty of good will here."

"Toda, my friend, thank you. You two have been great all along."

"We're not giving up before the big battle. We too have been bracing for such an event. We are not backing off now. Not in a million years."

"Which means one thing and one thing only! If necessary, you have the knowledge, expertise and experience to make Safe Haven for Israel work. I say it again, if necessary. That's all I can say. You can do it all by yourselves with the full cooperation of all Bulgarian authorities. I, on the other hand, have to be here. I have to wage my battles from here. I cannot do it from Sofia."

"But you can send Sarah and Aya, just for precaution's sake," Rovine said.

"Sure, I'll do just that. I'll speak to them and I'll call you to tell you what we've decided. I want them to be safe and I know they will be safe there with. And I also know you'll take good care of them."

"Great. You can call anytime, you know that Ruben. Anytime. Luckily, Jerusalem and Sofia are in one and the same time zone."

"*Shalom,* brother."

"*Shalom,* brother" Ian said.

"*Shalom,* Ruben" Rovine added.

40

SOFIA, BULGARIA

24 JULY 2020

SHORTLY BEFORE MIDNIGHT

Even though it was late, Dani was unable to sleep. He rolled out of his bed. He sat on his desk and opened his laptop. He clicked on the SkyCall icon to find out whether any of his friends were online. Aya's status indicated she was online. He opened a chat window and began typing.

"Hey, Aya, you still there? Your status shows you're online."

"Yes, Dani, I'm here but it's getting late. I should have been asleep by now. My parents don't know I'm still up..." Her response arrived almost immediately.

"I heard my parents talking to your father earlier this evening..."

"I know, he told me."

"They told me, too. Besides, I've watched the late-night newscast. I have an idea now of what's going on in Israel."

"Unfortunately from the news you only get a tiny fraction of the whole picture. It's scary, Dani. It's frightening to see how a conflict spirals out of proportion in a matter of hours. From noon until late evening, things went from bad to worse. I'm not even sure I'm going to school tomorrow. My mom said she wouldn't let me go."

"Aya, you know you can always come to Sofia. It's safe here."

"It's up to my parents..."

"Sure, but you can also tell them how you feel."

"Thank you for your concern, Dani."

"Aya, there's one thing I want to talk to you about."

"What is it?"

"I've received a message."

"What kind of message?"

"Well, I'll send you a copy... it's this:

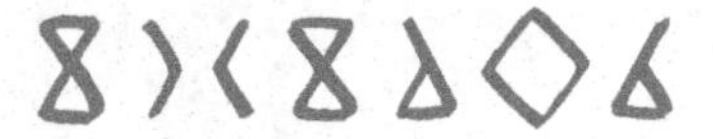

"What on earth are these symbols?"

"I have absolutely no idea. But they remind me of something familiar. They somehow resemble the pigpen symbols I use with my schoolmates, yet most of them are totally unknown to me. Below the symbols there was another one – a kind of pictograph strikingly resembling David's Star. Again I have no clue what it is."

"Do you have any idea who sent all these symbols to you?"

"The nickname below the message reads The LaW."

"That doesn't ring a bell."

"Will you help me decipher it?"

"Sure, Dani. My curiosity is now totally aroused! But how are we going to understand what they mean?"

"Do you know what?"

"No."

"It's just struck me you should go to Rapha and ask him."

"Why Rapha?"

"I remember he spoke to us about some ancient symbols. You show him these. He knows so much there's a chance he might know something about them as well."

"You're right. He did speak about symbols. All right, I'll certainly pay him a visit."

"When can you do that?"

"Tomorrow."

"Great."

"Dani, I just heard my mom come in. . .I'll talk to you later!

"Okay – talk to you later. Good night, Aya..."

"Night, Dani..."

Aya's status instantly changed to offline.

******

After his brief chat with Aya, Dani decided to continue browsing the Net for any clues that could help him decipher the string of symbols. He had already tried to decode them by checking some cryptography websites and nothing had come out of it. He now decided to dig deeper. The excitement of curiosity had just replaced his former drowsiness. Now he was as fresh as a steaming pumpkin pie coming straight out of the oven.

41

JERUSALEM, ISRAEL
25 JULY 2020
BEFORE NOON

"Here you go, Rapha," Aya said as she heaved two heavy paper bags of groceries on the table in Rapha's kitchen.

"Oh, dear Aya. I feel so bad because I have to ask you to get my groceries in such times of great turmoil and peril!"

"Now, Rapha, you know that we are the closest people you have. You should in no way feel guilty about asking such a small favor of me!"

"But I hear of violence in the streets. It's not safe outside, Aya, especially for a girl like you."

"Don't worry, Rapha. I wasn't alone. My dad went with me to the grocery shop."

"Where is he now?" he asked worried.

"Downstairs, waiting for me."

"Oh, poor child, you should have invited him upstairs. Please call him up. I would like to invite you both to a cup of tea."

"All right, I'll call him," Aya said and took out her SkyPhone. She invited Ruben to Rapha's flat.

In a few moments, Ruben walked in the doorway, a big smile on his face.

"Rapha... It's been a long time since we last met," Ruben shook hands with the older man.

"It is true. Thank you for helping Aya help me!"

"That's the least I could do for her and for you, Rapha."

"Long gone are the days when you used to come here as often as your daughter comes now." And that was true. Years before, Ruben used to come to Rapha's apartment and they discussed at great length various traits of the ancient Jewish mysticism.

"I miss our conversations, Rapha."

"You know I am always willing to have one with you," Rapha said and smiled. "And I am always here. Nowhere else left to go. But you look good, my boy. Still fighting the hawks?"

"Yes, Rapha, always fighting them. The battle hasn't grown any bit less fierce than before. Quite the opposite in fact."

"Same old story but I gather the doves are getting stronger with time."

"You being the strongest of them all," Ruben said kindly and full of admiration for the man who had once inspired the creation and aided the inception of Peace Now.

"Tea?" Rapha offered.

"With pleasure."

"Me, too," Aya chimed in.

"Of course, you too, Aya. I wouldn't think for a minute you wouldn't drink a cup –"

"– Of your most delicious mixture of teas, right?" Aya interrupted playfully.

"Yes, certainly," Rapha said and began pouring tea from the steaming kettle into mugs, he had placed in front each of them.

Sipping the hot tea, Aya said, "Rapha, I want to ask you something. Last night I talked to Dani. He told me he had received a strange message full of some mysterious symbols."

"What kind of symbols?" he asked calmly.

"Look," Aya said and handed him her SkyPhone. On its large screen, Rapha could clearly make out the string of the symbols and also the pictograph Dani had sent Aya.

"Where did he get these?" Rapha's voice was full of alarm.

"He received them," Aya explained.

"Who sent them to him?"

"Somebody calling himself The LaW."

"I see." Rapha didn't want to reveal his surprise.

"May I take a look?" Ruben joined in taking Aya's SkyPhone and as he saw the odd looking symbols he added, "I have no idea what they mean."

"Aya, I almost forgot. Could you please go down to the first floor, to Ms. Herzl and bring the mail for me? She called earlier saying I had received a letter."

"Certainly, Rapha," she said while standing up briskly and heading for the door. Both men saw her off with their eyes. When she went out, Rapha spoke first.

"Ruben, my boy, I thought the time for your last lesson would come much later than today."

"What do you mean?" Ruben was unable to understand.

"I taught you all the lessons but one. The last one I was supposed to deliver to you before I die."

"What last lesson? I thought you were through with the lessons long time ago," more incomprehension in Ruben's voice.

"These," Rapha said pointing to the screen of Aya's SkyPhone.

"What are these? Some scribbles I guess."

"These are symbols from King David's secret cipher."

"Wow, are you sure? I've never heard of it."

"Yes, I am. In times of war, King David needed safe communication with his dispatched units. Having received a divine revelation one night, he came up with twenty-two symbols - one for each letter of the Hebrew alphabet. The symbols consisted of straight horizontal or diagonal strokes - not a single vertical stroke - forming several kinds of basic geometric figures. The symbols were derived from the structure of Magen David, the Shield of David, with which all soldiers were armed. They were easy to write and especially to memorize because the inner part of the shield had its structure in the form of the six-pointed star visible. It was easy to look at the structure of the shield and sketch out the symbols in order to memorize them."

"So these are some of his symbols?"

"Yes."

"Do you know how to decipher them?"

"I know how to read them."

"What do these say?"

"If you observe them, they are in two groups - one consisting of three symbols while the second of four. Together they read מגן דויד."

"Magen David."

"Exactly."

"How about the pictograph below the symbols?"

"Look at it carefully. It is almost identical to David's Star but not quite -"

"Two of the short horizontal bars are missing."

"Good observation, Ruben. Indeed, they are. Do you know why?"

"No idea."

"Because this pictograph is a kind of monogram - it combines all the symbols above. Take a good look and trace the symbols." It took Ruben a few moments to begin to recognize how the symbols in the string had been interwoven.

"Amazing! You are correct," Ruben exclaimed while Rapha was showing him how each symbol had been incorporated in the monogram.

"I don't understand anything. Why would Dani receive these symbols and the monogram?"

"There's always a reason."

"What reason?"

"I don't know but I can assure you, there is a reason why this particular boy has received them and not any other one. You must find out why."

"All right, but how?"

"What's his full name?"

"Dani Magdev."

"This, Ruben, is the clear-cut answer to your why question."

"I don't understand."

"You will. In the aggadah it is said that when somebody receives the symbols, the day of the Messiah and end of times is coming."

"This is crazy, Rapha. What end of times? What Messiah?"

"Listen, Ruben, we don't have much time. This is serious. I have to transmit my knowledge of the symbols to you before anything happens to me."

"Nothing is going to happen to you."

"I know better. Take Aya home and come back. It won't take long. Hurry now."

42

GAZA, PALESTINE

25 JULY 2020

EARLY EVENING

Dr. Ramzi Rasil and his colleague, Dr. Mohammed Hakim, were walking down one of the main streets in Gaza in silence. Dr. Rasil was a 45-year-old respected and highly experienced cardiologist. Dr. Hakim was a 49-year-old surgeon with many years of experience at one of the local hospitals whose brother, a Palestinian hawk, had gone high up the Hamas military ladder. Both doctors headed the Gaza branch of Peace Now. They fought for peace with all means available. Risking their lives was only one of those means. They were two Palestinian doves.

Throughout the day and at a low-key secret location, important political and military Hamas functionaries had been bitterly bickering over the current situation. Early in the morning, orders for indiscriminate shelling against Israel had already been dispatched to nests of militants scattered across Gaza. In the meantime, at the secret location, the functionaries were squabbling and trying to devise a retaliation plan in case in ten days' time the Temple Mount and Land of Israel Faithful Movement actually carried out the ceremony they had announced would take place. Most of those present were in favor of Israel being hit hard. "No mercy for Israel" some of them had shouted out during the meeting. But they knew of the immense might of the Israeli Army. They knew if they launched a full-scale attack on Israel deploying all the man- and gun-power they had at their disposal, Israel would wipe them out in a matter of hours. Most of them were fundamentalist enough to accept the grim perspective of being washed away from the face of the earth. What many of them feared was such a grim fate for their families and children.

At some point in the early afternoon, one of the soldiers entered the room and announced the arrival of the younger brother of commander Naif Hakim, Dr. Mohammed Hakim, accompanied by another doctor; they both wanted to join the meeting. Commander Hakim puckered his brows because he knew Mohammed had been lost all too long ago to the other side, the enemy camp, and he deeply despised him for that. Naif stood up and walked out of the room under the watchful eyes of everyone present.

"What are you doing here, Mohammed? You know you have no business here!" Naif scolded his younger brother.

"The situation is getting worse and worse by the hour. If we don't make the right moves now, Brother, we may never have another chance," Mohammed said calmly.

"You don't have to worry about that. We've gathered here precisely to make the right decisions!" Naif was angry.

"I just want to say a few words to everyone in there," Mohammed said pointing with his head to the nearby room from which Naif had emerged.

"I cannot allow such a thing to happen. You must be out of your mind. How dare you?" Naif exclaimed in disbelief at the nerve of his brother.

"I have brought with me my colleague Dr. Rasil," Mohammed continued, still speaking calmly.

"I know very well who your friend is. He stole you from us and sold you to the other side of our Israeli oppressors. You would have made a fine soldier, Mohammed. Rasil has absolutely no right to be here. Scumbag!" Naif hissed at Ramzi with anger and glared at him with hatred.

"Why?" Mohammed asked still composed.

"Because your minds have already been brainwashed by those dovish Israelis."

"Oh, don't be so naïve, Naif! We ask only for peace. Do we ask too much?"

"It depends on the cost, Mohammed. Peace at any cost is no peace at all. We will never be slaves to the Israelis."

"Wrong. You are wrong. Peace at any cost is better than any of your wars. You already are slaves to your fundamentalist views!"

The last remark of Mohammed's seemed to send Naif's temperature to the boiling point.

"Don't tell me I am wrong. I decide that for myself. And don't ever dare talk to me about my wars. They are not mine. They are the wars of my oppressed people. You have no right to be here. You are already in the enemy camp!" Naif was shouting with rage, his face contorted in an expression of malevolence.

Mohammed's eyes opened in disbelief at the words of his brother. "Your oppressed people? Don't you get it, Naif? By denying peace to your people you oppress them, not the Israelis. You and your hawkish fundamentalist clique. You don't allow Palestine to live in peace," Mohammed shouted these words right in his brother's face. Naif couldn't restrain his rage and punched Mohammed hard in the face. He collapsed to the ground. Naif was still out of control and began to kick Mohammed in the stomach. In a madman's fury, Naif said, "Pray you are still alive, Mohammed. You should have thought about your wife and children before selling yourself to the Israelis. Dog!"

Three soldiers rushed in. One used the muzzle of his rifle to push Ramzi to the door while two others picked Mohammed up and began dragging him. The two doctors were literally thrown out on the sidewalk and left there. Ramzi tried to help his friend stand, but Mohammed was in convulsions and couldn't get up. They sat on the ground and leaned back against a fence.

"They are insane hawks in there, Mohammed. They are suicidal," Ramzi said looking at the face of his colleague and friend distorted with pain.

"I know this. That's why we came here to put some sense into them but now I see it is a lost cause. My brother has been lost to the fundamentalists, forever."

"I cannot understand them, Mohammed. Why is Hamas still shooting and shelling at Israeli settlements? Hamas has to stop that right now and for good. It has to return to the negotiating table and altogether give up arming more and more militants. Brutal force doesn't lead us anywhere. Haven't those hawks realized that after all these years?"

"No, they haven't, unfortunately. They have to renounce violence forever but they will never do it. And think about it, Ramzi. Who are we? Refugees in camps, yet another weapon in the hands of nationalism-fuelled Arab fundamentalists, that's who we are. I say no to violence. We should be fighting our cause not with aggression and bloodshed but peacefully at the negotiating table."

"I cannot agree more. They can call us names and the paid dog servants all they want. This won't change anything because we know what the main problem of Palestine is," Ramzi looked at his friend, took a deep shaking breath and continued. "With absolutely no power or choice over their destiny ordinary Palestinians have been held hostage by a clique of Hamas hawks. Yes, there were elections. Yes, some claimed they were fair and not rigged. But we know the truth that bares its vicious teeth at us - we know that the politicians the Palestinians vote for usually dance to the tunes of local and foreign fundamentalists."

******

All that happened about an hour earlier. Now it was evening and there were still a lot of people in the poorly lit streets. The two doctors were walking, still in silence, and too preoccupied to notice the crowd along the sidewalk. They were both sunk in their thoughts as one was leaning on the other for support. Electricity, among many other things, was a scarce and expensive commodity in Gaza. A dog barked behind an iron gate as they walked past.

At a road junction they bid each other a silent farewell and walked off in opposite directions. Still submerged in thought, Dr. Rasil failed to notice the two figures that emerged from the corner and quietly fell in behind him, getting closer every step. He swerved left down a narrower street and was approaching home, the neighborhood he had grown up in. He stopped in front of a green metal door, unlocked it and went in. He began climbing the stairs that were opposite the entrance. At that very moment, he was suddenly dealt a heavy blow with a large object. He had no time for last thoughts. He dropped face down like a felled tree. Two strong fingers of a masculine hand checked his carotid artery. Dr. Rasil's heart had stopped beating. He was dead.

43

SOFIA, BULGARIA

26 JULY 2020

EARLY MORNING

It was about six o'clock when Ian's SkyPhone rang. Eyes still closed he reached out and grabbed it. When he picked up it was Ruben, all distressed, calling to inform about Dr. Rasil's brutal murder.

"Oh, Ruben, this is really sad news. Dr. Rasil was one of the staunchest supporters of peace in Palestine. Things won't be the same without him..." Ian responded with great anxiety in his voice, now fully awake by the news. As Rovine shifted in the bed, awoken by Ian's voice, he immediately switched on the SkyPhone's loudspeaker.

"I know that, Ian. I hope this is no sign of hawks taking over doves in the Palestinian camp although it definitely seems so. In each case, we are lucky to have the other dove, Dr. Hakim, alive."

"Lucky? Do you really think so?" Ian asked in disbelief.

"I hope so. Look, the killers left him alive because his brother is a high-ranking Hamas functionary. Threatening him with a knife at his throat was a last warning of sorts. You know as much as I do if Dr. Hakim continues to openly advocate peace, he'll share the fate of Dr. Rasil. His brother won't hesitate the second time. There are powerful people out there in the Palestinian camp who do not want peace with Israel, who are fundamentalists to the core of their very being," Ruben said disconcertedly; Rovine was now attentively following the conversation having heard some of its key words.

"I think I know what you mean, Ruben. Now I can only hope Dr. Hakim won't give up his peace mission and collaboration with Peace Now."

"I must try to keep him in our camp, no matter what."

"Yes, you'll have to do your best but it's not going to be easy. Dr. Hakim has a wife and children. The family always comes first," Ian said.

"True."

"It should be that way," Rovine said. "Your own family always comes first."

"Ruben, you know that the peace talks in Camp Boyana are continuing despite the clashes and violence," Ian said.

"I know. The government has decided not to give in to provocations coming either from our or from the Palestinian camp. They will continue with the peace negotiations no matter what."

"Hillary Clinton has welcomed this decision as the most reasonable under the circumstances."

"But the violence is escalating by the day, Ian. They are trying to contain it at one place but shortly afterward it erupts at another. It's sprawling like a malicious virus."

"I understand..." Ian nodded thoughtfully.

"War can break out any day, any hour. It's all so uncertain."

"You have your other home here, Ruben."

"I know and I am constantly thinking about how to do things best for my family."

"Whatever you decide you can count on us."

"Thank you, dear friends. Ian, Rovine, now that the two of you are on the line, there's one more thing I'd like to speak to you about. Yesterday, Aya showed me a message she had received from Dani."

"What message?" Ian asked puzzled.

"He hasn't shown us anything, Ruben," Rovine chimed in.

"I am sure he hasn't but that is not the point. Ask him, he'll show it to you. The point is I'd like you to ask him to let you know if he ever gets any other messages like the first one."

"But what is this message?" Ian was unable to understand.

"You'll see it. Just call me if he gets another one."

"All right, no problem, Ruben," Rovine promised.

"Now I have to go," Ruben said abruptly.

"Please give our warm regards to Sarah and Aya," Rovine chimed in.

"Thank you, Rovine. We'll keep in touch..."

"Will do," Ian said as he and Rovine said goodbye and hung up.

******

"Dani, breakfast is ready!" Rovine called from the kitchen.

"I'm coming, Mom," he replied from his room.

"Now you can speak to him," Rovine turned to Ian.

"Good idea..."

"Here I am. Mmm, something smells delicious!" Dani entered the kitchen.

"Dani," Ian looked at him. "What kind of message did you get the other day?"

"How did you find out about it?"

"From Ruben."

"It means Aya told him."

"Is it a secret or something?" Ian was suddenly a bit suspicious.

"No. It's right here in my SkyPhone. Look," Dani showed them the message.

"Some symbols?" Rovine said.

"Strange looking symbols and what is this? It resembles David's Star," Ian said.

"They look a bit like the pigpen ones but are different and I have no idea what they mean. Yes, and there's the star as well," Dani said.

"Who sent them to you?" Ian asked.

"You can see the name of the sender below. The LaW," Dani replied.

"Who's he?"

"I don't know."

"Why didn't you tell us?"

"I thought it was some kind of prank, Dad, that's why."

44

SOFIA, BULGARIA
26 JULY 2020
LATE EVENING

"Why do you think that message Dani got is so important for Ruben?" Rovine asked Ian as they got into bed.

"I don't know but it seems it is, otherwise he wouldn't have asked about it."

"It's strange Dani didn't tell us in the first place. He told Aya but not us."

"Ah, it's okay. As he said he thought it was some kind of joke. Besides you know how much he likes Aya. It's only natural he shared with her first."

"Yes, I guess you're right."

"But the symbols in the message got me thinking..."

"What do you mean?"

"When I saw them in the morning they instantly reminded me of characters I had already seen elsewhere."

"What characters are you talking about?"

"Characters from The Stone Book of the Bulgarians. I found a copy of the book in the university library in the afternoon. Inside I found a table of ancient Bulgarian letters compiled by Dr.

Petar Dobrev – the prominent scientist who devoted his life to the study of the ancient history and language of the Bulgarians. And do you know what I stumbled upon?"

"I have absolutely no idea."

"I encountered six ancient Bulgarian letters whose structure allows them to be, so to speak, interwoven in the graphics of David's Star. Look at them," Ian showed Rovine a piece of paper with six symbols on it while below them were the symbols from Dani's message.

⧖ ⧖ ◇ X V A

"Wow..." Rovine exclaimed.

"Three of the ancient Bulgarian letters are equivalent in structure to three of the symbols Dani got the other day. Isn't that amazing?"

"Indeed. Do you know what the ancient Bulgarian symbols stand for?"

"The first two symbols..."

"The pair of identical symbols, you mean."

"Yes, well, they stand for the Bulgarian letter E, equivalent to the English E. The third and fourth symbols stand for the Bulgarian letter C, equivalent to the English S. The fifth symbol in the string stands for the Bulgarian letter Ъ, equivalent to the English sound of 'u' in words such as 'buck' or 'luck'. The last symbol is a kind of diphthong AA corresponding to double As in English. Hence, with the correspondence to English, we've obtained a string of seven letters from the English alphabet: A-A-E-E-S-S-U."

"Do you think that whoever sent Dani the string of symbols had the ancient Bulgarian letters in mind?" Rovine was puzzled.

"I doubt it. Otherwise I would have found them all in Dr. Dobrev's table. I only found three matches."

"So it means they are different ones."

"For sure, they are but the important point is that each of the ancient Bulgarian symbols I discovered fits in the graphical structure of David's Star."

"So, in a way, Dani's message inspired you to a new discovery."

"Exactly…"

"I'd imagine that during the day you went the whole length of unscrambling the string of seven letters you obtained through the table, right?"

"You guessed it but in fact, it wasn't difficult at all to unscramble them. Once the letters are put in the correct order they simply read: *Sea Esau.*"

"Something like Sea (of) Esau?"

"Yes," Ian said looking at her. "We should rather ask ourselves why such phrase can be derived from David's Star in the first place," Ian offered.

"It must be pure coincidence."

"Well, I very much want to agree with you but I can't. It simply doesn't smell like coincidence to me. In each case, I'll call Rabbi Loew first thing in the morning." Ian switched off the bedside lamp and kissed Rovine. She wrapped around him and tenderly kissed him back.

45

SOFIA, BULGARIA

27 JULY 2020

EARLY MORNING

When Rabbi Loew picked up his SkyPhone the following morning, he was pleasantly surprised to discover he was having a conference call with Ian, Rovine and Ruben Openheim. Ian told them about his latest discovery of the ancient Bulgarian letters and explained about the phrase he had uncovered after unscrambling them. Rovine was seated next to Ian as both sipped their morning coffees.

"In historical aggadah, Esau has always been seen as a figure aggravating violence and metaphorically speaking, he has become an epitome of violence," Rabbi Loew began and then added. "Therefore a phrase such as Sea of Esau would translate as –"

"Sea of violence," Ian cut in, having a sudden rush of insight.

"That's right," the Rabbi agreed.

"But that's what we've been submerged into these days...a sea of violence all across the state of Israel..." Ruben was worried.

"Sadly, this is true as well, I must admit it. However, the insight we've received through the ancient Bulgarian letters seems to give us hints about currently unfolding events regarding the eternal struggle between the twins – Jacob and Esau," Rabbi Loew explained.

"What do you mean?" Rovine asked.

"As the Biblical narrative describes it, Jacob and Esau have been locked in a constant struggle against each other ever since they were in the womb of their mother, Rebekah. It is said that since then, and especially after Esau was tricked into giving up his birthright and hence leadership of Israel to Jacob, the two brothers and the two separate families descending from them – Edom and Judah – have been in a constant struggle. The Edomites were always portrayed as violent, uncultivated, barbaric and marauding people who were enemies of the kingdom of Judah. In due time, the Edomites became the collective archetype of all enemies of Israel," Rabbi Loew calmly explained.

"So can we say we are currently witnessing yet another clash of the never-ending struggle between Jacob and Esau?" Ian asked.

"Yes, you can put it that way – Jacob against Esau, Judah against Edom, or Jerusalem against Bozrah."

"Bozrah?" Rovine asked unable to follow.

"Yes, the ancient capital city of Edom, the kingdom of the descendants of Esau. Actually in latter Jewish history, the Romans were considered descendants of Esau. Still later, it so happened that all enemies of the Jews came to be considered as Esau's descendants," the Rabbi said.

"But why this never-ending struggle? Is it really never going to end?" Ian asked puzzled.

"It will end, of course, in Bozrah, at the end of days when the Messiah will arrive," the Rabbi stated.

"What do you mean in Bozrah?" Ian asked.

"In Hebrew, the word *bozrah* (בצרה) means 'sheepfold'. The city of Bozrah is related to the prophecy of Micah in which he predicts what shall happen when the Messiah arrives at the end of times. This is how Micah speaks about that most prodigal of events in Micah 2:12," Rabbi Loew said and began reciting by heart:

I will surely assemble, O Jacob, all of thee; I will surely gather the remnant of Israel; I will put them together as the sheep of Bozrah, as the flock in the midst of their fold: they shall make great noise by reason of [the multitude of] men.

"And this is how Micah continues in 2:13," the Rabbi said and continued reciting:

The breaker is come up before them: they have broken up, and have passed through the gate, and are gone out by it: and their king shall pass before them, and the LORD on the head of them.

Then Rabbi Loew continued explaining. "Bozrah was a pastoral city and as its name, sheepfold, already suggested the main occupation of its inhabitants was the breeding and trading with sheep. According to Micah's prophecy in the Old Testament however, Bozrah will be the place where the final score between the two brothers - Jacob and Esau - will be settled.

That is why we have spoken since then of the Bozrah deliverance, when the Messiah will arrive there as breaker, or as the one who will break the sheepfold, *bozrah,* in which the people of the covenant - the children of Abraham, Isaac and Jacob - will be kept prisoners and shall let them pass through it, led by their God, YHWH."

"Thank you, Rabbe. I think there's yet another thing left we need to do," Ruben said. "We have to take the string of ancient Bulgarian letters transliterated to English: A-A-E-E-S-S-U. Then we'll have to find the Phoenician letters corresponding to each transliterated English letter. Once we do that we'll have to convert the Phoenician letters to their Hebrew equivalents."

"Interesting idea," Rabbi Loew commented.

"At the end, we'll have to unscramble them to see what we'll come up with. Agreed?"

"Yes," Ian said.

"Let's do it now and speak shortly afterwards," Ruben suggested.

"The seven English letters correspond to the following string of Hebrew letters which you can write down," the Rabbi said and began dictating, "Aleph-aleph-he-he-vav-shin-shin."

"We'll speak in half an hour, all right?" Ruben asked.

"In half an hour," Rovine said. Then they all hung up.

******

"We found a number of singular words," Ian said when half an hour later, all four of them had resumed their conference call.

"I also found many," Ruben said.

"But we need to find one coherent phrase," Rabbi Loew reminded them.

"Well, the closest to a coherent phrase I got is *He' 'esh Shaveh* (הא אש שוה) -"

"Lo, behold the fire of Shaveh," the Rabbi translated from Hebrew and continued explaining, "Shaveh is the plain also

known as the King's dale, where, near a fire set precisely for the occasion, Melchizedek, king of Salem and the most high priest of God, met Abraham and blessed him."

"So we have the phrase," Rovine concluded hastily.

"No, dear Rovine, this is not the phrase we are looking for. Among the many words you have come up with, there are three which give us an exact meaning."

"What are these words?" Ruben asked, beginning to grow impatient.

"*Eshshah vav sha'ah* (אשה ו שאה) meaning 'fire and devastation'," the Rabbi explained.

"How are we supposed to understand them?" Ian asked.

"In the context of the eternal struggle between Jacob and Esau, the approaching final battle between the two brothers will be marked by eruption of fire and total devastation. This is what we are witnessing across Israel and the Palestinian territories at the moment – fire and devastation from which millions and millions of people suffer."

"So, Rabbe, you think something big is about to happen?"

"I don't think, Ruben, I know."

"When?" asked Ruben, with ever more growing excitement.

"I don't know when exactly but I am sure the star holds the answer. It is there, right in front of our eyes. We just need to see it, to uncover it."

"We failed miserably the first time," Ruben spoke with a tinge of frustration in his voice.

"Oh, it wasn't your fault, Ruben. It was Uri Zohar's excess of self-confidence and hasty conclusions. You don't put whatever into whatever to get whatever you want to get. No. He had it wrong from the outset but Professor Epstein and I told you in advance that nothing would happen on the 20th of May, didn't we?"

"You did."

"So now all of us have to roll up our sleeves and get back to the star and try to find the new date," Rabbi Loew said in an encouraging way. They all said good-bye and promised to hold another conference call, should anyone come up with anything novel related to any kind of date.

46

SOFIA, BULGARIA

27 JULY 2020

EARLY EVENING

Deeply shaken by the latest revelations made by Rabbi Loew in the morning, Ian couldn't stop thinking all day about the knowledge hidden in David's Star by means of interwoven letters and symbols. The knowledge seemed endless, all-encompassing. He was convinced the star held one of the biggest secrets, too – the date of the final battle of Jacob and Esau in Bozrah. So he was looking for a date. A *date*.

Unable to concentrate much on his work in the office throughout the day, part of his mind was frequently reeling back to the star. Almost all the time he would mentally sketch out one sign or another from the graphics of the star. The rabbi had been right – they couldn't so frivolously manipulate the Roman numerals to get whatever they wanted. Uri Zohar, however, had done just that. Ian already knew whatever had come out of the star, had appeared in a straightforward manner. So if there were any date interwoven, it would be in a proper way without manipulations, just like all the words and phrases they had already uncovered.

In a sudden gush of inspiration, Ian made an outstanding discovery. He rushed home to share it with Rovine.

******

"Wait, wait, if it is really as big as you say it is, then I suggest we call Ruben and Rabbi Loew before you tell me. They also need to hear it," Rovine said to Ian, who was bristling with excitement.

"Actually, you are right. We have to call them right away," he said as he grabbed his SkyPhone and began to dial Ruben's number. When he picked up and was on line, Ian rang Rabbi Loew. After a few buzzes the Rabbi picked up as well and all four of them were connected in a conference call. Ian began as excitedly as he had first spoken to Rovine when she got home.

"So, Rabbe, you said in the morning we should be looking for the date when the final settling of scores between Jacob and Esau would take place, right?"

"I did say that," the rabbi agreed.

"Looking for an exact date, that is, looking for numbers and being a mathematician myself, I decided to find out if there were any other numbers interwoven in David's Star beside the Roman numerals we had already found. The natural question for me was where to start. I realized I had only one option – the numerical systems that had been used in the land of Israel throughout the centuries..."

"Why, this is the most logical approach. I should add the only possible and admissible approach," the Rabbi nodded in approval.

"My reasoning goes as follows. We have already discovered the Roman numerals. Why? Because at the period of the Roman domination of Israel, they were the predominant numerical system used. For purposes of communication and trade, Roman-dominated Israel made best use of the Roman numerical system."

"Correct, Ian. It was so anyway."

"Thank you, Ruben. Uri Zohar's distortion of the Roman numerals made most of us believe we were dealing with the year 2020. But we all know that figure is written in another way and with different Roman numerals than the ones we have discovered. My next question, therefore, was about those who dominated Israel before the Romans. Who were they?"

"The Greeks, of course," Ruben chimed in, already keyed-up himself.

"It is interesting to point out here that at that time, the numerical system used by the Greeks was called Acrophonic numerals."

"Acrophonic?" Ruben seemed lost.

"Yes, just as ancient Israelites used their letters as numbers so did the ancient Greeks. The earliest alphabet-based system of numerals used by the Greeks was called Acrophonic Attic numerals. The Greeks began using it in 7th century B.C.E. By the time they conquered the Levant, the system had already gained popularity and had been extensively used across the Greek-dominated world. Once again, for purposes of communication and trade between Greeks and Jews, the latter made best use of the numerical system of the former."

"What did you discover, Ian?" Ruben was clearly on the very edge of his patience.

"Surprisingly, I discovered that according to this Acrophonic Attic system, X corresponded to 1000. Since David's Star has two wings there also are two Xs..."

"So we've got 2000," Ruben said.

"This is twenty years ago," Rovine concluded hastily.

"Along with the two Xs, I also came to discover the symbol Δ. It equals 10."

"Hence, adding-up the numerals, we end up having 2010," Ruben said.

"It makes no sense. This was ten years ago," Rovine again.

"Of course it makes no sense because I haven't finished telling you everything I've come to discover," Ian said. He shot a quick surreptitious glance at Rovine. She seemed to have grown too impatient to contain herself. Then Ian continued. "If you take a closer look at the graphics of David's Star you will see it actually consists of the merger of two opposite-pointed triangles. So if you take the downward-pointed symbol and turn it upside down, you get a second Δ, hence a second 10. In the end, the two Xs give us 2000 while the two Δ give us 20. Hence 2020 is my answer to the question which the year at stake really is."

"Brilliant," Ruben exclaimed.

"Indeed," Rabbi Loew agreed.

"So the Acrophonic Attic numerals give us the exact year," Ian said.

"But we still don't know the accurate day and month. Do we have a solution for that?" Ruben's curiosity probed further.

"Unfortunately, the Acrophonic Attic numerals don't hold the answer to that question, Ruben, as all of them are exhausted with the year."

"There must be some clue of sorts," Ruben pressed on.

"We've got a clue but we will have to change codes for that and I'm not sure how accurate such move will be. As you may know, the usage of a single code is consistent when encoding a message. Uri Zohar made the mistake of mixing codes and what did he get? We got it all wrong. Right, Ruben?"

"Yes, Ian, you have a point. Let's then take the month and the day as a separate message. In this case tell us what the clue is, no matter how inconsistent with the year it may initially appear."

"With this provision made I can say the following... To our aid come the ones who replaced the Greeks as the dominating power in Israel – the Romans. Before I tell you anything further, I'd like you to see a sign I have sketched out of the graphics of David's Star. Just give me a second to send it to you," Ian said and began browsing the menus of his SkyPhone. When he found the picture he was looking for he sent it to both of them. He gave them another moment to look at it before he spoke.

"So what do you think you are looking at?" Ian asked.

"It looks like a monogram to me," Ruben said.

"I clearly see an A," Rovine said.

"And there is the V below the A," the Rabbi joined in.

"And on the left you have the Roman numeral X," Ian concluded.

"O, my God," Rabbi Loew exclaimed.

"Wow, we've got X Av – the 10th of Av. This should be the correct date," Ruben spoke haltingly, disbelief in his voice.

"Yes, Ruben, the 10th of Av 2020," Ian cut in.

"But this year the 10th of Av falls on the 31st of July. This is in a few days' time!"

"What is the 10th of Av?" Rovine asked.

"Av is one of the months in the Jewish calendar," Rabbi Loew began explaining to answer Rovine's question. "In Judaism the 10th of Av is known as *Tishah be-Av* – the day of mourning and fasting that commemorates the destruction of the first and the second Temples. According to the Prophecy of Jeremiah, the First Temple – the building of which had been prepared by King David and carried out by his son King Solomon – was destroyed by the Babylonian king Nebuchadnezzar in 586 B.C.E. exactly on the 10th of Av. According to the Jewish historian Josephus Flavius, the Romans destroyed the Second Temple in the year 70 C.E. That happened again on the same date – the 10th of Av. So the date became an official day of mourning and fasting because a number of calamities throughout Jewish history happened on it."

"There is more to what you are saying, Rabbe," Ian cut in.

"What is it?"

"When I discovered the exact year and date earlier today, I permitted myself to check 2020 as a Strong's number. In the Strong's Concordance, 2020 corresponds to the Biblical-Hebrew noun *hatstalah* (הצלה) which means 'deliverance'. I'd also like to point out the curious fact that the noun *hatstalah* was used only once in the Hebrew Bible, in the Book of Esther. Listen to the crucial part of Esther 4:14," Ian said and began reciting by heart:

'For if thou altogether holdest thy peace at this time, [then] shall there enlargement and deliverance [hatstalah] arise to the Jews...'

"The way I see it is that The Temple Mount and Land of Israel Faithful Movement sees itself as an individual entity heroically confronting the enemy, in the face of Arab neighbors. By staging the laying of foundations for the Third Temple, the movement offers to provide means for the deliverance of the Jewish nation," Ian paused for a moment and then resumed.

"For the Temple Mount Movement, Israel has every reason to exist in Palestine. By divine decree, recorded in the Holy Torah, Israel was given the right to inhabit ancient Palestine. Then there was the Babylonian exile followed by a return. Then there was the Roman exile that lasted for over 2000 years. It too was followed by a return in 1948. In the time of absence, the Arabs moved in and settled in Palestine. They've been living there ever since. After the Roman exile, however, troubles for Israel did not cease. For those 2000 years of exile, Israel was constantly persecuted and expelled from places where it sojourned. Oftentimes those persecutions and expulsions were violent and ended tragically. And they didn't end in the 20th century."

"This is so," Ruben agreed, "When under Hitler's command the Holocaust against European Jewry began to take place across the Old Continent, Israel had no alternative but to find any means possible to return to its motherland of Palestine. Bitter struggle made that possible and the state of Israel was born in 1948. For many of us, religious and secular Jews alike, the creation of the state and the return to the land of our forefathers equaled divine *hatstalah* and rebuilding of the Third Temple. But there is another aspect as well. The creation of the state was Israel's response to centuries of humiliation, persecution and extermination."

"Let us not forget that the founding of the state of Israel in 1948, was our way of shouting out loud to the rest of the world,

'No more exile, no more persecution, no more genocide against us!' Rabbi Loew joined in with agitation in his tone of voice.

"But then Israel faced another enemy - the hostile Arab states which didn't think it right to do justice to events, such as the expulsion of the Jews from Israel by the Romans that took place over 2000 years ago. What happened, they claimed, had already happened. But one can't expect to illegally evict and expropriate a family from their own property and many years or centuries later to be surprised when descendants of that family tried to reclaim that illegitimately confiscated property. This is called restitution or reparation. Hence what the Arabs didn't want to admit they knew - sometimes justice could wait a very long time until it was rightfully served," Ian said, exalted by the explanation he delivered and in which he so strongly believed.

"You have understood many aspects of our life in Israel correctly, Ian," Rabbi Loew said.

"Indeed," Ruben agreed.

"And so the movement wants to make us believe that the 31st of July 2020 will be the date of the final *hatstalah* then?" Rovine asked puzzled by this revelation.

"It seems so. The coinciding of the date of their ceremony and of our discovery is quite extraordinary," Ruben said.

"But look at what that announcement for the staging of a ceremonial laying of a marble cornerstone of the Third Temple on Temple Mount itself sparked - instant anti-Israeli riots across the Palestinian territories and the Arab neighboring countries. Jacob challenged Esau. Jerusalem challenged Bozrah," the Rabbi said, concerned.

"I can draw only one sound conclusion from all this," Ruben said. "We've discovered an important date. How important we don't know yet. But judging by the events already unfolding and by all these anti-Israeli riots and clashes with security forces, it is a pretty important one. For one reason or another, this date has been interwoven in the graphics of David's Star. We've come to discover it before it has taken place. This means we've turned up a warning of sorts and we have to do something before that date, something about peace, something to avert war. I am thinking here of the verse in Esther, of holding our peace together, so that there's deliverance to all of us."

"You are right. But this also means we've got no time," Ian said.

"No, we don't." There was a shade of angst in Ruben's voice.

"Adding Bozrah and deliverance, we finally get to a phrase such as the Bozrah deliverance," Ian chimed in.

"Which, in all likelihood is believed to take place on the 31st of July 2020," Ruben said in awestruck tones.

"The date is not believed, Ruben, it is downright interlaced in the graphics of the David's Star," Rabbi Loew said.

"Well, there seems to be people like the members of the Temple Mount and Land of Israel Faithful Movement who believe the resolve of the final score between Jacob and Esau will take place on the 31st of July. I believe it is no coincidence they chose precisely this date. And there is more to that. The fact that an event of the magnitude of anointing the cornerstone for the Third Temple to be built on Temple Mount, if not prevented or avoided, will surely incite a war between Jacob in the face of Israel and Esau in the face of Israel's enemies," Ruben spoke softly.

"You're saying that in a few days' time, the end of days will come?" Rovine was incredulous.

"All I'm saying is someone's been trying to instigate Jacob against Esau in an attempt to provoke a final settling of scores between Jerusalem and Bozrah," Ruben said and then fell silent. That revelation made everyone thoughtful. It was scary to imagine a full-scale war laden with so many scores for settling. It wasn't difficult to imagine how fierce, violent and brutal such a final war could be. None of them wanted to delve into further speculation on the matter. At the same time, they all realized time was running out and Friday 31st of July 2020, 09:00 AM was approaching fast, too fast in fact.

"If such an event should ever take place, it will be the gravest disaster the state of Israel has known since its restoration in 1948," Rabbi Loew said.

"But what should we do then?" Rovine asked.

"I don't know but I am pretty sure the answer has been interwoven in the star, friends," Ruben said assertively. "There's one thing we can do once we've been invited inside the ark of knowledge that David's Star is, and that is to go further and dig deeper. We've come thus far because of the star so the answer must surely be hidden embedded in it. And perhaps with the answer, we'll stumble upon the vital key to peace."

Then they all bade each other farewell and the conference call was over.

47

SOFIA, BULGARIA

27 JULY 2020

SHORTLY BEFORE MIDNIGHT

Dressed in his pajamas, Dani was already in bed, chatting with Aya on his laptop. He was able to type pretty fast, his fingers moving rapidly across the keyboard.

"So your father told you the message from The LaW was a prank?"

"Something like that. He said you shouldn't worry about it."

"Prank or not, I just wanted to know what it meant, Aya?"

"Do we always want to know what pranks are intended to mean?"

"Perhaps not, but this message didn't seem like a prank to me."

"But why are you so keyed-up about it?"

"Because an hour ago I got a second one."

"A second message from this mysterious LaW?"

"Yep."

"Another practical joke?"

"I don't think so. I can see one practical joke, but two? For what reason? Especially if the one at the receiving end of the joke didn't get it. I'm telling you, Aya, this is not a prank."

"Then what is it?"

"I don't know. You'd better ask your father. He might have an idea."

"Send me the message."

"All right. Just a sec."

"I'm here."

"There it is:

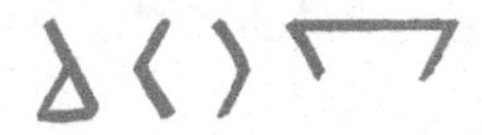

"I've got it. The symbols are weird. I'll ask him first thing in the morning. Sweet dreams, Dani, :-X"

"Sweet 2u2, :-X"

48

JERUSALEM, ISRAEL
28 JULY 2020
MORNING

Ruben, Aya, and Sarah were seated at the breakfast table, enjoying their fresh fruits and bagels, and cheese. The TV was on with the morning news cast. Another wave of clashes and violence had swept off the country during the night.

"Dad?" Aya turned slightly toward her father, drawing his attention away from the screen. "I spoke to Dani last night and he told me he had received another message with those strange symbols…"

"When did he receive it?" Ruben calmly cleared his throat and succeeded in concealing his surprise.

"Hmm, yesterday."

"What are you two talking about?" Sarah looked up from the newspaper section she was reading.

"It's about Dani. He's been receiving some weird messages."

"Did he send you the message?" Ruben asked still giving the impression of being more interested in his breakfast.

"Yes, he did. It's here in my SkyPhone."

"Can I take a look at it?"

"Sure," Aya said placing her SkyPhone next to the plate of her father.

"Ahah, I see."

"What is it?" Aya leaned forward, puzzled.

"Another prank."

"Come on, Dad, it just can't be. Who would do this twice?"

"I don't know, Aya, there are all kinds of geeks out there," Ruben said and at that very moment a deafening explosion burst the windows of the Openheim's kitchen. As the millions of tiny glass shards rained down, Ruben managed to topple the chairs of Aya and Sarah with an inhumanly fast reflex, almost the kind Neo displayed while dodging the bullets of Agent Smith in the Matrix. Then the three of them fell down to the floor.

As the noise from the explosion quickly faded, Ruben heard the screams of Aya and Sarah but it was as though through earplugs. His eardrums had been damaged. He jumped to his feet and helped Sarah get up first. Then both held Aya under the arms and lifted her. She couldn't stand on her feet. She was in shock, her body shaking uncontrollably with terror. Her pupils were dilated and tears poured down her cheeks like raging miniature floods.

Even with his damaged ears, Ruben could hear shooting outside. Two bullets hit the kitchen dish drainer, breaking several plates and spraying more shards around. Still on the ground, Ruben turned to Sarah and shouted out as loud as he could "Run!" His voice sounded muffled to himself. Sarah heard him and started quickly crawling out of the kitchen. Ruben grabbed Aya mightily and began pulling her toward the bedroom, at the other end of the corridor.

******

According to one witness, the suicide bombers wedged their van packed with an estimate of over 200kg of explosives between the two buses full of students and blew themselves up. There are only 6 survivors and they are in critical condition. The death toll is 63 casualties on the bus alone and another 12 in the adjacent apartment buildings... (channel changed)... The surrounding apartment buildings along Derekh Hevron have been seriously damaged with all of their windows shattered, entrance doors and hinges torn off, huge chunks of concrete chipped off their walls... (another change of channels)... CNN has received a notification that this morning's explosion in a neighborhood not far from the Temple Mount in Jerusalem has been most harshly condemned by the Palestinian authorities who are currently holding peace negotiations in Sofia with the Israeli government... (channel changed)... No one has so far claimed responsibility for this atrocity. All outlawed terrorist groups are still silent... (channel changed)... The Israeli government has condemned the suicide bombing and has openly blamed Hamas for it. The US President Hillary Clinton expressed her grief publicly over the loss of so many innocent lives of young children and offered her most sincere condolences to the affected families. She swore she would put an end to the violence...

Ruben switched off the TV. It was all quiet now outside. It was past midnight. The ambulances had long gone their sirens wailing off down the street and so had the fire engines. Now only the forensic investigators were doing their job efficiently.

It was early evening when the family had returned from the hospital. Thank God, none of them had sustained any serious damages. Ruben's loss of hearing was temporary. But Aya had experienced tremendous shock, the doctors had said. Now she needed rest. Sarah was holding her in the bed.

Ruben and Sarah had had a chance to speak albeit briefly. They had decided that Aya and Sarah would fly to Sofia first thing in the morning. There Aya would be able to recover in calm and without any stress as the doctors had advised.

Ruben grabbed his SkyPhone and dialed Ian's number. He told him everything that had happened and also informed him about Aya and Sarah's arrival to Sofia.

"This is not all, Ian," Ruben said with concern. "I don't know if you are aware of the fact that Dani has received a second message with symbols."

"No, I'm not. He must have missed telling me. Is it again this LaW?"

"Yes."

"What has he written this time?"

"He has sent four symbols which read Zion."

"Mount Zion? The ancient one or the modern one?"

"Yes."

"The ancient one or the modern one?"

"I'd bet on the first, of course."

"This means the City of David."

"Exactly."

"And The LaW hasn't sent anything else? Just this?"

"Yes, just this."

"No pictogram as the last time?"

"No but this is enough."

"What do you mean?"

"It is simple, Ian. It means we have to go to Mount Zion."

"We?"

"Actually, not we, only Dani but we are going to accompany him there."

"Are you suggesting we should fly to Israel?"

"I am afraid so, brother. I thought it over and over again. You have to come."

"It's so dangerous, Ruben. Why?" Ian was in more denial but Ruben went on telling all he had learned from Rapha about David's secret cipher and about the events that would precede the advent of the Messiah.

"Ian, listen to me, this is not a game. This is serious. You must come."

"I understand. I'll call you tomorrow. And don't worry, I'll pick up Sarah and Aya from the airport," Ian said and they hung up.

******

"It was Ruben, right?" Rovine asked whispering, the bedside lamp still on. It was nearly one o'clock in the morning. Ian turned slowly to her.

"Yes," and he went on to tell her the horrendous disaster that had befallen the Openheims earlier in the day.

"Is Aya all right now?" Rovine asked, deeply concerned.

"She is stable for the moment. Sarah is bringing her here tomorrow..."

"Oh, this is good. This is the right thing to do. I'll call Sarah first thing in the morning."

"This is not everything."

"What is it?"

"Ruben told me Dani had received a second message with mysterious symbols."

"Dani hasn't mentioned anything to us."

"No, he hasn't but that is beside the point now."

"What do you mean?"

"Ruben said the situation in Israel was getting completely out of hand..."

"And?"

"He consulted some people there. They think this thing with Dani's messages is not a prank."

"Oh, come on, Ian. You know as well as I do that there are so many Internet geeks out there. They do pranks all the time! It's their way of entertaining themselves."

"I know it looks that way. But I'm telling you this isn't a prank."

"Why are you so sure?"

"Because Ruben has translated the symbols in the first and the second messages."

"And?"

"The first message Dani got read Magen David whereas the second said Zion."

"What do these two mean beyond their obvious meanings?"

"I don't know. We don't know why Dani got the messages in the first place. But we have to find out. We have to pursue it further in order to understand."

"Pursue it further? But how?"

"By going there."

"Are you serious, Ian? Just tell me that!"

"That's why I am discussing it with you."

"What is it there to discuss? Huh? Israel is almost on the brink of war. What is there we have to discuss? We cannot go there!"

"I didn't mean we."

"Then who?"

"Just Dani and me."

"Oh, great, and what am I supposed to do here? Going gray while worrying about you two there?"

"But we have to."

"Have to? Really?"

"Yes, really."

"Tell me then, how is it that you have to go? As far as I remember our project is over and that's great because millions of Israelis might need to flee the country and settle here, including the Openheims."

"Look Rovine, we've embraced the idea of peace in Israel in general, not only in its particular manifestation of building housing for possible Israeli refugees."

"I agree but what else can we possibly do?"

"Look, we embraced that idea many years ago. Now it's the call of duty to carry things through to the end."

"But this thing with the symbols has never been part of the project and it looks more like a game to me, to be sure, and to Dani as well."

"The thing is, it's not a game, not any longer. It's for real, Rovine. You know Ruben and you also know that he wouldn't tell me gibberish, would he?"

"Tell me then who in the whole wide world will take these messages seriously?"

"Besides us?"

"Besides Ruben and you?"

"Look, Ruben told me he'd called a few high-ranking people and he told them about the messages. He also told me that they wanted to know what the messages meant."

"And you think you can help?"

"I do."

"And you think anyone would believe Ruben after the fiasco with Uri Zohar? Ruben put his name on the line and sorry to say it but he failed bitterly."

"He was led to fail."

"Wording."

"It's not."

"Who led him to fail?"

"Uri, of course."

"I see and now you're going to tell me that Ruben has still some stashes of credibility left, aren't you? Ian, please, get realistic, it's not a Swiss bank this thing with the credibility. You can't expect interest on it. You fail once miserably, you fail for good."

"Oh, come on, Rovine. Don't be so harsh in your judgment.

Ruben is a well-respected citizen. He's got much more credibility left. Besides, it wasn't exactly his fault."

"But he was the one to blow the whistle, wasn't he? You know the saying, once a failed whistle-blower –"

"– Always a failed whistle-blower."

"Well, so you know it."

"I knew you'd say that."

"Look, Rovine, it is no mere accident Dani has been receiving those messages. We just need to get down to working them out. If we properly decipher them we stand a chance."

"You fully understand that in the meantime you are getting into something you don't fully comprehend."

"I will comprehend it."

"Will you? This is not the pure science conducted in ideal conditions. This is –"

"Esoteric cognition," he cut in sharply.

"There we go again. Why do you always have to wind things down to your favorite esoteric sciences?"

"Because its esoteric cognition we are dealing with here. We've been dealing with it ever since we stumbled upon the Cyrillic letters."

"That's great, really great, but now we have to deal with real-life serious issues, Ian."

"Like war."

"Yes, like war. From what I gather from CNN, it's a near war zone out there in Israel. Switch on the TV and look at it, look!" She nearly yelled pointing at the large flat HD TV screen in their bedroom. Then she continued.

"Ian, darling, don't you understand? I am worried about both of you. I can't just send you out in a war zone. I'd go mad. You may get killed, both of you and I love the two of you. I love you as much as I love Dani. You are my family and my life. I cannot imagine living without you, do you understand?"

"Rovine, sweetheart, I know that. I love you and Dani the same way. You two are my life as well. I don't want to take chances with the life of any of us but I have this gut feeling, this deep-seated intuition that we're going to be fine despite the risk," he said hugging her gently. Her eyes welled up with tears.

"But it's not like you are solving a puzzle in the Sunday newspaper."

"Oh, Rovine, sweetheart, you think I don't realize that? I know that perfectly well but I also happen to know that we simply don't have any amount of this precious commodity called time. We have to act fast and act right now. We've got to go. The situation in Israel is deteriorating by the hour."

"I can't believe you're saying that, Ian. I really can't."

"This is a test for us, Rovine. We've gone that far in preparing for an event. Now the event is happening and we're backing off. How cowardly!"

"But Ian, my darling, this is not a test. It's for real now, and if you go to Israel you may die, not only you but Dani, too."

"I won't let anything happen to Dani."

"Easily said but hard done in a war zone. Let's leave Dani here."

"We need him, Rovine. You know that. He is the link. He's been receiving the messages. I am sure it is no sheer accident he is the one to receive them."

"What makes you say that?"

"This mysterious person calling himself The LaW. He's chosen Dani for some reason. I think that along the deciphering of the messages we might get to know why Dani, why not some other kid."

"It might be because he was the first one to discover the interwoven letters remember?"

"Never thought of it but what you're saying sounds absolutely plausible. Anyway, we don't know for sure. Not knowing means there might be more letters. Again we don't know that yet. We need Dani. Besides it is not only about the letters, it is also about the messages, Rovine. We need him."

Ian spoke in terse sentences to make his point as clear as he possibly could. Rovine was looking at him all the time. She knew that in a way he was right. They had embraced the cause of aiding the peace process in Israel and now they had to do what duty required - help Ruben because helping him meant helping Israel. However, sheer accident, that's what it was, had brought Dani on board, too. Her motherly instincts were putting up a fierce resistance to the idea of taking Dani to Israel.

When she saw Ian's determination she looked down and said, "So are you ready to risk his life for the cause we've embraced?"

Looking straight in her eyes, Ian placed his two arms on Rovine's shoulders. Then he spoke.

"I am ready to die protecting him. I won't let anything happen to him. I promise you. We will be all right. Really. Trust me. Besides we can always hop on the first flight home."

"I know."

"Look, Rovine, I understand your concerns. They are mine, too, you know. But we've embraced the peace in Israel as our highest cause. We cannot back off now."

"I know we can't," she said and grew quiet for a few moments. "How long?"

"Just a couple of days and if things get worse we fly home immediately. I promise you. We will even take Ruben with us. I won't let him stay there no matter what."

"Of course, we're not going to let him stay in the battle zone while his family is here. So you promise you'll come back the minute you see it gets too unsafe."

"I promise. So are we together in this?" he asked her.

"We are, darling," she said and kissed his lips lightly. It was her way of saying she'd go the whole mile with him. "You are my man, you know that. I trust you and love you."

"Thank you for your love and understanding," he said kissing her back tenderly. Then he switched off the light and they hugged tight. Staying hugged for a long time was one of the ways they expressed the love they had for each other.

49

SOFIA, BULGARIA
29 JULY 2020
EARLY MORNING

Ian got into his son's room early in the morning. He sat on the bed and stroked Dani's head. The boy shifted slowly and opened his eyes. He read anxiety on his father's face.

"What is it, Dad?"

"Something terrible happened yesterday to Ruben, Sarah and Aya."

"What?" Dani asked and sat upright in his bed.

Ian told Dani the bad news.

"How are they?"

"Thank God, they are physically okay."

"And Aya?"

"She's had a nervous breakdown. The shock was too immense for her. The doctors said she needed calm to restore. They are arriving today on the morning flight from Tel Aviv."

"Oh, that's great. They'll be safe here and I'll have time to go out with Aya. I'll introduce her to my friends. You'll see, Dad, she'll be all right in no time."

"Dani, you don't understand, sweetheart," Rovine joined in as she entered the room. She had heard Dani's words as she was approaching the open door of his room. "Aya has gone through a great shock. She'll need calm and rest for a couple of weeks, at least."

"I think going out with friends will be better for her than staying at home."

"Don't rush things with her, okay?"

"Okay, Mom. Are we picking them up at the airport?"

"Of course," Ian said and added, "Hurry now, get dressed and come downstairs for breakfast. We have to get there by nine."

"I'll be ready in a minute," Dani said as he jumped out of his bed.

"Dani, there's one more thing I have to tell you."

"What is it now?"

"You've received a second message from this secretive LaW."

"Yes, I have."

"And you didn't tell us but you told Aya first."

"I was going to..."

"When?"

"It's just that I didn't think it was such a big deal."

"It is. It is a very big deal. Actually so big we are taking the evening flight to Israel."

"We?" Dani's mouth fell open, gaping in disbelief.

"You and I."

"But, Aya's family is coming here."

"Ruben is not coming. He is there waiting for us."

"Why? Has he already deciphered the second message I got?"

"He has."

"And what does it say this time?"

"It reads one word only – Zion."

"But there's a fresh conflict going on in Israel, Dad."

"I know but we have to go to Israel and find out why you've been receiving those messages and what they mean."

"How long, Dad?"

"Just a day or two. Then we'll be back and you'll have plenty of time to spend with Aya," Ian said looking at his blushing son. Dani's hopes to be with Aya had been obvious to his father.

50

GAZA, PALESTINE
29 JULY 2020
NOON

In order to blend with the crowd of downtown Gaza, Ruben Openheim, was disguised as a Palestinian as much as possible. He was walking as briskly as he could toward the house of Dr. Mohammed Hakim. He knew the address because he had visited him on several occasions in the past.

There were lots of people in the streets. They were in a hurry, rushing from one shop to another. They were busy increasing their household food supplies because in this time of escalating conflict Palestinians knew from experience they couldn't rely on shops being open regularly.

Ruben was pretending to be window-shopping as he looked into one shop or another. He knew there were Hamas sentries on almost every rooftop and he also knew he was taking a great risk if he appeared to be doing things out of the ordinary. Every now and then he stopped by a shop window, looked inside for a moment or two and then moved on.

"Did anyone see you come in?" Dr. Mohammed Hakim asked as he let Ruben in, poked his head out carefully and looked left and right, just to make sure his guest hadn't been tailed. Then Mohammed closed the door and meticulously adjusted the thick privacy curtain over the glass.

"I don't think so," Ruben replied.

"Good. I am happy you got here safely," Mohammed said as he greeted him.

"There are a lot of people with guns in the streets. Last time I was here it was different."

"I know but we are on the brink of war with Israel."

"I tried my best to look like everyone else though."

"Let's go to a room in the basement. There we can speak undisturbed."

"Where's your family?"

"You'll meet them later. They are out now, shopping for food."

"You let them go alone?"

"They are together with our neighbors. It's okay, really," Mohammed led the way down a narrow stairwell and opened a door to a spacious room in the basement. The day light was seeping through the transparent curtains of two very narrow windows placed high above and just under the room's ceiling. "You see it is fully furnished. In times of peril, we spend our nights and days here out of harm's way."

"Oh, you've got everything here. A stove, a fridge, a TV set..."

"We even have an electric generator when the power fails."

"So you've got it all tucked in this room."

"I told you. We often have to spend long hours here during the conflicts. Ruben, Ruben," Mohammed said looking at his friend, "You know you're risking your life by coming here. I admire your courage."

"I had to see you in person, Mohammed. As you see, it seems yet another war is pending over Israel and Palestine, the bitterest and toughest of them all."

"Yes, unfortunately, I see it, Ruben."

"But we cannot allow such war to take place. Both Israel and Palestine desperately need peace, a long-lasting one, for many years to come."

"Especially we need a long period of peace so that we have time to build and rebuild houses and gain in prosperity."

"I know but in a way, we also owe it to the memory of the passionate Emil Grunzweig. You remember him, don't you?"

"Of course, I do. It was February of 1983. He was killed by that horrendous grenade at our peaceful demonstration in Jerusalem in front of the office of the then prime minister of Israel Menachem Begin. My God, now that I think of it, that was 37 years ago."

"And little seems to have changed since then."

"Little, Ruben, very little."

"But this has to change. Grunzweig's was a life lost in the fight for peace but it wasn't a life lost in vain. We shall never forget his death and what he stood for."

"How are we going to change this deadlock we've been gripped in for decades?"

"There are ways, Mohammed. For a starter, Peace Now has begun organizing groups of staunch activists many of whom have already started protesting against the impending war. Just like in 1983."

"What makes you think these protests will reach their desirable goal?"

"Because we are not just protesting now. While the protests are going on, we are building a strong case in favor of peace."

"What case? Based on what?"

"Here's the most shocking revelation, Mohammed. Our case is built on the ancient military cipher invented by King David."

"Really? What cipher? I've never heard of it."

"It is a very long and interesting story," Ruben said and went on to tell him all he knew about David's cipher. Then he told him how Dani Magdev had miraculously begun receiving messages written in David's cipher.

"But this boy is not Jewish, right?"

"No, he is Bulgarian."

"Why would a Bulgarian receive such messages?"

"Just like you, I have no clue as to the answer of this question, Mohammed, but to tell you the truth, this is really not important. The important thing is that his parents work with us and they've informed us about the messages. Actually, the boy and his father, Ian Magdev, I think you know him..."

"I do know him, yes."

"Well, they are arriving this evening at Ben Gurion Airport in Tel Aviv. Ian told me that Dani had received a second message sending us to the original Mount Zion, on top of Ir David."

"Sounds like a kind of hide-and-seek."

"Maybe, but I believe that in the next few days, we will have enough information to build our case in favor of peace. You see, each message adds an additional bit to it."

"What makes you think the boy will get more messages?"

"The fact that he got a second message after we solved what the first meant."

"How do you plan to do it all?"

"The case should be one last demonstration of possible peaceful coexistence between Judaism and Islam, between Israelis and Palestinians right here in Jerusalem and Gaza and, of course, across the Holy Land. If we solve the problem of Jerusalem through its peaceful division between Israelis and Arabs only then do we stand a chance to finally avert war. As you know very well, Israel wants peace..."

"And so do so many Palestinians whose voices unfortunately remain unheard."

"Exactly, Mohammed. That's where you should step in."

"What do you mean?"

"Peace won't be served on Israel or Palestine's plate if both Israel and Palestine don't fight for it."

"This is true but..."

"I'm sure all this sounds a bit shocking to you especially coming from a sworn pacifist. You already know me very well, Mohammed. When I say fighting I mean putting all our energy and efforts into the cause we've embraced, which is finally reaching lasting peace. This means helping ourselves first, and by ourselves I mean the Israelis. Then helping the Palestinians by making them understand peace will only be possible if, and only if, they unite. As long as Palestine is torn to fractions fighting one another, there is no hope for a peaceful solution with Israel. The Palestinians have to accept us the way we are much the same way we, the Israelis, have to accept them the way they are. This is one of the primary tasks of Peace Now. But the Palestinians have to unite themselves first - this is the basic prerequisite for peace because they are now still torn to fractions."

"Indeed, we are, although you know there are people from within the Palestinian territories who submit to those very views you've just outlined."

"There are such people but sadly, hardly anyone pays any heed to them, am I right?"

"You are."

"This is why I have to ask you to do the unthinkable."

"Which is?"

"To speak with your brother," Ruben said as he read the dread that ran across Mohammed's face. "Change in Palestine has to come from within those who rule it and your brother is one of them."

"But he threatened to kill me last time we met. I have a family, Ruben. What will happen to them if I get killed? Don't get me wrong, I'm not worrying about my life but I'm worrying about theirs."

"I know, Mohammed. But someone has to worry about the lives of all Palestinians. Listen now, I am working on that case, on that last argument in favor of peace. If we succeed in building it, which we will, we'll have to use it to demonstrate the value of Israel and its people and to negotiate the total cessation of hostilities and the achievement of permanent peace in the region. We should all be able to live together peacefully, each group in its own section of the city."

"And this should apply for the rest of the divided territories, right?"

"Absolutely."

"I'll do my best, Ruben. I can't promise you much now but I promise you that I'll speak to my brother."

"Don't get me wrong, Mohammed, I am not talking religion here, I am talking politics. The problem between Israel and Palestine has been stripped stark naked of its religious garments and has been subsequently clad solely in a secular outfit. And this is how it should have been from the outset."

"I've realized that already. Religious fanaticism on both sides didn't bring any good result. It only brought more hatred and havoc. We should have no reasons to hate one another, Ruben. The hell with religion if it turns us against one another."

"Can't agree more with you, my friend. And let me tell you one more thing, the God of Israel has long ago become secular."

"What do you mean?" a tinge of shock in Mohammed's voice.

"He understands the new ways in the world and He has accepted them. But He has remained staunchly religious in his commandment for justice and righteousness. If He would appear here and speak to us, He would tell us, live the way you please but while doing that, the justice you do to yourself, do also to the others in a corresponding measure."

"Of course, this would mean to live in a way that what I do for myself I can do for the others and what I don't do to myself, I don't do to the others either, right?"

"Yes, this is so."

"And if I went to my brother and spoke to him about the prospects of peace from within Palestine, this would be doing justice to myself, my family and my people, right?" Mohammed looked Ruben straight in the eyes anticipating an answer.

"Yes, it would be."

51

BEN GURION AIRPORT, TEL AVIV, ISRAEL

29 JULY 2020

LATE EVENING

The EL AL flight from Sofia to Tel Aviv arrived on schedule. Dani liked the cakes on board and spent much time listening to Israeli music.

When Ian and Dani came out, Ruben was already waiting for them. He greeted Dani and the two men embraced each other. It was very emotional.

"Thank you for coming, my friend," Ruben said, his eyes welled up. "It's been a rough twenty-four hours. In an instant, the whole world could have shattered to pieces for me and my family. It's a terrible feeling, Ian, just imagining it."

"I know, I know. I'm happy none of you was injured in the blast."

"True! I am glad you came," Ruben looked at Dani and shuffled his hair. "So Dani, are you ready for a big adventure?"

"I always am, Ruben. Dad told me we were going to try to decipher the messages. Is that true?"

"Absolutely! I heard you like decoding messages," Ruben smiled at Dani's enthusiastic response. He and Ian had decided not to inform Dani of the seriousness of the whole situation by presenting the whole story as an intriguing adventure rather than the matter of life and death it actually was.

"I do but I only have experience with the pigpen cipher."

"This is no small thing. You never know when such knowledge may come handy, Dani. Let's go now."

"Is it safe to travel?" Ian asked Ruben, whispering while Dani was out of earshot. Ruben only nodded in confirmation.

When they drove out of the airport parking lot, none of them noticed the black inconspicuous sedan that kept a measured, but steady, distance behind them. Discussing the current situation, they drove all the way from Ben Gurion Airport to Jerusalem on the highway. When they got to Ruben's apartment, they didn't notice the black sedan pulling over to the curb, not far behind them.

52

JERUSALEM,ISRAEL
30 JULY 2020
OUTSIDE OPENHEIM'S APARTMENT
PAST MIDNIGHT

"They got in, Adah. I guess we'll have to spend the night out here in the car," Agent Chasin Weissman said to his colleague Agent Schwartz. Both of them had received a late-evening call to resume surveillance of the arriving Bulgarians and Ruben Openheim, their host.

"After all, it's our duty to protect them, if necessary."

"But you have to admit it is rather strange for a father to invite his son to a potential war zone."

"Strange or not, this is none of our concern."

"Would you do something like that to your own child, Adah?"

"I can't answer that question. I haven't become a mother yet."

"This is a hypothetical question."

"I don't like such questions because they bear little significance to the reality of things. Listen, Chasin, I'm sure they have a perfectly good reason for coming to Israel at this particular time. Besides, following them we have to find that reason but you know that inasmuch as you've received the instructions."

"Yes, I have."

"So who's taking the first two-hour shift?" she asked looking at him.

"I'll take it. You try and get some rest. It's going to be a long night and a long day tomorrow."

"This neighborhood seems quiet now after the bombing the other day."

"You are right. I hope this is a good omen."

"So do I," she said and smiled at him. "I truly hope we have an uneventful set of shifts."

53

JERUSALEM, ISRAEL
30 JULY 2020
MORNING

To get to the City of David, Ruben, Ian and Dani made a detour and entered the Old City from the Jaffa Gate. There were very few tourists and almost all of the souvenir shops were closed down, especially the ones run by Arabs. The Old City was on the fringe of turning into a ghost town, the crowds of tourist having been scared away by the unfolding events. The conflict between Israel and Palestine had rapidly escalated. Every night the Israeli army made incursions into the Gaza and the West Bank to clear these two areas from extreme Hamas militants incessantly shelling at Israeli settlements. The death toll on each side of the border was slowly but steadily rising and so was the fear and terror.

The three men walked past the Citadel, down the narrow streets of the Armenian and Jewish quarters to get to the Dung Gate. Once there, they went through and started down the side-walk of Derekh Ha'Ofel Road. Then Ruben suddenly stopped.

"Below is the ancient Mount Zion, also known as the Strong-hold of Zion or the City of David," Ruben said to Ian and Dani while drawing an invisible line with his hand to show them its limits. "This is the mount on whose top once stood the Jebusite stronghold initially conquered by King David. Just below the archaeological garden and across Derekh Ha'Ofel Road once also stood the palace David built for himself and made his per-manent place of residence after proclaiming the stronghold of Zion the capital of the Kingdom of Judah. Now that you saw the City of David from above, let's walk down Derekh Ha'Ofel Road to the heart of ancient Zion," Ruben said and they began to climb down the narrow sidewalk.

As they were walking down the street, they could see the archaeological excavations taking place just below the junction between Derekh Ha'Ofel Road and Ma'Alot Ir David Road and in a place that had formerly been used as a parking lot, as Dani read aloud from his Lonely Planet guidebook of Jerusalem. They continued climbing down. None of them noticed the inconspicuous black sedan that had pulled over under a fig tree before the entrance to the Ir David complex.

They got inside and walked past a small olive garden - to its right, a couple of water fountains. They got onto a wooden platform where the ticket stand and souvenir shop were. Once they bought the admission tickets, Ruben led them to a staircase leading below the main wooden platform. There they saw the remains of King David's Palace. Large stones were scattered about revealing the remnants of magnificent ancient foundations. There was an explanation board to the left of the platform immediately below the staircase. On top of the board, there was a large picture of a column capital that once was part of the palace structure.

"Look, Dad," Dani said, pointing to the column capital. "There are three Cyrillic Λ letters in its middle - each tucked within a larger one."

"This is an architectural design, Dani, but looking at it your way, you might say the three letters are tucked in one another," Ian agreed. Ruben looked at what Dani was pointing at but to his great surprise he didn't see the Cyrillic L letters. He instantly recognized three *he*s from the King David's military cipher. When he calculated their numerical value, they yielded 15. Translated into Hebrew numerals 15 was letters *yod* and *he* yielding *Yah* - the two-letter Hebrew name of God. Ruben was not surprised so much at the discovery as he was at the ingenious way God's name had been inscribed on the column capitals of David's palace. Then they moved on to the lower levels of Ir David.

"This here is the famous stepped-stone structure which served as a supporting wall for the palace of King David," Ruben said after they had descended a series of stairways to a relatively large platform and were looking at a bulging wall of massive ancient stones.

"Why are we here?" Dani suddenly asked after the three of them took a seat on one of the benches in the booth before the stepped-stone structure.

"Because of what the message read - Zion," Ruben said, Dani was still looking at the stone structure.

"You told me that but I still don't understand what made you think we were supposed to come here."

"We thought the sender wanted to draw our attention to this place for some reason," Ian interjected.

"Even if you could assume that, the message didn't indicate it in any way imaginable. It contained just a name, like the first message. It read Magen David, right?" Dani was still puzzled.

"Yes, it did," Ian confirmed.

"But we didn't go anywhere, did we?"

"That's because Magen David is not a particular location. It is a symbol," Ruben clarified.

"And precisely this might be the case with Zion. I think we shouldn't be looking so much at the proper place but rather at its name. Perhaps, and this is only my imagination now, The LaW wanted us to consider it just as a name. I don't think we are supposed to look for anything in particular here. We just need to concentrate on the name."

"Go on," Ruben urged Dani trying to follow his point.

"How is Zion spelled in Hebrew?" Dani unexpectedly asked. Ruben looked at him and then pulled a small sheet of paper and a pen out of his inside coat pocket and wrote Zion in Hebrew.

"Four letters," Dani observed as he held the sheet.

"*Tsade, yod, vav,* and *nun,*" Ian clarified to his son.

"What does the name mean?" Dani inquired.

"A sunny mountain," Ruben replied.

"How interesting," Dani remarked and just at that moment, he heard a buzz. Its source was inside the pocket of his jacket. It was an indication that he had just received a message. He drew out his SkyPhone and checked the message.

"It's another message from The LaW," he said to Ruben and Ian. They both abruptly stopped talking and looked at him.

"What does it say?" Ruben asked impatiently.

"I don't know. Once again it contains these strange symbols. Look at it," Dani handed Ruben his SkyPhone.

"It reads Moriah - the name of the continuation of Mount Zion northward to Temple Mount," Ruben explained after he deciphered the message and pointed in the direction of the archaeological garden.

"Do you mean that we are now standing on top of Moriah?" Ian inquired.

"Well, not exactly but I'll explain. Give me your Lonely Planet guidebook," Ruben said. Once he got the book he opened it on a page showing the map of the Old City of Jerusalem. Then he continued with his explanation.

"The Jebusite stronghold that was conquered by David was the original site of Jerusalem. This site has the form of a spearhead, which you can clearly see on drawings depicting the ancient City of David, and it cuts into the surrounding hills thus forming the Tyropoeon Valley on its west, the Hinnom Valley on its south and the Kidron Valley on its east. What you see below us is the spearhead-shaped Mount of Zion gradually descending south to its tip at which the Hinnom and Kidron Valleys meet. Ma'aleh HaShalom Road and its continuation Derekh Ha'Ofel Road that are here," Ruben's finger traced lines on the two-page map of the Old City and the City of David, "are the site of the ancient Ophel - a depression that separated the City of David from Mount Moriah. Now you can't see that depression because it had been covered with debris. Nevertheless throughout the centuries, people continued to make the distinction between Zion/City of David and Mount Moriah on whose top once stood the First and the Second Temples. Geographically speaking though, they are one and the same mount now."

"What does Moriah mean as a name?" Dani inquired.

"Chosen by Yahweh," Ruben replied.

"And how is Moriah spelled in Hebrew?"

"*Mem-vav-resh-yod-he,*" Ruben wrote the five letters on Dani's sheet of paper.

"So, by putting the two names together, Zion Moriah, I'd get a combination like this: A sunny mountain chosen by Yahweh." Ruben and Ian exchanged glances. They realized something had begun to crystallize in Dani's mind. Although still blurred, it was gradually emerging and taking proper shape.

"You have to bear in mind, Dani that the name Chosen by Yahweh has a very important meaning. The site of Moriah was chosen by God as the place where Abraham was commanded by Him to offer his son Isaac as a sacrifice."

"I know that episode, Dad, I've seen some depictions of it on the Internet."

"Well, then you know what I'm talking about. I'm just telling you the reason why the place is called 'chosen by Yah.'"

"And later on that very same place, Solomon erected the First Temple. Still later, after its destruction, the Second Temple was built on top of Mount Moriah," Ruben clarified.

"Moriah is one word and you translate it as Chosen by Yah. Why is this so?" Dani inquired.

"Hebrew is a very unique language. It allows for combinations of all kinds of words into names. For instance, the name of our country Israel means 'God prevails' but it is composed of the verb *sarah* meaning 'to contend' and 'to have power' and the noun *El* which is one of the names of God. In a similar way, Moriah consists of the verb *ra'ah* meaning 'to choose' and the noun *Yah* standing for one of the abbreviated forms of Yahweh – the name of God."

"I see," Dani said submerged in thoughts. Then he asked, "Does *vav-yod* mean anything?"

"No, it doesn't."

"Hm," Dani sighed.

"But the reverse, *yod-vav* does mean something - *Yav.* It is like *Yah,* another shortened version of the name Yahweh."

"Now I see," Dani said, his face beamed.

"Ruben, you told me Moriah read *mem-vav-resh-yod-he.* Tell me is there a Hebrew word that spells *mem-resh-he?*"

"Yes, there is. It reads *morah* and it means 'sadness', 'grief' and 'bitterness'."

"What are you up to, Dani?" Ian asked looking at his son.

"You see, if you notice the noun *morah* and the name of God, *Yav,* are both contained in Moriah. Letters 1-3-5 and 4-2," Dani said and showed them a small table he had drawn on one of the Notes pages in his Lonely Planet guidebook.

HE	YOD	RESH	VAV	MEM
ה	י	ר	ו	מ
5	4	3	2	1

"Oh, yes, you are right," Ruben exclaimed.

"If you put them together you'd get a name like Morahyav meaning 'the grief of Yav'."

"Unbelievable," Ian uttered.

"It makes sense, Ian," Ruben turned excitedly to him. Then he added in a moment of revelation, "Mount Moriah has been a site of bitter conflict for so many centuries now that Dani has also discovered it's the place of God's grief."

"If we discover that secret of Morahyav hidden within the name of Moriah now, it most probably implies that the God of Israel has in all likelihood ceased to want to return to Temple Mount. Why? Because Temple Mount, as you've just said, has been the source of harsh contention for so many centuries now. This should be made clear to all religious Jews, Ruben," Ian said, a serious expression on his face.

"This way there's a chance for the conflict to end," Ruben picked up and smacked his forehead, "And all Jews and Arabs will be able to live peacefully right in the heart of Jerusalem - the City of Peace. Why? Why would they live in peace?" he asked and began answering himself, "Because the Jews would no longer crave for re-conquering Temple Mount. They would have their own... Wait a minute. If Jews renounced Temple Mount what would they be left with?" Ruben left this question hanging in the air. He was puzzled. Something didn't add up. He spoke again. "Ian, you, as well as I, know that all Orthodox Jews would deem insane the giving-up of Temple Mount. You remember what happened to Yitzhak Rabin - he just wanted to bring peace through reconciliation."

"I do remember and, yes, you are absolutely right, unless -"

"Unless, someone clearly and convincingly demonstrates to them that it is futile to fight for Temple Mount when there's a more sacred site in the heart of Jerusalem for Jews," Ruben spoke interrupting Ian. Dani was just looking at them, turning his head from one then to the other. His mind was still spinning combinations of the five Hebrew letters.

"Let's be realistic, Ruben. Think about it, which would that site be?" Ian asked looking straight into his eyes.

"We have to find out whether such site may possibly exist," Ruben said, excitedly.

"Ruben," Dani turned to him, "Is there any Hebrew word spelled with letters *tsade-nun*?" Ruben looked at him, drawn out of his thoughts and still processing Dani's question.

"Mmm, yes, there is. It is *tsen* and means 'a shield'. Why?"

"Look," Dani showed them another small table he had drawn in the meantime.

ן	ו	י	צ
4	3	2	1

"The name Zion is spelled *tsade, yod, vav,* and *nun,*" he continued. "Right in the middle of it, there is *Yav* - 2 and 3 - the shortened name of God - which is surrounded, protected, shielded by 1 and 4 or *tsade* and *nun* which form *tsen* - the Hebrew word for shield. When you put the two together you'd get *tsenyav* or 'The Shield of Yav'."

"Unbelievable, Dani, this is unbelievable," Ian exclaimed.

"Zion is the Shield of God. This is mind-boggling. Revelatory. And you don't speak Hebrew, do you, Dani? Of course, you -" Ruben, stunned, rhetorically asking, not expecting any answer for he knew, Dani didn't know Hebrew, or did he? Then it hit him.

"Don't you see it, Ian? Zion, the place David conquered and chose as his stronghold and residence, has always been and will always be the most sacred place for all Jews. This is the place we, Jews, have to cherish most. This is the place we have to restore to its former glory, to polish the shield of God to a perfect sheen. We need not look any farther. God has left the answer encoded to us for all eternity in the name of Zion.

"We've been after Temple Mount, fighting for it, shedding our blood for it, dying for it in our thousands. Whereas God, many centuries ago, showed David which was the most sacred place on earth for Jews - Mount Zion - His shield. David conquered it and turned it into the stronghold of Judaism and everything Jewish. You should also know that long before the construction of the First Temple, the Ark of the Covenant had been kept hidden in the palace of King David which was somewhere right above us," Ruben said and pointed at the stepped stone structure and what was above it. "Only later did Solomon choose Moriah, where he built the Temple and moved the Ark to the Temple's Holy of Holies. Afterwards, Jews erroneously began to believe where the Holy of Holies was that was the

of this incredible stuff, they'll have enough to steer the ship of Israel into a new course." Agent Adah Schwartz said calmly and glanced at her reflection in her powder compact's mirror as her forefinger smoothed her arched, jet-black eyebrows. Then she looked at Chasin, her eyes getting to his very essence.

"But this will be impossible."

"Look, Chasin, you only need to study our history to see great changes were brought by particular individuals and their skills, knowledge or intuition. Take King David for example." She closed her compact with a loud snap and replaced it in her shoulder bag. Her composure added an extra drop to the pool of his nearly overflowing restlessness.

"This hasn't always been for the best of Israel."

"Sure, but try to see the big scheme."

"I'm trying."

"Not sure you are because in the big scheme of things, this recent discovery by Dani Magdev may turn out to be the ship of Israel's Gibraltar Strait leading out into the wide open ocean. Just imagine what it would be like if the conflict between Israel and Palestine were to end. Then imagine the Palestinians having their sacred sites alongside ours, and this without any hatred, envy and skirmishes. Just imagine what peaceful coexistence in which all the religious differences are respected would mean for the children you and I haven't had yet, Chasin."

"Well, I can try to imagine all that..."

"Wait, Dani is speaking again."

55

JERUSALEM, ISRAEL

30 JULY 2020

IR DAVID'S COMPLEX

NOON

"Dad, Ruben, Look! I just received another message from The LaW!" Dani was excited. Ruben looked at his SkyPhone.

"It reads one word only: Gihon," Ruben said after decoding the message.

"What does that mean?" Dani asked.

Ruben was lost in thought for a few moments. "This is the spring at the foot of Mount Zion – the only source of water for the Stronghold of Zion. It's down below," he said pointing at its direction.

"Why would I receive something like that now?"

"There must be a reason," Ian said.

"I agree," Ruben confirmed.

"Perhaps it's in invitation. It sounds like an imperative to visit the place."

"I think you have a point, Ian."

"Where is Gihon?" Dani asked.

"It's down below. Let's go." Ruben started briskly off to the stairway leading down to the entrance of the Warren's Shaft. Ian and Dani followed suit – Ian pensive while Dani was still holding his SkyPhone in one hand and the guidebook in the other. None of them noticed the man and the woman in dark suits who were watching them from one of the landings high above.

"Can you write down Gihon in Hebrew for me, Ruben?" Dani requested as they were climbing down. Surprised, Ruben abruptly stopped, took the guidebook and wrote the five Hebrew letters composing the name of Gihon – גיחון or *gimel-yod-heth-vav-nun*.

Then the three of them moved on.

******

They had their tickets checked and walked into a small entrance hall. There were pictures of archaeological finds and a few text boards. Dani's attention was caught by a picture of a bronze statuette – depicting the fist of a king. The caption dated the bronze to the 10th century B.C.E. – the time of King David.

"Dad, Ruben, look at this!" Dani motioned them closer. "Look at the way in which the fingers are clenched."

"Well, it's a fist, Dani. How else should the fingers be clenched?"

"But it's not the typical tight fist ready for a fight. It's a bit loose."

"What's your point, Dani?" Ruben stared at the picture.

"To me it resembles the letter *samekh*. Look at it!" Dani said as Ruben and Ian gazed at the photo of the bronze fist.

"If we assume that fist was clenched in a *samekh* then we could only infer a reference to the meaning of the 15th letter in the Hebrew alphabet."

"Which is what?" Dani asked, his curiosity now fully aroused.

"It's a verb meaning 'to support', or 'to sustain'."

"If we then take the fist to represent a hand sign for might…"

"…Then the whole meaning would be 'to support with a fist!'" Ruben interrupted Ian.

"A worthy expression of a king," Dani added.

"You see, Dani, the very shape of *samekh* is a circle. So everything inside that circle is protected, shielded. Hence we may take this hand gesture of a letter to stand for the Hebrew word *sohirah* beginning with *samekh* and meaning 'a shield'," Ruben explained still looking at the photograph.

"To support with a shield, as it were, with might. It makes sense," Ian declared.

"Mind you," Ruben continued, "*samekh* also stands for the first letter of the Hebrew word *sowd* meaning 'a secret'. Then we get something like *sohirah sowd* –"

"– The shield of [the] secret," Ian translated, and Ruben nodded in agreement.

"Once again we come up with a reference to a shield," Dani remarked and added, "*Sohirah David.*"

"Let's move on," Ruben urged as he exchanged a look with Ian. Both men were surprised at Dani's original way of combining letters and discovering things.

They started going down the steep flight of stairs of Warren's Shaft. The walls of the tunnel hewn through solid rock were jagged, traces of chisel scrapings all over. Nooks, crevices, cracks, the narrow tunnel was very steep. Then they got to a spacious underground hall housing the remains of the fortifications of the Gihon Spring.

A great deal of concrete had been used to erect new supporting walls for the hall. They walked on to a small opening leading to a narrow landing. To the right, there were metal bars – beyond them they could see the Kidron Valley. To the left, they saw a board showing the water level in the Hezekiah's Tunnel – the one that led the waters of the Gihon Spring to the Shiloah Pool. Approximately 70cm of water covered the tunnel. Flashlights and water shoes were required to make that 45-minute one-way walk through the 533-meter-long tunnel running deep below the City of David.

"These narrow steps lead down to the mouth of the Gihon Spring. Shall we go?" Ruben asked, a hint of urgency in his voice. They started down and on the left, they passed by the opening to the water-free 400-meter-long Canaanite Tunnel which was at a higher level than the Hezekiah's one. Then they squeezed through an opening to a very narrow metal-grid landing – below them, the waters of the Gihon Spring were gushing forth.

"So, this is the spring!" Dani exclaimed with amazement.

"Indeed, for many centuries this was the only source of water that sustained life above, in the City of David."

"It's so narrow in here," Ian observed.

"Ruben," Dani asked, "Can you tell me whether there's a word in Hebrew spelled with the letters *gimel-heth-nun*?"

"Mmm, no, there isn't."

"Then how about a word spelled *gimel-nun*?"

"*Gan,* the Hebrew word for 'garden'."

"Is there any Hebrew word which consists only of the letter *heth*?" Dani asked further.

"No, but *heth* being the eighth letter in the Hebrew alphabet is usually associated with the word *chay* meaning 'life'," Ruben explained.

"How is *chay* spelled exactly?" Dani inquired.

"*Heth-yod,* why?"

"I think I've come up with something," Dani said.

"What is it?" Ruben was eager to learn.

"Look at this," Dani said and held up a table he had just drawn containing the name Gihon spelled in Hebrew.

ן	ו	ח	י	ג
5	4	3	2	1

"That's right."

"Look at this," Dani said and held up a table he had just drawn.

"If you take the second and the fourth letters – י and ו – you'll get *Yav* – one of the names of God. Then if you take the first and the fifth letters – ג and ן – you'll get *gan,* the Hebrew for 'garden'. Hence *Gan Yav* or The Garden of Yahweh. But in their midst is חי or *chay* meaning 'life'. So in the middle of the Garden of God is life. If you slightly change the manner of reading the rearranged letters, you can easily read *Gan Chay* or The Garden of Life."

"But in this case, there's one letter *vav* that remains unused," Ruben remarked.

"What does it mean?"

"It's a connection and it means 'and'," Ian explained.

"There you go then, Gihon contains the phrase *Garden and Life,*" Dani exclaimed and then added, "So in each case whether you read it as 'in the midst of the Garden of Yav is Life' or 'Garden and Life' the name Gihon points to one and the same thing – the Garden."

"This reminds me of Genesis 2:10," Ruben said.

"What is it?" Ian asked looking at him.

"And a river went out of Eden to water the garden," Ruben quoted.

"And this river is gushing forth right beneath our feet," Ian added.

Each of them looked down and into the mouth of the spring. Dani was closest to the narrow opening. He was curious to see the mouth of the spring hidden below the iron grating. He got down on his knees and tried to peek under it and straight into the mouth of the Gihon Spring. The gap between the chiseled wall and the grating was too narrow to see anything. He got out his SkyPhone, adjusted its camera settings and shoved his hand under the grating. Then he took a picture, the flash reflecting sharply off the surface of the water. He checked what photo he had taken. There it was, the mouth of the spring – very flat and narrow, the surface of the water quite smooth for the noise it made. Dani's attention was caught by something on the plane side of a stone protruding from the left of the mouth. He zoomed in. His eyes got wider with disbelief.

"Dad, Ruben, I think there are four symbols chiseled out onto the stone. Here, look at them," Dani said and showed them the brightly lit screen of his SkyPhone.

"Where are they exactly?" Ruben asked Dani.

"They are engraved on the side of the mouth of the spring," Dani explained.

"I'm not sure I am able to discern them." Ian was trying to focus on the details of the picture. Then he handed the SkyPhone to Ruben.

"Oh, yes, Dani, you're right. There are some symbols. It's difficult to make them out because of the flash but they are visible!" Ruben was astonished.

"Let me see again, Ruben," Ian took the SkyPhone in his hand.

"Gosh, these really are the symbols we've been deciphering these days," Ian exclaimed.

"Yes, the same symbols I've been receiving from the mysterious LaW." Dani verified.

"Exactly the same," Ruben agreed.

"What do they read then?"

"They read *elefpeh,* Dani," Ruben said astonished.

"*Elefpeh*?"

"Precisely, Ian," Ruben confirmed.

"Why are you so surprised, Dad?"

"Let Ruben tell you the story," Ian said.

Ruben was pleased to tell Dani the story about the strange non-existent Hebrew word that once adorned the door of Manasseh, the progenitor of the tribe of the same name.

"Why here, Ruben? This is what I cannot understand." Ian was definitely puzzled.

"I have absolutely no idea."

"How do you spell this word in Hebrew?" Dani inquired. Ruben took Dani's Lonely Planet guidebook and wrote on one of the empty Notes pages the four letters it was composed of: *aleph-lamed-peh-he* (אלפה).

"Wait a minute," Ian exclaimed, "Rabbi Loew told us that *elefpeh* read as *El* and *Peh* which translates as The Mouth of God."

"Or now that you are saying it," Ruben cut in, "It reminds me that the combination of letters *peh-he* also reads as the Hebrew adverb *poh* which means 'here'."

"*El poh,*" Ian said in amazement.

"God is here," Ruben translated for Dani.

"And we find this ancient word chiseled out on a stone by the mouth of the spring. Isn't that odd?" Dani asked.

"It is not odd because as a noun, *peh* also means the mouth of a spring," Ruben began but then in a sudden revelation he said, "Wait, wait a second!"

"What is it?" Ian asked intrigued.

"We find the inscription *God is Here* actually right here at the mouth of the spring, you see where I'm going with this?" Ruben was getting himself all keyed up.

"Mmm, I'm not sure I do," Ian said shaking his head.

"In ancient times, this was the only spring supplying the City of David with water. There was no other source for the inhabitants of the Stronghold of Zion above us."

"So, what's your point?" Ian pressed him.

"I'm thinking of three consecutive verses in the Torah."

"Which ones?"

"The ones describing the creation of man. Here is Genesis 2:6-7-8: *There was only spring-water which came up from the earth, and watered its whole surface. And now, from the clay of the ground, the Lord God formed man, breathed into his nostrils the breath of life, and made of man a living person.*"

"Oh, I begin to understand."

"There was only one spring, this one, The Mouth of God or God is Here, and its water flowed on the surface and made from the soil mud or clay. And God took from it, because He is Here and formed man and breathed *chay* into the nostrils of man and made him a living person."

"Ruben, up there, on the signboard that we read it was written that throughout the centuries, Gihon had been known by several names: The Fountain of Yahweh, The Fountain of Israel and The Fountain of Life," Ian spoke rapidly.

"All at the same time while Gihon contains hidden another name Garden and Life or Life in the midst of God's garden."

"So, from what you are saying it means that the garden, the fountain and the place of creation have to be found at one and the same location, right?" Dani asked trying to keep up.

"Yes, right here, at the Fountain of God, the Mouth of God," Ruben said passionately. "Adam was created around Gihon. This chiseled inscription in the symbols of David's cipher is a confirmation of that. What is more, Gihon is the spring which watered the garden for which we have many names: Eden, Ginnah Pele, Gan Yav and Garden of Life," Ruben spoke excitedly.

"This is amazing," Ian was awestruck.

"This spring and the valley of Kidron which once hosted the garden of God are the most sacred places for us, Jews. This is it," Ruben said and grew quiet, his mind racing with the thought of what they might have discovered.

"So this is the answer we've been looking for."

"Absolutely, this is it, Ian. This revelation is what we've been after. This place here, right before the beginning of the Hezekiah's Tunnel, this tiny spot is the most sacred place for Israel."

"Wow! Amazing," Dani exclaimed.

"What's next now?" Ian asked, concern in his voice.

"Now we have to act. We have to make our discoveries public and I'll have to fill in the government. Let's go," Ruben said with determination and bent to walk back through the narrow opening. Ian followed him. Dani looked around one last time. To him, the walls of the little cave looked so ancient. They were damp and gouged everywhere with scratches. He stretched his hand and touched the cold rock. It felt so jagged. Just as he was about to bend his head to go out he noticed something carved onto the rock: two thick Latin letters - J and H - below them there was a number - 921.

"Dani, are you coming?" Ian called him out.

"Dad, Ruben, come back..."

"What is it?" Ian asked from outside.

As they returned, Dani showed them the letters and the number.

"J and H seem to be an abbreviation to me," Ian offered.

"An abbreviation of what?" Dani inquired.

"Say, of a name."

"Like Jonah," Ruben suggested.

"Or like Jeremiah," Ian clarified.

"Wait a second! This might be a reference to the books in the Old Testament," Ruben said in a burst of revelation. He took out his SkyPhone and logged online. He checked the Book of Jonah and discovered it only had four chapters. Then he immediately tried out the Book of Jeremiah. It had a chapter 9. He opened verse 21 and read out loud:

For death is come up into our windows, [and] is entered into our palaces, to cut off the children from without, [and] the young men from the streets.

"Wow, what is that macabre verse supposed to mean?" Dani asked puzzled.

"I don't know," Ruben said as he looked up.

"Neither do I," Ian chimed in. They hurried off.

56

JERUSALEM, ISRAEL
30 JULY 2020
THE OLD CITY
AFTERNOON

On the way home from the City of David, Ruben made a couple of phone calls and arranged to be picked up by a government vehicle and taken directly to the Knesset - the Israeli parliament.

"I'm meeting with the government officials, Ian," Ruben said after he finished with the phone calls. "I have to inform them of what we've discovered. I'll try to convince them to rethink the entire situation with the peace talks in light of these new findings. I hope they'll see the significance of all we've come up with."

"It is your responsibility to do so, Ruben."

"I'll take you home...please wait for me there," Ruben said looking at Ian.

Just as the three of them were walking down a narrow, deserted street and were about to make a right turn at the next corner to reach the Jaffa Gate, two men jumped out of a shadowy doorway unnoticed behind them. The two men were dressed in loose-fitting clothing, their heads and faces covered. Each of them drew a large knife and rushed stealthily forward, their weapons raised in a threatening position.

At that moment, a muffled popping sound was heard; the two assassins instantly dropped to the ground, out cold. Two figures that of a man and a woman in dark suits dragged them back to the opposite side of the street.

As Ruben, Ian and Dani turned right toward the Jaffa Gate, Dani looked back, but didn't see anyone in the street.

Outside Jaffa Gate a black limousine was parked, the engine running. The person in the passenger seat got out of the car, opened the rear door and motioned for Ruben, Ian and Dani to get inside the automobile. Then the limousine drove off.

57

JERUSALEM, ISRAEL
30 JULY 2020
OPENHEIM'S APARTMENT
AFTERNOON

Ruben dropped Ian and Dani off at the apartment and left in the black limousine to meet with the members of the government. Dani was a bit hungry and Ian decided they needed a break with tea and cookies. He set the kitchen table with cups and saucers and placed the cookie jar in the center, close to Dani's right hand.

Just as Ian was pouring the tea, Dani spoke up, alarm in his voice.

"Dad, I just got a message."

"From your mom?"

"No. From the LaW."

"Who, then?"

"The LaW..."

"What does it say?"

"This time it's different. It's just a sequence of numbers. Eighteen-ten-six-fourteen."

"Let me see," Ian grabbed Dani's SkyPhone.

"What could it possibly mean, Dad?"

"If we take the numbers as standing for letters then we'll get R-J-F-N."

"But that sequence doesn't mean anything."

"You are right. Let me try another time. With my knowledge of Hebrew, I see that 18-10-6-14 corresponds to the Hebrew letters *tsade-yod-vav-nun* or... Zion."

"Once again 'Zion.' I wonder why The LaW would send me the name twice?"

"Good question and I believe it is for a reason."

"What reason?"

"Perhaps, and I'm guessing here, but since The LaW sends numbers, he requires you to do the math."

"What do you mean?"

"To sum them up. Add them all together and you get 48."

"What then?" Dani was puzzled.

"Good question."

"What do you do with 48?"

"I can't do much except translating it back to the Hebrew numerals it is composed of."

"Which are?"

"The letter *mem* that equals 40 and *heth* that equals 8."

"Do these two letters yield any Hebrew word once put together?"

"Hm, I've got to check," Ian said and went to the bookshelves in the living room. He grabbed a Hebrew dictionary and began leafing through the pages.

"Bingo," he exclaimed shortly afterward.

"What?"

"The word is *moach* and it means 'marrow.'"

"Marrow?"

"Certainly not in the literal sense. Marrow also means 'essence.'"

"So once *moach* is put together with Zion, we get the phrase *Moach Zion*..."

"...Meaning 'the essence of Zion,'" Ian cut in.

"Okay, but what's that essence?"

"I guess it's what we've discovered today but to make sure perhaps it's best we speak to Ruben," Ian returned the heavy dictionary to the shelf.

Dani's SkyPhone beeped again. It was another text message. From The LaW. Again a sequence of numbers. Or nearly so. 6-10-14/18.

"This is a real riddle, isn't it, Dad?"

"Indeed, because there's no such Hebrew word starting with

vav - 6 - and then continuing with *yod* - 10 - and *nun* - 14."

"What about 18 - the separate *tsade*?"

"I have no clue what it could possibly mean without the other three letters," Ian said. Father and son stared at the numbers in silence, thinking, their brains trying all kinds of combinations and possibilities.

"Dad, I've got an idea."

"What is it?"

"What if the last message is a mathematical problem. Look at it. 6 minus 10 gives -4. Next -4 minus 14 gives -18. Then divide -18 by 18 and you get -1."

"The so-called 'negative one'. This is really brilliant, Dani. But what should we do next?"

"Luckily, you are the one into mathematics. You can try something with this negative one. I can't think of anything else."

"I'm thinking..." Ian said submerged in thought.

"Got another idea, Dad. You remember the first letters I discovered interlaced in David's Star were ours, the Cyrillic ones."

"Yes, so?"

"Let's try to substitute the numbers in the last sequence with their Cyrillic correspondences since the Hebrew substitutions yield nothing."

"Fair enough."

"In this case we get the following string: Е-Й-Н/С."

"Ein S...this really sounds like the Bulgarian transliteration of, wow, *Ein Sof*."

"What is that?"

"One of the names of God but I know hardly anything else about it. We should ask somebody who may know," Ian said.

"I think I know somebody who can help."

"Who?"

"Rapha."

"Wasn't he the elderly man you and Aya helped with the groceries?"

"Yes, that's the man. Last time we were here he told us so many stories. He knows a lot, Dad. He surely knows about this name as well."

"Well, let's call him."

"No need. We can go to his place. He lives close by."

"Dani, we are supposed to wait here for Ruben. It's not really safe to walk around."

"Big deal, Dad. Rapha is really around the corner. In no time we'll be at his place. We'll speak to him and we'll come straight back here afterward. We have to know what The LaW wants to say to us. Besides, Rapha can rarely go out and he may need some help. We need to check on him anyway," Dani said.

Reluctantly, Ian agreed with his son. They got ready and went out.

58

GAZA, PALESTINE
30 JULY 2020
AFTERNOON

Dr. Mohammed Hakim received a call from Ruben Openheim early in the afternoon. The latter informed of ground-the breaking discoveries and gave him clear instructions what to do next.

Mohammed approached the house of his oldest brother, Hamas commander Naif Hakim. He had called earlier and asked to meet him in private. Naif had sneered at the request but had finally yielded, albeit very reluctantly.

There were several pick-up trucks parked before the entrance of the house. They were packed with armed militants holding their Kalashnikov assault weapons and seemingly ready to leave the instant such orders arrived. There were also armed guards walking around. One of them stopped Dr. Hakim and asked him for his papers. The guard of course knew who the man before him was but wanted to humiliate him by exercising his bit of petty authority. Glaring at him arrogantly, he let the doctor in.

Naif was sitting on a large sofa in the spacious living room of the house. The shades behind him were half drawn and he was watching the news on television.

"You're watching CNN," Mohammed was surprised.

"Of course, this is the only way, one-sided, enemy-sided as it is, to follow what our traitors in Sofia are doing. You don't expect me to watch the biased channels of our Israeli enemies, do you?" Naif said looking at his brother haughtily.

"You shouldn't detest me for who I am and what I've chosen to fight for."

"You are a despicable wretch, that's what you are."

"I will say it again, you don't have to hate me."

"You are weak, and loathsomely pathetic. You're good for nothing. Why have you come? What do we have to talk about, you and I? We've got nothing to discuss. You are the enemy. You're no longer my brother."

"Cut it out, Naif, I am and will be your brother forever, whether you like it or not. Listen to me now," Mohammed said, anger in his voice but also deep-seated determination. Naif didn't say anything, just looked at him with a scornful expression. Then Mohammed continued.

"Hate me all you want. I don't care. I've come here for one reason and one reason only. You know I work with Peace Now..."

"... The sterile bitches even avoided by the stray dogs in their own camp," Naif interrupted with a derisive laugh.

"They've made ground-breaking discoveries about the most sacred site of all Israel. It's not and has never truly been Temple Mount. It's always been the City of David. If Peace Now succeeds in convincing the Israeli government, Israel will withdraw from the area and will drop all claims of return to Temple Mount."

"This is nonsense. You can't come here and try to sell me gibberish. I told you already, your sterile bitches are avoided by their own dogs. Nobody notices them. Nobody pays any attention to them and listens to them anymore. Why should I?"

"This is not true. Not at all. Peace Now is a well-respected and well-known organization in Israel," Mohammed objected.

"How do you expect a bunch of losers to convince the entire government of the enemy to retreat from Temple Mount and to abandon all demands of return? Have you forgotten about the Israeli ultra-Orthodox? "

"The Israeli government listens to its people."

"Not when they make insane proposals."

"But when they are sane, they listen to them."

"Tell me, where is the sanity in what you are saying? A retreat from Temple Mount? Not in a million years, that's how I see it. Jews have always wanted to destroy our mosque and rebuild their Temple."

"Listen, Naif, Israel wants to live in peace."

"But they also want to rebuild their Temple, don't they?"

"Some of them do."

"Yes, the ultra-Orthodox. They just don't get it that their temple is gone, gone for good. It won't come back, ever."

"Different people believe in different things. Listen, Peace Now has discovered the most sacred site for all Jews is the City of David - the true Zion - below which the Gihon Spring is situated and where the Garden of Eden once was."

"Bullshit! This is insane. This won't rebuild their Temple."

"Of course not but this is precisely the point - not to seek rebuilding of the Temple. The task of Peace Now is to demonstrate to the Israeli government what the findings have held hidden for so many centuries - references to the creation of Adam, to the location of the Garden of Eden, to the true Zion, where David kept the Ark of the Covenant for quite a long time and where he wanted to build the First Temple. Peace Now is already speaking to the government and is expecting its response."

"Why are you here, then?"

"Because if the Israeli government decides to retreat, this will be a huge concession to us. I'm telling you all this because I want you to be ahead of events and be ready to act accordingly. If that happens we should also be prepared to respond adequately."

"What does adequately mean to you?"

"First we have to cease fire, totally and unconditionally, and we have to condemn all acts of aggression against the state of Israel."

"What aggression are you talking about? The bombs and the shelling are just an expression of our indignation."

"There are civilized ways to express indignation and killing innocent people has never been and never will be one of them."

"Mohammed, you are going too far. My speaking to you is already an expression of being civilized. Your corpse could have been tossed out as food for the stray dogs by now if only I had ordered so. You are lucky that I think of your wife and children who would be so miserable without you."

"What about the family of Ramzi? Aren't they already miserable?" Mohammed snapped angrily. Naif chose to ignore the reference to the killing of Dr. Ramzi Rasil.

"You've read the message of this Temple Mount and Land of Israel Faithful Movement. They want their Third Temple but if they go further with their stated plans, we'll surely be plunged into war," Naif said in a flat voice.

"That's why Peace Now is talking to the government at the moment, to try to avoid war by proving it's altogether wrong for Jews to crave for a return to Temple Mount. Wrong and unnecessary. They should instead return to Zion which has always been waiting for them throughout the centuries.

"Don't you see it, Naif, if all of us found our most sacred places to retreat to, we would stand a chance of peaceful coexistence based on respect of one another's confines. This way all religions will be able to live side by side in the heart of Jerusalem. What's more, if that happened, the city could become a paradigm for the rest of Israel and Palestine. All we have to do is uproot hatred because it halts the progress of our bilateral relations. Hatred only breeds more hatred – that's its vicious circle. It's like rapidly developing cancer. Once Palestinians stop hating the Jews, and you very well know there are many among us who don't hate them and never have, they, in turn, will stop hating us."

"Why aren't they the first to stop hating us?"

"Why shouldn't we be the first?"

"It sounds so simple to you, Mohammed. You, idealist!"

"And in a way it is simple."

"No, it is not. We can't stop hating the Jews overnight."

"Yes, we can if so only we want. People can learn a lot of things. You shouldn't let most of the Palestinians be driven by the agenda of hatred with the argument that it has always been that way. Things can change."

"The peace with Israel requires too many compromises."

"Well, Naif, any political compromise is infinitely more valuable than the loss of even a single human life. I'll put it simply. Peace equals life for us. Hatred equals death."

"Oversimplified."

"It's all about what people like you, leaders, tell the rest of the Palestinians, like me. If you keep on speaking the language of hatred, we don't stand a chance. You have to start speaking the language of peace, only then do we stand a chance. The Jews are no monsters as you and your companions portray them. But I am sure that deep inside you know that very well, too. They have suffered much more than we have throughout the centuries. Some of them have even survived the Holocaust – the worst of all man-drafted catastrophes in mankind's history to befall a targeted group of people. Then many of those survivors learnt how not to hate the Germans. The Germans of today are not the Germans of nearly a century ago. Times have changed and are constantly changing. The Palestinians have all too long been speaking the language of hatred. What has all this speaking led to? Nothing, just more misery and suffering. You, my brother, stand before the greatest opportunity of your life. You can choose to be like all your predecessors and continue chanting the songs of hatred. Or, you can choose the songs of peace and make Palestinians sing them in harmony. We badly need a change of hearts and minds. You have the power over Palestinians to bring about that change. Our future and the future of the Palestinian lands is in your hands. I leave it to your conscience to decide."

Mohammed looked deeply into his brother's eyes a few moments, then stood up and left without another word.

59

JERUSALEM, ISRAEL
30 JULY 2020
RAPHA'S APARTMENT
AFTERNOON

"Who's there?" Rapha's feeble voice was barely audible from behind the front door of his apartment.

"Rapha, it's me, Dani Magdev from Sofia," Dani spoke loudly so the old man could hear him. The door cracked open and Rapha appeared.

"Oh, Dani, it's you," he said.

"Yes, Rapha, and this is my father, Ian Magdev."

"Come in, please ... nice to meet you Mr. Magdev," Rapha shook hands with Ian as he entered.

"I've heard a lot about you from my son."

"You have a very bright kid, you know," Rapha said and patted Dani on the shoulder. "Please come to the kitchen. What brings you here?"

"I wanted to see how you are. Is there anyone who's helping you now with the groceries?" Dani asked.

"My neighbor goes to the shops from time to time. We stay mostly indoors these days. It's not very safe to travel around the city. I watch the news regularly, so I know."

"Well, that's why we are here. We can go to the grocery store and the pharmacy if you need anything," Dani said eagerly.

"I do need a couple of things, thank you. But tell me first, where is Aya?"

"She's in Sofia with her mother. I don't know if you know about it but a bomb exploded a few days ago in front of their building," Dani went on to explain what had happened to the Openheims. The news came as a severe shock to Rapha. He asked a few more questions which Dani answered as composedly as he could.

"Yes, I heard the explosion but didn't know what befell the Openheims, poor Aya. And what are you doing here in these times of great turmoil in Jerusalem?" Rapha asked surprised.

"We've arrived because I've been receiving messages from somebody nicknamed The LaW," Dani began and went on to tell Rapha the whole story with the messages and the discoveries they had led to through what had been encoded in the names of Moriah, Zion and Gihon.

"The last message Dani got," Ian said after Dani had finished, "was made up of numbers only. Once we deciphered them we got an entire string of Bulgarian letters. Amazingly, they stand for Ein S..."

"You mean *Ein Sof*," Rapha said in anticipation.

"Exactly. And we want to know more about that name of God," Ian said.

"*Ein Sof* is a very unique philosophical concept. It is also known as the Negative One," Rapha said while Ian and Dani became instantly alert because they had already discovered that connotation.

"Could you explain to us?" Dani asked.

"If we accept that One is a thing, then Negative One is a nothing. In other words, if One is something existent, then the Negative One is the same One but prior to its existence."

"I'm not sure I'm following you, Rapha," Dani was puzzled.

"Look, my boy, it is not so difficult to comprehend. Before Creation, God had no form, that is, no manifestation. However, after he created Adam, God, so to speak, self-manifested Himself through His creation. Then God used Adam as a chariot with which He descended to the world He had created. He first arrived at the place where He created Adam. But at all times, God is and has remained 'without end' or endless, infinite, as Ein Sof literally translates."

"Could you write down how *Ein Sof* spells in Hebrew?" Dani asked. Rapha took a sheet of paper and wrote אין סוף on it.

"So, in a nutshell, *Ein Sof* is God before Creation and apart from it, am I right?" Ian was intrigued.

"You can put it that way, yes."

"Rapha, does the combination of letters 3 and 4 yield any Hebrew word?" Dani asked and showed Rapha the small table he had just drawn.

ף	ו	ס	ן	י	א
6	5	4	3	2	1

"What a neat table! You mean *nun* and *samekh*?"

"Precisely."

"They yield the word *nas* meaning 'a sign'."

"Good," Dani said, "And how about 1 and 6?"

"They yield *aph* which means 'a face'."

"I see. 2 and 5 yield *Yav*. So if you put them all together, you'll get a phrase like 'a sign of the face of *Yav*'," Dani said.

"Or 'a sign of the wrath of Yav' for *aph* also means that," Rapha added.

"And all this is contained in *Ein Sof,* how interesting, indeed!" Ian commented thoughtfully.

"Yes!" Rapha exclaimed. "There's one more possibility. If you take 6 and 1 and not the other way as before, you'll get the Hebrew adverb *pa* meaning 'here'. Hence the whole phrase would read 'here, the sign of Yav'."

"The question then would be where this 'here' is, right?" Ian asked.

"Good point," Rapha agreed. "We've got only one solution... *Ein Sof.*"

"I thought we'd already exhausted its potential," Ian said.

"Rather, we've just started exhausting it. I suggest we calculate its numerical value for a starter," Rapha said.

"Which is?"

"Adding 711 to 866 –"

"And you get 1577," Dani cut in.

"Exactly, but what do we do afterward?" Ian wondered. "Wait a minute, we can take 1577 as a Strong's number, can't we?"

"There you go doing it all by yourself, Ian," Rapha said and smiled.

In the meantime, Ian took out his SkyPhone and began browsing the Internet for a possible answer. After he found it he said, "1577 refers to Gamul (גמול) –"

"– Who was a priest and leader of the 22nd course of the Temple's service as instituted by King David," Rapha interjected.

"Dad, can I see how Gamul is spelled in Hebrew?" Ian handed Dani the SkyPhone.

"So, when did Gamul live?" Ian asked Rapha while Dani was busy writing something down.

"Actually, he lived in the time of David."

"Rapha, look at this small table," Dani said and showed him yet another of his hand-drawn tables of letters.

ל	ו	מ	ג
4	3	2	1

"This is a very interesting way to extract hidden meaning from Hebrew words, Dani."

"I'm fascinated with how much is hidden in a single Hebrew word, Rapha. So, that's how I came up with the tables. They make it easier to spot concealed words. Could you tell me whether 2 and 3 yield any Hebrew word?"

"In fact they do. It's *mow* meaning 'water'."

"How about 1 and 4?"

"That's the Hebrew word *gal* meaning 'a spring'."

"So once put together, the two words would yield 'a water spring', right?"

"That's correct," Rapha confirmed.

"Dad, I think we've got the answer. Today we were at Gihon Spring so it must be the place to which the phrase 'here, the sign of God' refers to. The LaW didn't send us those numbers without a reason. I am sure he wanted to show us even the name *Ein Sof* refers through a series of connections to Gihon and hence ultimately to Zion. This is another confirmation of all our discoveries," Dani was very excited.

"I think you are right."

"We have to tell Ruben about it when he comes back."

"We definitely will," Ian agreed.

"Thank you, Rapha, for the enlightening conversation," Dani said. Ian thanked Rapha as well. Afterward, father and son left. They wanted to get home before Ruben returned.

60

JERUSALEM, ISRAEL
30 JULY 2020
OPENHEIM'S APARTMENT
LATE AFTERNOON

On the way back from Rapha's place, Dani and Ian didn't talk much. Dani sensed his father was anxious and in a hurry. Once they got home, Dani asked him what was bothering him.

"You see, Dani," Ian said as they entered the kitchen and he began preparing a snack, "with the help of the mysterious LaW, we've made some extraordinary discoveries, any one of which could steer the course of Israel's history into an altogether new direction. It's just that I don't understand..."

"Dad, listen, I know it seems complicated because there's a lot of politics and diplomacy involved but to me we're just vehicles to all these discoveries which appear at this moment in time exactly as expected. I've got the feeling people here have been waiting for something like this to happen for a very long time. Well, now what they've been waiting for has actually happened and they'll just have to act and behave accordingly."

"It's not that simple, son."

"On the contrary, it is simple. What's needed is an act of will. Most of the fundamental changes in history have occurred precisely because single individuals have had the will to enact something and thus change things, right?"

"Yes, this is true but the situation with Israel and the Palestinians is much more complicated."

"More complicated? Think of David and how he won against the much stronger Goliath and afterwards the whole history of Israel changed for good. I guess all I am trying to say is that small can change big. It has to be that way so things happen for the better."

"'Small can change big' – nice way of putting it," Ian smiled.

"We are small, you, Ruben and I, even your organization Peace Now is small in comparison to the whole of Israel but this shouldn't discourage you from acting altogether."

A bullet suddenly crushed the kitchen window and thumped loudly into the wall on the other side of the room. Ian instinctively grabbed Dani's arm and pulled him down to the floor as a second bullet hit still lower and perforated one of the kitchen cupboards.

"What's going on? What's going on, Dad?" Dani shouted terrified.

"Calm down, Dani," Ian slowly began to crawl to the balcony's glass door to get a look at what was going on outside. He crept slowly, his body close to the floor, and they heard a loud commotion outside and several muffled shots. When Ian reached the glass door leading to the balcony, he ventured his head beyond the protection of the cupboard. He saw nothing but two shadows disappearing in the direction of the light coming from the setting sun. Then calm was restored and so was silence. He retreated behind the cupboard and crawled back to Dani who was shaking.

"It's all right, Dani, it's all right. The danger is gone," Ian said trying to reassure his son by hugging him tight. Dani's body was trembling violently. A few silent minutes passed. Then the shaking gradually receded. Still hugging his son, Ian retrieved his SkyPhone from his pocket. He dialed Ruben and told him what had just happened.

A quarter of an hour later, a black government limousine stopped by the building where Openheim's apartment was. Six security personnel came out and took over the surveillance of the perimeter from agents Weissman and Schwartz. Then two of them led Dani and Ian out and hurried them in the limousine. Father and son didn't have the vaguest idea of all that had happened. They didn't see the assailants nor did they see the agents.

In another quarter of an hour, Ian and Dani were driven to Rabbi Loew's house in the outskirts of Jerusalem. There they were in safety.

61

JERUSALEM, ISRAEL
30 JULY 2020
THE KNESSET
LATE AFTERNOON

There were few people in the corridors of the Knesset when Ruben entered the building. An assistant was walking briskly before him. When they reached their destination, the man opened the door and Ruben rushed in. It was a spacious conference room where the Israeli cabinet held some of its daily work sessions. Ruben cast a quick look around at the few members of the Israeli government who were present. They were seated around a long rectangular table. The Israeli flag with its huge Star of David hung on one of the walls.

On a large screen on the other side of the table, Ruben could see the remaining members of the cabinet and the Israeli President who were all currently attending the peace talks in the Boyana Camp in Sofia. All eyes were on him and were full of anticipation.

"You said it was urgent, Ruben. Please proceed," the President said with familiarity. Many years before, the president had been a political mentor of Ruben and the two knew each other well.

"Indeed it is. I'll get to the point right away. Gentlemen, I haven't come here to speak to you about the series of startling discoveries, my team and I have made. They are now confirmed for a fact," Ruben calmly began his address to the government and the President, "I've come here to tell you about the most important and the most shocking of them... Temple Mount is not the most sacred site on the face of the earth for us, Jews," Ruben said and paused, allowing his words to reach his exclusive audience. Ministers exchanged bewildered looks. The claim was indeed shocking, to say the least, and the statement had been served all too abruptly but Ruben had no time to beat about the bush.

"There is no other place but Temple Mount," one of the ministers snapped disrupting the awkward silence that had befallen.

"Which is this other site?" another minister asked. Before replying, Ruben looked slowly around as though to get a full picture of his audience. Then he spoke.

"It is, as it has always been, Mount Zion with its Gihon spring and Garden of Yav."

"Do you mean Gan Yav?" one of the ministers asked, utterly shocked.

"Yes, I do." Ruben said.

"How can you possibly know about it?" the same minister asked.

Ruben went on to explain how he had come to know about Gan Yav and then shed light on the hidden knowledge in the names Zion, Moriah and Gihon. "I'll now suggest to you another point of view, another story, a different way of looking at our discoveries. What is Zion, it has become clear - it is Tsen Yav, the Shield of God. But what is Gihon? It contains Yav - one of the names of God, the creator of life on earth. Gihon however has more to offer. It also contains the name of the Garden of God planted and populated with life and, last but not least, life is tucked right in the middle of the first two. And this is ingeniously preserved through the infinite possibilities of combining Hebrew letters. Gihon, the first spring, is God and life, both of humans and animals, in the first garden. The spring and the garden watered by it together create the best conditions for life. And, it is said, God created life there, in the garden and by the spring. And He considered life sacred. More, He considered it the most sacred of all His creations – life, or chay as we say it in Hebrew, as the most ultimate value. And it has been so for us since times immemorial. We've always held life at its highest esteem." Ruben paused, intentionally so. Then he resumed speaking.

"Now we are presented with a unique opportunity. We have a chance to cast our history in an essentially new mold since we returned to Israel after WWII. We should no longer put up with the role of victims of history mourning that it had tramped us under its relentless wheels. We should no longer build massive arms arsenals under the fear of war for the justification of our very existence in this land. Moreover, we should no longer let ourselves be lured to wage wars we later have to label defensive to account for the atrocities that regrettably accompany every war. To put it differently, we should no longer turn into Esau whenever he bullies and harasses us. Instead we should at all times remain Jacob, who was renamed Israel, and has always been considered a prototype of righteousness. This means we should never permit ourselves lose our own humanity. For what is war, gentlemen?" Ruben left this question hanging in the air for a brief moment. "War is the destruction of the most precious and sacred gift we are endowed with from our very beginning – the gift of chay. Throughout history mankind has waged all kinds of wars. And there are no just wars except the ones fought against deliberate and determinate invaders, against those enemies who threaten the very existence of a group of people, of us. Only then, in fighting to protect our own lives and those of our families and fellow-countrymen, only when attacked and in self-defense against imminent threat of losing one's life, are we justified to kill if necessary to save lives. But the Second World War didn't just show us war was one of the worst evils that could occur to men. It showed us, and by us I mean all the generations that followed and will follow, that one of the oldest pieces of human knowledge, that of killing, could be taken to the highest pinnacles of perfection – the pinnacles of well-planned and well-calculated mass killing of millions of people that was the Holocaust.

"Do you know what the worst thing about the Nazis was?" Ruben looked slowly around. "They worked against the extermination of the Jews because they hated us. And they hated us because we were alive, living, full of life. Hence they worked against the annihilation of life by defiling its sacredness. Killing for killing's sake. Period. They sneered at life and pretended killing was something banal, ordinary, a casual routine determined by strict schedules for execution. In their robot-styled perfection in the extermination of the Jews, many of the Nazis even exuded the wicked feeling of superiority in destroying life before one's very eyes.

"We've heard about it from Holocaust survivors, many of them our relatives, and we've seen it on pictures and in documentaries – in the truckloads coming out of the death camps the gassed corpses formed one huge pile in which names, origin, profession, denomination and faith all had vanished, worse still, ceased to matter. What had remained was the horrifying act of desecration of life and the cold face of death. And emptiness, of course. The kind of frigid emptiness that sneaks out of its foul pit after the forced departure of life. The kind of will-less emptiness which saps the very purpose of life. The kind of lifeless emptiness which only death leaves behind because death, as always, greedily gorges on one's will to live.

"Gentlemen, we are not justified to desecrate life only because we want to live in our former home after we have returned to it from a long absence. Nor are the Palestinians justified in condemning our return and killing us for that. We have as much right to live here as they do. Period. We are not the ones to teach the Palestinians what's wrong and what's right but we are the ones who can show them that by acting accordingly. Only by doing what's right can we show them what's wrong. Therefore, neither of the two sides is justified in constantly doing what's wrong - killing the other. Both sides are absolutely obliged to accept each other's presence and learn to live with it. Accept thy neighbor. This has been our most topical commandment for a very long time now. This is the commandment that shows the only way to a peaceful and prosperous future. No more war, no more killing, no more hatred, no more tit for tat, no more dread, and no more deadlock. One of the two sides has to make the first step. Now we have a chance to do that. Let's not miss it."

Ruben's words definitely steered the spirits. But it was essential for him to maintain the momentum. He continued.

"With the latest revelations on the significance of our symbols David's Star and Zion, the issue of righteousness has been brought back under the spotlight of attention but this time in the light of justice. It's time we did justice to ourselves, to Israel, to our history, to our land and most importantly to our future. Let's stop seeing Israel as futureless for it is not. Neither is Israel only chained to its past. For, you know, we had future after 586 B.C.E., 72 C.E., 1492, and especially after 1945. We knew we did. We've always fought for our future and our history has plenty of examples to illustrate that. But the Magdevs from Bulgaria have helped us realize that the fertile soil of our past is where the bud of our future will find the best conditions to grow. What we need to do, now that we are standing in the midst of our fertile field, is only plant that bud and this is entirely up to us. It's not up to anyone else, least of all the Palestinians."

"What do you propose?" a question came from one of the ministers who could clearly be seen on the screen.

"Let's abandon all wailing and mourning over the losses of the two Temples, over all the losses we've suffered throughout history for that matter. What we've lost, we've lost. Period. Let's leave Temple Mount to the Arabs. It has been theirs for many centuries now and we should let it remain theirs. Instead, let's return to Zion, the real one, the stronghold that once was conquered by King David - the Zion that has been with us all along, throughout all of our history and in our hearts amidst joys and sufferings. Let's restore Gan Yav, or Ginnah Pele as others know it, in the foot of Mount Zion and around the spring of Gihon in the Kidron Valley. Let's populate it with plants and trees as it was once created during the first six days of creation. And then, once we do that, let's immerse in its sacredness for nature and *chay* are the two biggest presents Adam received at his creation. They are our presents, too.

"By returning to Zion and the garden, we return to our roots. At the same time we leave Temple Mount to our Arab neighbors. It has become sacred to them and they venerate it. We have to let them continue to do so and only this way can we live side by side in peace. If we announce that we shall never have claims to Temple Mount, we stand a pivotal chance in history to give a head start to a healthy peace process."

"What makes you think that?" The President asked. Ruben looked at him straight in the eyes and then spoke.

"By abandoning all claims to Temple Mount we will show the Palestinians that we are able to make an enormous and unthinkable concession by current standards. We will show that we are ready to make previously inconceivable compromise for the sake of permanent future peace and peaceful coexistence. And this matters, not only to us but also to the Palestinians. This renouncing of claims will be heard because there are reasonable people among the Palestinians as well. I know that because I have worked with some of them. One of them even recently lost his life fighting for peace in Palestine as did our Emil Grunzweig for the just cause of peace in Israel."

Ruben intentionally paused for a moment to let his words do their job. Then he resumed his speech.

"Let us be the first ones to make this huge concession to the peace between them and us. We've got nothing to lose but, hopefully, much to gain. Sitting and waiting is no excuse for not acting. Only by taking things in our own hands do we stand a chance of changing the status quo and of turning things for the better. We must be active. It is our obligation. Why? Not because we are the Chosen People in the sense of a Master Race. No, no, no. We are the Chosen People because we have been selected out of all other people and we have been endowed with a mission - to set the example for the rest. If we fail to do that, if we don't set the right kind of example we are not Chosen People and the Chosen People will be those who set it. In this sense the Palestinians have an equal chance to become the Chosen People if only they choose to set the example."

A short pause and then Ruben continued.

"We, Jews, are accustomed to and very well know what it means to change. What's more, we now have to change."

"In what sense?" one of the ministers asked.

"We have to understand that what once was - I mean the way the Land of Israel once was - will never be again. Never. We cannot restore the kingdom of David. Nor can we restore the First or the Second Temples. Most importantly, we don't need to restore them. They are tucked safely in the Tanakh and they are there to stay for all posterity. Some of us therefore have to reconcile with their unhealthy yearnings to restore the Israel of old, that is, the Israel of the prophets and of David and Solomon. Our discoveries come at a critical moment and are crucial for all those Jews who, in some way or another, still yearn for some restoration of sorts. Let's stop hankering for Temple Mount. Let's go back to Zion, I would say to them. If you want to restore Israel of old you could do it, and rightfully so, on Mount Zion. Because, we have to admit it, we cannot simply disregard all those Israelis who yearn for restoration. They are many. They are among us. They are some of us. But they are not all of us. So those among us who are still yearning would best do so by returning to Mount Zion. The State of Israel was not founded with the aim of restoration of Biblical Israel. It was founded so that Jews could return to their homeland because the State of Israel is the Land of Israel - the two are inseparable and are identical. So by reconciling with our unhealthy yearnings for restoration, we'll be able to best understand the realities of today."

"What realities are you talking about?" a question came from another minister on the other side of the screen.

"They are the fact that the Palestinians inhabit the Land of Israel much the same way that we Jews do. They are part of this land today and will be in the future and we have to get used to this fact. At the end it is simple. They are not our enemies and we are not theirs. We are just two peoples who have to find a common way to live together and share one and the same land. That's all.

"Gentlemen, it is up to you to decide but bear in mind the historical crossroads we are currently standing at. Your move now will decide the future of many Israeli and Palestinian generations. This is the heavy load of duty and responsibility you have to carry on your shoulders. For humanity's sake, we have to make the first move otherwise the eye-for-eye and tooth-for-tooth skirmishes with the Palestinians will never ever end. We have to show them and the rest of the world that we are forever committed to peace. This is up to you for peace is our only future. Toda raba," Ruben said. There was silence all over the room and beyond in the room shown on the large flat screen. Ruben Openheim, the modest chairman of Peace Now, didn't know it at that moment but he had delivered the most passionate and sincere peace speech of his life. At that moment he didn't know how he had managed to stir the spirits of many important Israeli officials. But he had succeeded and that was what ultimately mattered.

62

JERUSALEM, ISRAEL
30 JULY 2020
AT RABBI LOEW'S HOUSE
EARLY EVENING

Rabbi Loew was really concerned about what Dani and Ian had gone through. The three of them were sitting on the terrace overlooking the garden. Rabbi Loew was fond of gardening and local plant species and throughout the years had managed to make his version of a neatly ordered botanic garden. There was a tall palm tree at the opposite end of the garden whose top was now bathed in warm colors by the rays of the setting sun.

"I'm wondering whether that was an open act of aggression against us or if it was just random shooting," Ian said and drank from his glass of fine Yarden wine. The bottle had come from the rabbi's small collection of carefully selected Israeli wines.

"Who would have wanted you killed? Think about it. Few people know you in this country. I think it was random shooting for such incidents sadly still occur," Rabbi Loew said to his guests sitting on a chesterfield across the table.

"I want to believe this whole thing was an accident."

"Look, Ian, unfortunately these days things have gone for the worse in Israel. Sadly, since the very inception of this country, there has been a constant danger of regular law-abiding citizens becoming accidental witnesses or victims of atrocities committed by brainwashed suicide bombers and terrorist groups openly operating in neighboring Arab states and advocating hatred against us. Regrettably, this was what happened to you tonight. And it is even more regrettable when children are involved. Dani should never have witnessed such an act of open aggression against innocent guests to Israel such as you are."

"Yet he did," Ian said.

"I'm okay, Dad. Really." Dani had already calmed down.

"Another inexplicably coincidental thing were the muffled shots. I'm positive because I heard the popping. Then two shadows appeared out of nowhere and to my relief calm was suddenly restored. Unfortunately I couldn't see any faces."

"Somebody has to prevent the general public from any acts of open aggression and at the same time rebuff this foreign hostility at all times. We have such body - Mossad with its agents and operatives. They are the good guys despite the fact that sometimes they have to do things that are despicable in themselves. But this is only to achieve a higher end. It must have been some of them that restored the calm. I am sure of it. They are all around, constantly watching and protecting."

"A bit like Big Brother," Ian offered.

"The Good Big Brother, mind you. You have to understand the Mossad is a clandestine organization and there is a very serious reason for that. Israel is a maximum-security state and maintaining such kind of security requires a lot of manpower and undercover work. You have to know that the primary goal of the Mossad is to maintain public sanity by acceding to do the dirty work. Imagine if regular citizens had to witness random killings, brutal murders, executions, tortures, rapes and dehumanizing disgrace. The authorities cannot allow that. What would happen then? People would be utterly appalled and distressed, shaken to the core of their very being. Some would go insane. Others would sink into a deep and incurable depression. Still others would give in and commit suicide."

******

After the early evening dinner, Dani went to his room to take shower. Rabbi Loew and Ian went out on the terrace for another glass of fine wine, this time produced by Carmel winery located in the town of Rishon LeZion.

"When I think about it, this whole adventure began with the discovery of the interwoven Cyrillic letters in David's Star," the Rabbi said thoughtfully.

"You are right, Rabbe. Ever since that moment I've been asking myself what the ultimate meaning of David's Star is."

"You see, Ian, this is a huge and very interesting question and one that cannot receive a single and straightforward answer. Judaism is a very unique religion and I am saying that not from the standpoint of my position as a rabbi but as an ordinary man. It was the only religion in the times of old, which forbade graven images – no idols and their pictorial or figurative representations. So, naturally, what Judaism was left with was an abstract concept of God. And what is that concept? It speaks of God as omnipresent and omnipotent. God is the Great Beyond. He is beyond the perception capacities of the human senses, yet, He is also invisibly connected to the world He Himself has created. However, even in ancient times, the Children of Israel were not satisfied by this abstract concept, deprived of any representation. Because, after all, abstract concepts require abstract thinking and one can acquire such through education, most notably, through philosophy, logic, language and mathematics."

"You say the Israelites were not satisfied with the lack of imagery. What happened then?"

"They resorted to the most wondrous and most abstract gift they had received from God at the time of Creation – language. Think of the Hebrew letters, Ian. What are they? Purely abstract graphical representations of uttered sounds. Genesis 1:3: 'And God said: 'Let there be light. And there was light.' This particular line teaches us that God's uttered words were not mere sounds but had creative powers. The combinations of sounds that formed the Hebrew words Veyomer Elohim yehi-or vayehi-or of 1:3 had actually come to let light be. God gave us the alphabet of His creation – the alphabet that signified His language. He lent it to us. Neither His language nor His alphabet was a mere abstraction. On the contrary, both of them held potent creative powers. Actually, the alphabet was God's way of doing away with abstractions. Since all Hebrew letters corresponded to numbers, the latter stood in the same relation to abstractions as the former."

"*Aleph* is One. *Beth* is Two. *Gimel* is Three."

"Indeed! Since Judaism strictly banned the worshipping and use of any images and representations of God - otherwise called abominations - the ancient Israelites sought refuge in the most divine gift - the language of creation. They began coming up with names for God - El, Ehyeh-Asher-Ehyeh, Adonai, Elohim, Shekhinah, Shaddai, Ein Sof, Yah, Yav and the Tetragrammaton which gained highest value since it was unpronounceable - YHVH. Since times immemorial, the names of God have been the gates of access to Him. They've also stood for symbols of His presence. So, there were no images but a name, the Name, ha-Shem.

"There were also strict rules when the names of God could be pronounced. As you may know, ha-Shem became the form that could replace the pronunciation of any of the other names. The most sacred name, the Tetragrammaton, was rendered unpronounceable and the most stringent prohibition of its pronunciation was imposed. This was so because the ancient Israelite sages taught that the regular pronunciation deprived the Tetragrammaton of its divine powers. Therefore, it had to be protected and shielded off from the abuse of colloquial language and everyday use. Only the high priest of the Temple was permitted to pronounce the Tetragrammaton once a year during the prayer of Yon Kippur in the Temple's Holy of Holies."

"They shielded it off... how interesting!" Ian said pensively.

"You see Ian, David's Star, as it is known in English, is in fact Magen David - the Shield of David."

"I know but what does this shield protect then?"

"It protects the Name, the Tetragrammaton and everything else related to the history and spirituality of the Children of

Israel that you found encoded in its graphical texture. The star is an ark of knowledge protected by the shield.

"There's more. Magen David is the graphical sign closest to the abstract concept of an invisible God the pronunciation of whose name has been most strictly banned. It is not an image, not at all, nor is it simply a combination of letters. It transcends both. It has some of the graphical properties of an image - it consists of spatial lines that interweave and in doing so form letters, But it is neither solely an image nor is it a set of interwoven letters. Hence it is more than those two yet it is those two at the same time. But the important thing here is that its enigmatic character protects it - shields it off - from the world in order to retain and safeguard the divine powers it has been invested with," the Rabbi paused.

"And at the same time all these lines and letters are on constant display, before everyone's eyes, at any given moment," Ian added.

"Good point. I should put it this way. Think of David's Star as the visible sign of the invisible God, the equivalent of the unpronounceable YHVH. When we look at David's Star on our flag or in our synagogues, we all undoubtedly see it. It is there, right in front of us, right before our very eyes with which we clearly perceive its interwoven lines. Yet, in seeing it, we don't see what has been concealed within it, interwoven in it, beyond it. We only see the sign but as a sign it is a mere graphical representation. And yet, precisely in its graphicality - if I may use such a hastily coined word - so much is contained, everything you've come to discover concealed through language."

"Letters and their combinations."

"Exactly! No matter how abstract the concept of God may be, it is definitely not entirely detached from the world of creation - the one in which created beings and things exist. And how did God create? Through the language of creation! You very well know His first words: 'Let there be light and there was light.' That was the epitomical act of creation - through language.

Later, God gave language to the man He had created. Language was the link between the Creator and His creation and was the most wondrous gift the former could give the latter. It is extremely abstract, yet, at the same time, it can refer to very concrete things. In either case, language's reference to things calls for the felt presence of the things spoken about. When I speak to you about the Ark of the Covenant, you don't see it, we don't see it because it is not around, but its presence can be felt through our speech. Language also has the formidable capacity to generate the presence of visible, invisible, existent, non-existent, abstract, imaginary and concrete things. Once a name has been written, the presence of what it refers to is generated and, at the same time, also asserted. When you contemplate the four letters of the Tetragrammaton, you understand that the combination of precisely these four signs generates the presence of something referred to."

"So wherever YHVH appears, it generates the presence of God."

"Exactly. Now you have to bear in mind that the Hebrew letters are also numbers. And in this line of thought, numbers too may refer to concrete things. Both letters and numbers - through the correspondence to each other - have the miraculous potency of generating presences. The letter and the number are both signs of presence and connection to it. Through YHVH we feel God's invisible yet asserted presence and we also feel connected to Him. The plain *graphicality* of YHVH represents the point where two worlds meet, touch, connect, bind together, and knot into each other. For us, Jews, we need not see God but we need to feel His presence. That's crucial. For us, presence has always been more important than appearance. And the Tetragrammaton gives us precisely that - a sign of God's mighty presence. But so also has been the case with David's Star which has always been a generator of presence."

"But then it turns out that David's Star has the same role as the Tetragrammaton," Ian suggested.

"You could say that but at the same time you should know that the star is more than that for it is also an Ark. It is a container of graphical signs that is able to generate God's presence in many ways. It is, if I may put it that way, the Ark of the Covenant of Divine Presence. You saw this during our work with the others in the office of Peace Now. Through David's Star, God asserts His continuous presence and assures that the World of Creation is perennially bound to that of His own because He is the Author of everything." The rabbi made a pause. He wanted to let his words sink in. Ian could feel the presence and weight of the words that had just been spoken. Then the rabbi resumed.

"Judaism banned the use of images of God. Such weren't necessary anyway. However, Judaism resorted to language as the only attested link between God and man. Since the destruction of the First Temple and especially after the destruction of the Second Temple, the Children of Israel have needed something to mark the presence of God. Don't get me wrong, for us God has been invisible at all times. This is out of question. The question is that the Temple in Jerusalem fulfilled the role of marker of God's presence in this world. With the two Temples gone, many a Jewish soul felt the absence of that Divine presence. Jews needed a sign, a universal sign of the divine presence.

"When King David constructed his first shield, its internal structure consisted of two interwoven triangles. David came up with that structure under Divine revelation, the sages asserted. So, we can assume that he was the first human who was invested with the knowledge of the much deeper meaning and significance of the two interlacing triangles. At the time of David, the two interwoven triangles had not yet become a sign, much less so a symbol. They emerged as such later. David's Star rose slowly to prominence as the sign of Jewry among the scattered Jewish communities."

"I have seen it on many synagogues across Europe. I have come to observe that wherever there is a Jewish community, there's the star."

"With David's Star, God made a covenant between Himself and the Children of Israel about the course of their History. Everything interwoven in the star's graphical texture was to serve as a compass showing the right direction and the right course of history to all posterity."

"What do you mean, Rabbe?"

"When you contemplate the form of David's Star, you see it has six rays pointing at six different directions. With time, the association with a star gained prominence over the translation shield. Billions around the world today, know the sign as David's Star. We, Jews, too say that name when we speak the languages of the countries where we reside. The association of the sign with a star is not only inevitable but also very natural. And what is a star?"

"Something up there in the sky."

"True, but it is also something beyond, unreachable, yet, most importantly, visible. It is visible, like a visible sign. As such it is also something more - it is a connection between us, the ones who see it, and what lies between and beyond - the immense void of the Universe. We can perceive the mind-boggling immensity of the space only through the line of visibility a star provides. It fixes the distance up to which we can see with our naked eyes. And we can only see very, very little. The rest - the immense bulk of stars and galaxies - remains concealed beyond."

"Yet they are there."

"Absolutely but invisible, just beyond the scope of our seeing and at the same time also unseeing eyes. The Great Beyond has always been right in front of us but we've never really seen it. We hover below the face of the deep covered in darkness and we don't see. And then suddenly, a light flickers and then more of it. Hundreds of thousands of rays of light spring forth in all directions. And there is light. And all of a sudden, we find ourselves bathing in it. And all of a sudden, yes, all of a sudden, we see. And what we get to see is what has been hidden before.

And through seeing, we get to know. Through knowing, we find the link between Creator and Created. This way we are given the chance to glimpse at the secret of Creation. And the void is no longer empty and it is no longer unformed. Language lends a hand. There is a star. And it is bright. It is full of light that it emits generously, eternally, endlessly, no end, Ein-Sof, or, as you had revealed, 'here, the sign of Yav'. And there is no end to light as there is no end to God. And then, the unknowable and enigmatic Great Beyond instantly acquires a much higher degree of proximity to us. We feel it closer to us, more, next to us. It becomes the closest presence we have ever felt. It becomes us. It is us..." a long moment of silence followed as though everything had been said. No words were necessary, just silence and the all-engulfing invisible presence. That was all. Ian felt that such great unity with the Great Beyond, with Ein-Sof, could only bring calm and the feeling of all-pervasive belonging to this world. The evening star was above the horizon, visible, yet unreachable.

Then the rabbi's resumed speaking.

"You wanted to know the significance of David's Star. There it is – the invisibly visible and the unconcealedly concealed sign of God's presence. Wherever that sign appears, it immediately marks God's presence at that place and not only His presence but also that of His children. Yet, you now know, David's Star is not simply a sign of presence. It also is an ark containing an immense wealth of encoded knowledge of history, facts, places, people, and names. It is the Ark of coded and enigmatic messages. But that Ark only few chosen people have learnt how to open and read its contents, Ian. Only very few! And your Dani is one of them.

"Probably nobody will ever discover everything that has been hidden in it. Of that we can never be sure, of course. Probably, one day, somebody will. And that discovery will be the sign of the advent of the age of reason, hence, of the son of David."

"So the son of David is the epitome of the age of reason?"

"Yes. The advent of David's son will be when humankind reaches the climax of its capacities of reason. That is when humankind will be closest to God."

"There's one thing I don't understand. Why exactly my son? Why did he have to discover the letters?"

"Well, these are questions I cannot answer, Ian. If you want their answers you will have to find them by yourself," Rabbi Loew said and at this moment the doorbell rang. He stood up briskly and went to answer it. Ian remained on the terrace, flooded by a fresh wave of thoughts.

63

Rabbi Loew and Ruben came out on the terrace. Ian stood up to greet his friend. Ruben asked about the incident and Ian went on telling him in detail about what had happened. Then to change the subject, Ian asked about Ruben's meeting with the government. Ruben spoke with fervor about it and was still speaking when Dani stormed in holding his SkyPhone.

"Dad…Oh, Hi Ruben, it's nice you're here…"

"What's the excitement about, Dani?"

"I've just got a message from The LaW but I can't read it. It contains those symbols from David's cipher."

"Let me see it," Ruben took Dani's SkyPhone.

〈	〉	V	〉	⊔	δ	⌈
3	1	4	6	5	7	2

"What does it mean?" Ian inquired.

"*Ruwm Layishyav* (רם לישיו)," Ruben read aloud.

"The Elevation of the Lion of God," the Rabbi translated.

"What's that supposed to mean?" Dani asked.

"Rabbe, I have the suspicion I've heard the name *Layishyav* somewhere before," Ruben said.

"Are you sure? Because I've never heard it in my life," Rabbi Loew said puzzled, looking at Ruben.

"No, I'm not. I guess it's just..."

"Why don't we call Uri Zohar?" Ian offered.

"Why him? As far as I remember he didn't prove to be a very reliable source," The Rabbi inquired.

Well, he may have heard the name," Ian suggested and Ruben looked at him, thoughts racing through his mind.

"He's made one mistake but we're not going to hold him accountable for it till the rest of his life, are we?" Ruben turned to Rabbi Loew. Then, with a burst of determination, he took out his SkyPhone and dialed Uri Zohar's number. Uri picked up and the two men warmly greeted each other. Then Ruben switched on the telephone's loudspeaker, explained what message Dani had received and asked about *Layishyav*.

"In the Kabbalah tradition, *Layishyav* stands for the arcane equivalent of Ariel," Uri Zohar said.

"Why two names which mean the same?" The Rabbi inquired.

"They are not just names, they form a symbolic and shrouded relation," Uri answered.

"Would you please elaborate?" Rabbi Loew pressed on.

"There are basically two interpretations of the origin of the Hebrew name אריאל or *ariel*. The first one states that it consists of the root *ari* meaning 'to burn' while the afformative *lamed* implying 'hearth'. The second one states that *ariel* means 'God's mountain' based on the claim that it derived from the Akkadian word *arall* of the same meaning. Both interpretations are based on evidence. In ancient times, sacrificial altars were generally built in the form of truncated pyramids also called *ziggurats*. Now, the uppermost and most sacred level of that truncated pyramidal altar where one could reach God was called *ariel* and the whole structure of the *ziggurat* stood for a symbol of God's mountain."

"God's mountain?" Dani asked puzzled.

"This is Zion, Dani, the original site of Jerusalem," Uri said and then added, "The message you got says *Ruwm Layishyav* – the Elevation of God's Lion. Zion is a mount, that is, an elevation above the ground. Hence the message could have read with the same effect *Ruwm Ariel*."

"But it doesn't," Dani exclaimed.

"I assume you don't think this is by mere accident, do you?"

"I don't really know. Why is it by no accident?" Dani was confused.

"Most probably you don't know it, Dani, but the name with which the prophet Isaiah referred to Jerusalem was Ariel."

"Why was that?"

"In the Kabbalah tradition, Uriel is one of the four angels around the throne of God. In his vision, the prophet Ezekiel saw the four angels in the form of holy animals. The lion that he saw was Uriel who had been given a special role by God. During the times of the First Temple, when sacrifices were offered on the altar, it was Uriel who descended from the heavens in the form of a lion and consumed them. This was a sign that God had accepted the sacrifices. But that was not all. The appearance of Uriel as a lion on *ariel*, the top of the altar, brought about change of heart and penitence to those who could see him," Uri Zohar explained.

"Still I don't understand why doesn't the message simply read *Ruwm Ariel*?" Dani asked, even more bewildered.

"Had it been that case you would never have thought about *Layishyav*?"

"And why should I think about it?"

"In Kabbalah, numerical values of names and words are essential and there is a very mystical reason for that. The numerical value of the name *Ariel* is as follows: 1 [aleph] + 200 [resh] + 10 [yod] + 1 [aleph] + 30 [lamed] equals 242. The numerical value of *Layishyav* is 356. So we have 242 on the one hand and 356 on the other. The difference between them is exactly 114.

"Now, 114 is the numerical value of the Hebrew word עמד or *omed* meaning 'a place'. But it is also the numerical value of another word מעד or *moed* meaning 'an appointed time'. Which was the place? The top of the altar. When was the appointed time? When sacrifices had been offered on the altar."

"How interesting!" Dani exclaimed.

"This is not all. 242 is 2+4+2 or 8. 356 is 14. 8 and 14 stand for the Hebrew letters *heth* and *nun* which, when put together, yield the word חן or *chen* meaning 'grace' as God's grace. So when Uriel descended at the appointed place, atop *Ruwm Layishyav/Ariel,* and at the appointed time and consumed the offerings, the people were given God's grace and experienced change of heart and repentance. So whoever sent you the message, I am sure, wanted you to understand this complex relation between *Layishyav* and *Ariel* and everything it entailed. But you also told me there were some numbers under the letters, right?"

"That's correct," Dani said.

"Please send me the message so that I see them," Uri asked and Dani got down to sending it. In a few moments, a beep was heard coming from the loudspeaker. Uri had just received Dani's message.

"Just give me a second to make sense of it all," Uri said while the others sank in thoughtful silence. New revelations had emerged and everyone was busy trying to comprehend their significance. In a minute Uri spoke excitedly.

"Listen, *Ruwm Layishyav* is indeed a very unique name."

"Why is that?" Ruben asked.

"Because it stands for Jerusalem (ירושלים)."

"What?" Ian exclaimed in disbelief.

"Yes. Take a look at the message - רם לישיו. The numbers under the symbols are all mixed up, right?"

"Right," Ruben said.

"All you have to do is order the letters from one to seven starting from one which is *yod,* followed by two which is *resh* and so on until seven which is *mem,*" Uri explained.

"O, yes, you are right, *Ruwm Layishyav* is indeed Jerusalem" Ian said in awe.

"It is amazing what has been hidden in that name," Rabbi Loew said, surprised.

"Thank you, Uri. This has been a great help for us," Ruben said.

"I'm glad I could help. I mixed it all up once and I know it won't happen twice. If you need any further assistance, I am always available," Uri said and bid them goodbye.

Right afterward, Ruben's mobile rang and he went inside to pick it up.

64

"You sound worried, Mohammed," Ruben spoke into the receiver of the phone.

"I am. You remember I promised you I would speak to my brother. Well, I went to his house and did just that."

"I am listening."

"I told him what I thought was the truth about the entire situation in Palestine, right in his face. You've heard enough about him. You know how ruthless he usually is and how much more merciless he can be if he wishes. But I tell you back in his house the scale could have easily been tipped off-balance. I was on the verge of losing my life. He could have killed me for what I told him had I not been his brother."

"You shouldn't have risked your life. You should think about your family first, Mohammed."

"But I want to make a difference, Ruben. I want to provide a better future for my children. I don't want them to be the same casualties of a brutal war as I have been. I don't want them to be hostages to a constantly failing peace process. The Gaza and the West Bank are like two huge open-air prisons for the Palestinians."

"I know as well as you do that this is how people like your brother Naif see the Palestinian territories."

"Speaking of him, this is the news I want to tell you. He called me a short while ago and said he wanted to meet you in person. He said it was important."

"Me? Are you sure?"

"Yes, he said it explicitly 'the chief of your organization'."

"He told me he had received a call from our President who is now in Sofia."

"I know."

"Apparently your Prime Minister called our President and told him the Israeli government was rethinking its position on the Temple Mount in Jerusalem meaning it was considering a retreat from it and a permanent return to the City of David. Your Prime Minister said his government needed a bit more time to think and discuss things through because a rare window of opportunity for permanent peace had arisen. He requested a short break of the peace talks until the afternoon of the following day."

"Which is tomorrow."

"Exactly."

"When does he want to meet me?"

"Tonight."

"Where?"

"At the Erez Crossing. You'll have to arrange it, Ruben. Naif should be allowed just beyond our side of the gates. He has to receive all assurances he won't be shot at by the Israeli forces. You have to meet between the two gates – in the narrow no-man's land."

"I understand. I'll make a few phone calls and call you back with the details," Ruben said and hung up.

65

EREZ CROSSING
BETWEEN ISRAEL AND PALESTINE
30 JULY 2020
10PM

Ruben was picked up from Rabbi Loew's house by two government operatives, a man and a woman. He was driven in an inconspicuous black sedan to the place of the meeting. He arrived in time. Walking toward the gate he could see a lot of military border patrols to his left and right along the demarcation line. All street and border lights were on in anticipation of something ominous to take place. What Ruben couldn't see beyond the lighted area were the snipers at standby atop several houses and buildings. They were there as part of Mossad's standard precaution procedures.

He passed through the revolving metal gates. Once on the other side, he walked on under the blinding border lights and stopped in the middle of the no-man's land between the two border checkpoints. The revolving gate on the opposite side screeched with a rusty kind of squealing. A dark figure squeezed through. As the man came out in the lit open space and marched forward briskly, Ruben could see he was of average build and agile suggesting military training of sorts. The man had a thick black beard running up his jaws, the rest of his face being clean shaven. His eyes, as he ground to a halt just a meter before Ruben, were betraying his animosity. Ruben observed Naif looked so different from Mohammed. If he hadn't known he would never have believed Mohammed and Naif were brothers.

"Why did you have to mess up the head of our puppet president just now?" Naif spoke first, a frown on his face.

"I didn't mess up anyone's head," Ruben replied.

"Just yours, I guess."

Ruben did not respond to this uncouth provocation. It was much easier to insult back than to retain self-control. He let it pass.

"What is this talk of giving up Temple Mount? The Israelis have been after it all along and now, suddenly, you come up and say you should give it up. You've always claimed it's been yours."

"Not me. I've never claimed that. I claim something essentially different."

"I'm all ears."

"Together with a small dedicated team, we've come to discover that the most sacred place for us, Jews, has always been Mount Zion on whose top the City of David stands. The Temple Mount may have been sacred for us in the very distant past but it no longer is. The two temples have been long gone, vanished under the rabble of history. They are no more. History has closed the chapter with them."

"History also closed the chapter with you Jews, living in this land. You were exiled for the last time twenty centuries ago."

"True about the exile but wrong about history closing chapters. Mount Zion is still standing where it stands, to-date, isn't it?"

"Mount Zion may remain standing for another hundred thousand years, how does that give you the right to return and claim our land?"

"Because it has always been sacred for us all along, all throughout history and throughout our exiles and in spite of them. Mount Zion has always been there for us, waiting for each and every of our returns. And if we want to be true to ourselves, we have to admit it is the most sacred place for us."

"And so?"

"We renounce our claims for return to the Temple Mount and instead return to Mount Zion, to the heart of the City of David. We thus forever partition the sacred sites in Jerusalem between Jews and Palestinians so that each of us is able to visit them freely and worship without any constraints."

"But we've partitioned the sites long time ago. We've got Temple Mount. You've got the Wailing Wall."

"Sadly not an insignificant number of our own people still have claims of return to Temple Mount. These claims should be abolished altogether and for good because they create a lot of problems."

"You see this is your task, your obligation. You're really going to instigate a conflict because of some phony claims of return to Temple Mount and of rebuilding of your temple..."

"I am not preaching any rebuilding of any temple. This is what the Temple Mount and Land of Israel Faithful Movement is doing."

"All the same to me, still one of yours."

"What I'm advocating is return to Mount Zion – the City of David."

"You'll never succeed," Naif sneered.

"Sure, I won't if I don't have your cooperation."

"What do you want?"

"Well, if I succeed in making people have a change of hearts and renounce their claims of return and at this very moment you start pointing your finger at us mockingly, saying we're weak and hopeless and so on and so forth, the extreme elements within our own camp will surely resort to violence against you. That's how you're going to get a fresh conflict. I want you to refrain from mocking the Jews if they officially announce they are abandoning all attempts at returning to Temple Mount."

"I can't see that coming. This is impossible."

"Now this is your part of the deal. Your obligation."

"Will you be able then to stop your fanatics from the movement tomorrow?"

"This is my concern. My duty. My obligation."

"It's mine as well, at least for the moment."

"Think long term here. If we succeed in effectively partitioning Jerusalem, we stand a great chance of applying the same to the rest of Palestine, safely and securely dividing the land between Israel and Palestine. Only this way do we stand a chance to achieve lasting peace."

"The Gaza and the West Bank that you've given us are too small for our growing population, Mr. Openheim. We need more land. Do you realize that?"

"There are your good co-religionist friends from Jordan and from Egypt. They surely wouldn't decline helping their Muslim brothers from Palestine. You just need to negotiate with them and find some lasting solution for the Palestinians in the West Bank and in Gaza."

"Are you insane? We both know that Jordan and Egypt are two sovereign states –"

"– And so is Israel," Ruben cut in. "You have to understand that Israel is on the world map and is there to stay. You cannot wipe it out and you shouldn't think in such terms. You should think how to solve your internal problems because frankly you've got plenty of them. And you know what your biggest internal problem is? You haven't matured enough as a nation to achieve self-determination. What's worse, you project your problems on us, as though we are your problem. Israel is not the problem of Palestine. Remember that. Palestine, unfortunately, is its own biggest problem, worse still, its own victim. We fought you in several wars, won them fair and square and reclaimed our land. You have to accept that and live with it. Remember, to solve your big problems and the ones you have with us, you need to be very flexible and not constrained by dogmas and prejudices."

"I kill for such words, you, bastard. How dare you speaking to me like this?" Naif bared his teeth at Ruben. He was furious.

"You and I have to be able to tell each other when the white is white and the black is black. You get it? Otherwise it won't work and don't take my words as an offence to you. I don't seek to offend you. I'm just making things clear to you. And you need not threaten me. I know you are a killer but how far do you think you're going to get by killing? One day you'll get shot and then what? Another Palestinian life lost in vain. You've succeeded in climbing so high up your military rankings. You stand a great chance of changing the tide and making things for the better."

"As though I am listening to Mohammed. Now I see where he learned that kind of talk of peace, it was from you."

"And this is good, Naif. You have to be far-sighted. You have to try to see the future of this misery- and poverty-stricken land. Don't make the present your prison. Instead, open the metal-barred gate of the present's prison and step out. Once out, take a good look at the distance ahead of you and then go forward into the open field of the future. That's what I am offering you now – a chance to reach out for a future in which we could live in peace."

"What do you want in return?"

"The most important thing that I want from you is to totally and unconditionally renounce violence and military conflict. No more shelling, you understand? No event should ever make you take up your weapons."

"Are you insane? This is impossible?"

"No, Naif. Nothing is impossible. It's all a matter of will and discipline."

"Will your military do the same?"

"This is my end of the deal."

"I am a man of war."

"But I am a man of peace."

"So then, there's no way."

"On the contrary, there is a way. I want you to agree in principle on the idea of peace and to embrace it as your value as well. By shelling at each other we won't get anywhere. The past has proven it sufficiently. We mustn't repeat one and the same mistake over and over again. Palestine is not the victim of Israel nor is it the underdog in this conflict. Remember that as well. Two separate, independent and self-determined states living side by side. This is all I want."

"Will you stop the Jewish fanatics marching on Temple Mount tomorrow?"

"Leave it to me."

"How can I trust you?"

"You can't but I will tell you this - don't trust my words, trust my deeds. If I succeed in preventing the ceremony from taking place tomorrow, this will be the sign for you that my government and I will do what I've told you. Do you agree?"

Naif just nodded, turned abruptly and walked back to where he had come from.

66

JERUSALEM, ISRAEL
31 JULY 2020
IR DAVID
MORNING

A lot of supporters of The Temple Mount and Land of Israel Faithful Movement had already gathered at the Western Wall Plaza. The expectant hum of the exuberant crowd reverberated off the huge walls of the plaza and increased manifold. The people were high-spirited, eagerly waiting for the ceremony of anointing the cornerstone for the Third Temple to begin.

An ensemble of Levites was in the northern corner of the plaza. Most of its musicians were tuning their instruments, the sounds mixing with the hum of the huge crowd. It was surreal and ceremonial. The air was full of tense anticipation.

All around the plaza, the Dung Gate and beyond it, along Ma'aleh HaShalom Road and Derekh Ha'Ofel Road, there were S.W.A.T teams in place. A few military choppers were flying overhead. Agents in civilian clothes and earpieces were scattered among the crowd. The security was tight. It had to be, as usual.

Outside the walls of the archaeological garden, a bit further down the junction of Derekh Ha'Ofel Road and Ma'Alot Ir David Road, Ruben Openheim was atop a flatbed truck, holding a mouthpiece and giving instructions to an impressive assembly of supporters of Peace Now that had gathered before him. Shortly after midnight last night, he had come up with a plan how to counter and eventually thwart the march and the ceremony of anointment organized by The Temple Mount and Land of Israel Faithful Movement. He had discussed it with Ian and Rabbi Loew and then had spent the whole night calling people and organizing them for a protest rally the following morning. He hadn't slept at all but he didn't feel any fatigue. The adrenaline was doing its job.

Caught by surprise and uniformed of the rally, the police had tried to disperse the supporters of Peace Now who had gathered at a vital spot on the route of the ceremonial procession. But then, as they had surrounded the supporters, all police personnel had suddenly dispersed. They had been called off. Ruben was informed that one of the chiefs of police had received a phone call from a high-ranking government official. A direct order had been issued to let the Peace Now rally take place. Ruben's passionate speech delivered to the government had paid off.

The atmosphere around the Wailing Wall and the entrance to the City of David was getting tenser by the minute.

Holding the mouthpiece, Ruben was giving instructions. "Under no circumstances should you resort to violence. There will be provocations but we won't respond to any of them because we are a peaceful organization. We want peace. We should show everyone here we've assembled with peaceful intentions."

Ian, Dani and Rabbi Loew were among the people standing just below the truck's platform with Ruben atop. Ian checked his watch. It was five to nine. In a few minutes the ceremonial procession would start from the Western Wall Plaza and would slowly sneak its way through the Mugabi Gate. Then it would turn left down Derekh Ha'Ofel Road and then it would have to turn right down Ma'Alot Ir David Road. But the participants in the procession would not be able to continue any further for their path would be blocked by the participants in the Peace Now rally. Most of the police chiefs present were worrying a clash between the two groups was inevitable. None of them wanted violence to erupt amidst Jerusalem, especially one in which Jews were caught up fighting against other Jews. Something had to be done to avoid hostility.

"Defend yourselves if only you are attacked and have no other option. Let us show all Israel conflicts can be resolved without bloodshed," Ruben spoke firmly and calmly through his mouthpiece.

Just beyond the Mugabi Gate, the supporters of The Temple Mount and Land of Israel Faithful Movement lined up in a thick file behind a priest clad in ceremonial garments and all the movement's dignitaries. The Levite musicians commissioned for the event started playing, their drummer beating a low and slightly muted beat. The entire procession looked like a gigantic caterpillar which shivered for an instant under the drum's beating before it slowly lurched forward. It moved through the Mugabi Gate then sluggishly turned its bulky body left under the watchful eyes of a tight cordon of policemen lined up along each side of Ma'aleh HaShalom Road and Derekh Ha'Ofel Road. Behind either side of the cordon, there were thousands and thousands of ordinary citizens and bystanders, watching the event unfold. The time it took the head of the procession to cover the short distance to the intersection with Ma'Alot Ir David Road passed in growing anxiety for the security forces and the Peace Now supporters watching the measured and imperturbable advance of the caterpillar.

Then the moment came when the procession gradually turned right and down Ma'Alot Ir David Road. As its head straightened up, the priest and the dignitaries met face-to-face with the first lines of participants in the Peace Now rally. The huge caterpillar abruptly ground to a halt, its end still at the Western Wall Plaza. The live music stopped mid-blast. The drumming instantly died away. People from both camps froze to a silent standstill.

A short-trimmed middle-aged man whose dark skin was emphasized by a distinct white scar on his left cheek came out from behind the priest. "What is going on?" Caleb Medan tersely demanded. Somebody from the first line explained it was a peaceful rally held by Peace Now.

"This is a ceremony permitted by the Israeli government. We received the permit for it more than a week ago. You have no right to block the route of our procession," Caleb Medan shouted out furiously. Ruben heard him well. He put the mouthpiece to his lips.

"We are holding a peaceful rally, also permitted by the Israeli government. We have much the same right to be here as you do," Ruben spoke loudly and calmly from atop his makeshift platform. What he said noticeably further infuriated the man with the scar, now already blood red.

"Peaceful rally, nonsense. Why didn't you hold it yesterday or, better still, why don't you hold it tomorrow? Why exactly today? You're holding it because of us, against us," the scarred man yelled out loud. A wave of grunting approval issued from the thick caterpillar.

"I hope you realize there may be no tomorrow for Israel precisely because of your ceremony."

"So you admit your rally is against our ceremony."

"Our rally is against no one in this country, only against the insanity that sometimes seems to get the best of some of our citizens."

"I'll have you jailed for such words," said Caleb Medan, gasping with rage. Ruben placed the mouthpiece to his lips again. Then he spoke to the whole present multitude of people coming from all walks of Israeli life.

"This ceremony you are holding is against Israel, against the future peace of this country. What Third Temple are you people aspiring to rebuild? Israel doesn't need it. What Israel needs is peace – durable, permanent, long-lasting, never-ending peace. This up there," Ruben pointed in the direction of Temple Mount and the Dome of the Rock, "has become one of the holiest sites for our Palestinian neighbors. Do you see any Israelite Temple standing on it? No, of course you don't. There need be no temple of ours there and we needn't claim anything back. Why? The answer is simple – because of peace. If today we start claiming back Temple Mount by usurping it with some ceremonies of forthcoming rebuilding of a non-existing temple, we'll openly wage yet another war against the Palestinians and all other Muslims across the globe. Do we need that? No, we don't. What are we doing then? Serving like slaves to some century-old and deeply imbedded surges of nostalgia over an Israel that once was but will never be again. Forget about it. Israel of the Torah will never be again, people. Don't mourn over its loss. Mourn over the loss of six million of our people gassed to death in the Nazi concentration camps. Mourn over the loss of so many lives in this never-ending conflict with the Palestinians. Along with the mourning, be happy we claimed back most of our land and we returned to it after the Second World War. Rejoice over the fact that the extremists among the Palestinians haven't been able to fulfill their goal of destroying us as a nation and expelling us from our land. And then, look forward to the future of the state of Israel. This is what matters – the future, the one we are now forging, our future. Think of your children today and your grandchildren tomorrow. Think about their future. Do you want them to live in constant fear as we're living today? Do you? I'm confident you don't.

"Listen to this, people... The most sacred site for all those of you who seek the sacredness in our land is not Temple Mount –" a sudden burst of booing instantly issued from the caterpillar made Ruben stop for a moment. He didn't get disheartened.

On the contrary, he felt even more compelled to continue. He looked calmly over the huge multitude. He knew this was his moment.

"The Temple Mount is the holiest site for us," someone from the front of the caterpillar shouted out loud.

"The holiest site for us is and has always been the original Mount Zion on whose top we are all standing now. This here and further down is the City of David, the stronghold of Zion, the very first Jerusalem. The First and Second Temples sank under the rabble of history. But Zion didn't. Despite all vicissitudes of history it remained standing. Look at it... it is still standing to-date and it's the only remnant of Israel of old, the one most of you are hankering after. You can see it all around us now. It has been standing here all along and will be standing for all posterity. This is where we should return because Zion is our place -"

"Bloody Zionist," someone from the procession crowd yelled out ferociously.

"Let us proceed," another one shouted.

"We should channel our energy and aspirations here to Zion, to *Tsen Yav,* to the first Jerusalem, to *Ruwm Layishyav.* You see what is hidden encoded in the names Zion and Jerusalem. This here is our place - the one we should defend, rebuild and cherish dearly. And I am not saying these words as a religious man, which I'm not, but as a man of peace because peace means well-considered and reasonable compromise. We cannot have peace without compromise. You all have to realize that. This is the situation Israel and Palestine have been in for a long time now. And I'm saying all this for the sake of our future and for our people. We have to overcome our internal rifts stemming from our claims of returning to Temple Mount. We have to renounce those claims and leave Temple Mount to our Muslim neighbors, the Palestinians. And this will be no defeat. This will be the way to peace."

"The Palestinians are terrorists," someone shouted.

"Shame on you who said that...this view is so unfairly and blatantly wrong," Ruben said, looking at the people from the procession. "The Palestinians are not terrorists by default and all of you know it because all of you have met and spoken to Palestinians. Most of them also want to have peace with us but sadly there's a small clique within the Palestinian camp which always steers it in one and the same direction of bloodshed, fear and violence.

"You know what, this ceremony you are holding today. What is it? A provocation, no less than that. By constantly provoking the Palestinians we always get one and the same response - violence and suicide bombers. We punch and we get punched. It's as simple as that. We have to stop punching and be unwavering in this position over a long period of time but this should happen after we had aided the Palestinians in creating their state. Once the Palestinians have their state and we give them no reason to attack us, whatever of their aggression has remained will finally wear out. Why? Because, as a newly created state the Palestinians themselves will finally have to deal responsibly with their own internal problems before the eyes of the world and the international community. When they are a state and they attack us, we, as an independent and self-determined state, will have all the rights to defend ourselves accordingly. In the meantime and until the creation of the Palestinian state takes place, the question remains, whether we should keep on succumbing to circumstances of violence and acting like the Palestinians - tooth for tooth and eye for eye. Our mistake is that we've allowed our enemy to contaminate us with the virus of lack of moral standards and thus force us into moral and spiritual degeneration. Now we have contracted this virus and we don't know how to cure ourselves. Are we terrorists? Of course not. Do we want to become or be seen as such? What a foolish question. We have the military might to easily erase the Palestinian territories from the map of the world but if we do that we will prove we've become just like our Palestinian enemies. At present we're lacking the unshakable adherence to moral standards we so desperately need. And this precisely is our weakness. What's worse, we've been yielding to this weakness for far too long now. One of the direct results being that that Israel has itself created an image of a pocketsize Palestine as Israel's biggest and more feared enemy. Why, why, why? Palestine doesn't have anything even remotely equal to Israel's military might. Moreover we are ready to enter into battle with much larger and much more powerful states but at the same time we fear tiny Palestine to the core of our very being. Why? Well, there is an answer for that. We've created this fearsome image of Palestine because we need an external enemy to keep us internally intact, whole, undivided and unanimous in what a few of our politicians see as our common strives for the future. A few of us know that Israel fears it would disintegrate into tiny city-states each claiming its own independence and right to self-determination, each sworn to its doctrine and unwilling to compromise. This way our enemies, if they should ever decide to attack us, as they have done in the past, would easily be able to conquer us. And this, people, will be the end of the great Israel our grandparents created –"

"Traitor," somebody shouted out interrupting Ruben. The crowd picked up the word and made it into a maddening chant.

"Fear no one most but yourselves. Only peace is the way forward. Shalom," Ruben yelled in the mouthpiece in an attempt to make himself heard but the roar of the thousands of shouting voices could hardly be drowned. Ian, Dani and Rabbi Loew were next to the truck, just below Ruben. The eyes of all people were still on him. Just at that moment, a red spot burst on the white shirt of Ruben, slightly below his left chest. As if in a slow motion, he swayed a bit but managed to remain standing. His right arm clutched his left chest and was immediately covered by the gushing blood. He looked down to the bullet wound. Then he slowly looked up at all the people as though taking one last glance of this world, one last farewell. The shouting crowd had suddenly stopped yelling, its chant frozen mid-breath. Thousands and thousands of eyes were staring at him. Ruben swayed one last time. This time he lost balance, his body diving headfirst into the group of supporters below the truck. Ruben had been sacrificed on the altar of peace.

Loud screams of terror were heard. People were in shock, devastated, deeply traumatized. Panic set in and many of the people either threw themselves on the ground in fear of other shots or dreaded tried to run away from the scene of the brutal murder.

Just then something strange and unexpected happened.

The priest who was heading the ceremony of The Temple Mount and Land of Israel Faithful Movement suddenly rushed forward and made his way through the crowd of Peace Now supporters. When he reached the truck he grabbed one of the signboards and drew something hastily on it. Then he climbed on the truck's flatbed so that everyone could see him. Clad in original priestly garments, the same as the ones worn by priests during the times of the First and the Second Temple, the priest raised his two arms in a gesture of bringing peace and quiet over the crowd. He remained in this position. For a moment there, it seemed as though time had reversed to the eras of the Temples. People stopped and stared in silent awe. Then the priest picked up and raised the signboard he had drawn on with his left hand. There was a strange symbol on it. An upward pointed triangle with a line protruding from its left side and a smaller triangle drawn in its left corner. The priest lifted the mouthpiece with his right hand, for a moment there looked at the huge assembly below and then said loud and clear, "This is Ariel".

Ariel.
The burning hearth.
The top of the truncated pyramidal altar.
The flat top of the ziggurat.
God's Mountain.
The Lion of God. Layishyav.

The other name of the angel Uriel.
Yet another name of Jerusalem.

The word eerily reverberated in the air and as though it kept on resounding for several more protracted seconds. Ariel... Arie... Ari... Ar... A...

The original Mount Zion on which everyone was standing now was the stronghold of Zion that David conquered with cunning from the Jebusites. The stronghold in turn became the City of David, Ir David, the initial site of Jerusalem. And since time immemorial, Jerusalem was called Ariel - the Lion of God. And Ariel was also the top of the altar on which ancient Israelites offered sacrifices to God. And one innocent life had just been consumed by the invisibly descended Uriel on the ariel of the most primordial altar Jews had ever known. The people were standing there in silent awe.

Slowly the crowd began to disperse. But there was no shouting. No noise. People were silent, pensive, shocked, and disturbed. Nothing of what they had thought they had come for had lived up to their expectations. Yet at the same time, the murder, or sacrifice, and what happened after it was unusual enough to exceed all of their expectations. They were one people when they arrived and another when they left. Something had changed in the meantime but few were aware of that change at that moment.

Only slowly and gradually and after days, weeks and months had passed would they realize the events they had witnessed on that tragic 10th of Av had had a great impact on them and had brought about a change of heart and penitence. And what an extraordinary change that was!

THE END

Ma'aglei tzedek